KAKISTOCRACY

THE CONRADVERSE CHRONICLES

Book 2

ALEX SHVARTSMAN

CAEZIK
SF & FANTASY
ARC MANOR
ROCKVILLE, MARYLAND

✳

SHAHID MAHMUD
PUBLISHER

www.CaezikSF.com

ISBN: 978-1-64710-082-7

First Edition. First Printing

1 2 3 4 5 6 7 8 9 10

An imprint of Arc Manor LLC

www.CaezikSF.com

"Is ours a 'government of the people, by the people, for the people,' or a Kakistocracy rather, for the benefit of knaves at the cost of fools?"

—JAMES RUSSELL LOWELL

CHAPTER 1

I stalked the fae serial killer across Green-Wood Cemetery.

The maniac was seven feet tall, skeletally thin, and freakishly strong, given the apparent ease with which he carried the overstuffed burlap sack slung over his back, like some malnourished Santa. The sack shifted and swayed as his next intended victim tried to claw their way out, but the fae paid them no mind. His long legs carried him steadily past the headstones.

Even without the added burden of hauling about a fully grown person I barely managed to keep up with my quarry. I followed him at a respectful distance, fervently hoping the amulet I was using would shroud me from his heightened senses. I'd bought it via mail order, for top dollar from a second-rate sorcerer in a third-world country. He had assured me the amulet's magic would make me invisible to the fae. Given how rare such beings were in our world, there was no good way to test the seller's claim in advance. I had to hope for the best. The amulet did nothing to prevent the combination of September sun and New York City humidity from slowly cooking me in my own juices.

There was no one around, not even the ghosts of the dead. I was tempted to confront the fae there and then rather than try to keep up with his inhuman pace. I wanted to liberate his prisoner and make certain this lunatic could never abduct or hurt another living soul again, but patience and better judgment won in a close contest over impulse. I needed to follow him to his lair. There was a chance, however remote, that some of his previous victims were still alive.

It had been five months since Daniel Chulsky, the CEO of Abaddon, Inc., had asked me to save the world. I owed him a favor or five, so I said yes, but when I showed up ready to thwart whatever epic-level peril he had in mind, all he asked of me was to find the serial killer who'd turned my home borough of Brooklyn into his personal hunting grounds. This was a bit of a letdown. It's not every day that heads of mysterious and powerful corporations ask you to save the world, and when they do, you might expect a little more pizzazz.

I'd pressed Chulsky on why this particular scumbag was on his radar. He hadn't been forthcoming on the details, but he'd told me the perpetrator was fae, and a blood relative of some bigwigs in his realm to boot. Nepotism appeared to be alive and well across all species and planes of existence. "You're the right man for the job, Conrad," Chulsky had told me. "Do not underestimate its importance." He said I must capture the killer alive, and that Abaddon would then return him to the care of his fellow fae, so as to avoid an interdimensional incident.

None of that seemed particularly apocalyptic to me, but I was interested in the case all the same. Protecting mundanes (humans without magic) from the gifted (humans with magic) and from all sorts of arcane threats is what the Watch—the organization I belonged to—was created to do. It was my duty to find and capture the murderous fae. Squaring my accounts with Chulsky in the process was an added bonus.

That had been back in April. Months went by, and my quarry proved as elusive as he was brazen. The crazy bastard would walk up to a seemingly random person in the middle of a busy street, shove them into his oversized burlap sack, and disappear down some alley or backyard where there were no egresses. He used fae magic to step across the in-between and emerge elsewhere, which allowed him to easily avoid his mundane pursuers and confound human magic users like me.

A week or two later, the skull of his victim, clean of skin and muscle, would show up somewhere in the vicinity of where the poor soul had been abducted in the first place. Not the entire skull though; only the cranium. The jawbone would always be missing. This prompted the media to call him the Mandible Killer, once DNA testing connected the craniums with the abduction victims. The entire mess was catnip to the reporters. With each subsequent abduction, their headlines grew more macabre, more similar in tone and content to the pulp horror stories of the bygone era. The pressure to solve the case grew, both on the police and on me. I had to hope I'd get to him before the police did; there wasn't a whole lot New York's Finest could do to capture or contain a fae.

Having tried lots of different approaches that had yielded no results, I'd caught a break. An informant of mine had seen someone matching the fae's description in Green-Wood. After months of failing to so much as catch a whiff of the guy, I finally had the opportunity to catch him red-handed. All I had to do was wait for another abduction to be reported on police channels, then use a portal to arrive at the cemetery before the fae. Although the cemetery was by no means small, I had a pretty good idea of where the Mandible Killer might be headed.

As I panted and wiped sweat off my forehead, each step the killer and I took brought us closer to the Necropolis.

Green-Wood Cemetery rests on five hundred acres of what used to be a Revolutionary War battlefield. It was established in the early 1800s and became a final resting place for many New York luminaries. But it wasn't until the 1860s that a vast cavern was dug under the cemetery using magic, and the Necropolis was created. Its original purpose was to house the gifted who perished in the Civil War. The gifted abolitionists ensured that war heroes were interred in the Necropolis regardless of their color or species. Trolls and giants and all manner of creatures were allowed to be buried alongside the humans, so long as they'd fought for the Union.

After the war, the Necropolis became a symbol of integration among the gifted, and what few burial spots it had left were eventually filled with remains of respected members of New York's gifted society. By the turn of the twentieth century the Necropolis was full. It was a venerated but seldom-visited place. The sort of place a serial killer from another dimension who held nothing sacred might use for a hideout.

My hunch proved to be right. The Mandible Killer squeezed into an unmarked mausoleum that housed an entrance to the Necropolis. Since his kind could teleport at will, I wondered why the fae hadn't just teleported to the Necropolis entrance and saved both of us the trouble. Did he *enjoy* a brisk walk and some fresh air before he got to the killing? Was he too far gone to be logical? Or was it me who was being irrational, trying to ascribe human logic to an unhinged interdimensional interloper?

The mausoleum door was unlocked; the gifted were meant to have access to the secret burial chamber whenever they pleased, while any mundane who might accidentally stumble into the mausoleum wouldn't be able to perceive the descending granite staircase located behind a decoy stone coffin; the mundane minds would permit them to see only an unremarkable gray wall.

Unencumbered by such illusions, I followed the Mandible Killer down the stairs. My footsteps echoed in the silence of the subterranean chamber, despite my best efforts.

Perhaps the amulet's magic concealed my footsteps from the Mandible Killer, or perhaps the muffled screams from inside the sack drowned them out. Either way, he didn't appear to notice me as I descended into the baseball field-sized cavern. Ranks of tombstones lined much of the ground while the walls served to house a chessboard of plaques, each sealing off an urn with the ashes of some permanent resident of the Necropolis. Wards were in place to ensure the interred would enjoy uninterrupted rest.

The Mandible Killer had made himself at home at the far side of the cavern. As I quietly edged toward him, I began to make out the details by the dim, green-tinged light of the handful of eternal flames suspended on pillars scattered throughout, enchanted to burn continuously to both provide illumination and commemorate the Civil War heroes buried here. A dirty mattress with several springs sprouting at the edges lay on the ground. A plastic lawn chair that had one day been white stood next to it.

Evidence of the fae's grim workings extended in a wide semicircle from the spot where he presently dropped the sack and was examining something I couldn't yet see on the ground. Bloodstained items of clothing that must've belonged to his victims were strewn around, mixed with fast-food wrappers. The place stank of piss and rot. A child's yellow windbreaker with its right sleeve ripped off below the shoulder was hanging from one of the grave markers. I'd seen a lot of grisly stuff in my time, but this visual got to me; I had no doubt I'd be reacquainting myself with it in my nightmares for weeks to come.

I shook off the sense of dread I was feeling and got my adrenaline under control as best I could. I concentrated on the task at hand, cautiously edging close enough so that the killer couldn't teleport away. I grasped the charm Chulsky had given me tightly. It felt smooth and cool and calming in my fist as I crept toward danger.

Soon I was close enough to see what the fae was so focused on. Atop a silk cloth the size of a picnic blanket lay an assortment of knives, saws, and other sharp utensils that would've fit right in at a horror movie's prop department. The knives were probably made from fiberglass or some other material inoffensive to a species allergic to iron and iron-based alloys such as steel. It didn't make them look any less lethal.

The Mandible Killer picked out a wicked-looking machete and lifted it close to his gaunt face. Bits of blood and gore were caked along its blade. He turned toward the shifting sack with a content smile on his lips.

I willed the charm I was clasping to activate and dropped my concealment.

"That is a fish knife," I said. "Don't they teach table manners where you're from? Regardless, you won't be needing the cutlery today."

The Mandible Killer whirled to face me. Up close he couldn't be easily mistaken for a lanky human. His skull was a little too long, his cheekbones too prominent under the wispy beard. His unkempt albino hair too thin and delicate. His unnerving chartreuse eyes narrowed as he looked me up and down.

"Tomorrow's not looking likely, either," I added.

Whatever interplay between fight-and-flight syndromes took place in the fae's brain, fight won a decisive victory. By the time I finished speaking he was already lunging at me, machete raised. He was pretty fast, but I was no slouch, either. I sidestepped his attack and used his own momentum in a judo-like move to send him tumbling to the ground.

The fae rolled away from me and into a crouch, quickly recovering into a defensive position. One knee pressed into the dirt and his machete still in hand, the murderer whispered a curse under his breath. His words of power would have punched an unprepared opponent worse than a well-aimed uppercut, but I was wearing more trinkets than a fully decorated Christmas tree. The curse slid off me, its power sapped by my protections. All I felt physically was the equivalent of a light shove.

That's when he must've realized I was a more dangerous opponent than I looked, and his flight syndrome took over the driver's seat. He tried to open a portal and step through the in-between, several times in a row, as the haptic feedback from the charm in my fist confirmed.

"The fun rides are closed," I said.

He must've not liked that idea one bit, because the fae growled and then launched another attack, tackling me head-on before I finished speaking. He didn't have the mass of an offensive lineman, but he sure had the speed any quarterback would have envied. Even though I'd expected the attack, he managed to drive a bony shoulder into my jaw and the two of us rolled onto the ground.

In a fair fight, he might've beaten me, but if I ever found myself in a fair fight I actually had time to prepare for, then I'd be a terrible tactician and would deserve to lose. As it was, I wore an iron belt buckle and two wide iron bracelets like a gender-swapped Wonder Woman. I'd also inserted strips of iron into my pockets. In such close proximity, I could probably do more damage to my opponent by hugging him tight than by trying to punch and kick him. Which didn't stop me from punching and kicking him. The psycho murderer deserved it.

Despite whatever pain and suffering I was managing to inflict, the fae reciprocated by landing a good number of hits. I kept as close to him as I could so that he wouldn't be able to properly swing his machete—I briefly wondered again if its blade was cobalt, titanium alloy, ceramic, or obsidian: all non-steel options a fae could handle—but he bruised me well enough with his fist and the hilt of the machete to ensure I'd be popping ibuprofens later.

Entangled in close combat, we rolled past the smorgasbord of sharp utensils and crashed hard into an ugly brown pot the size and shape of a thirty-gallon trash can. Clay shattered loudly against the granite memorial plaques in the Necropolis wall and a plethora of mandibles spilled onto the ground.

I recoiled from the gruesome sight. I'd known the Mandible Killer must've been responsible for dozens of deaths, but the sheer number of trophies in that pot adjusted my estimate into the triple digits. I paid for being distracted. The fae landed a mighty sockdolager to my jaw. Pain intermixed with a renewed infusion of anger, and I lashed back at him, aiming a series of blows with my bracelets upward to the sides of his head.

He tried teleporting away again, which was futile and cost him precious seconds. I gained the upper hand, and soon he collapsed half-dazed upon the ground.

I retrieved a special pair of handcuffs. According to Chulsky, they'd cancel all fae magic—and not just their ability to teleport.

"Earth vacation's over," I said. "Next up is the slow and not-so-scenic cruise back to the fae realm."

As I attempted to clasp the handcuffs on him, the Mandible Killer twisted and kneed me hard above the ankle. He managed to knock me off balance long enough to scramble past me and half-tumble, half-run toward the staircase. His long legs carried him impossibly fast while I struggled to get back on to my feet. Even without using magic, he could easily outpace me.

There was no way I was letting him escape and add to his body count. Visions of a bagful of mandibles spilling from a clay pot swam before my eyes as I drew a pistol from the inner pocket of my trench coat and disengaged the thumb safety. Chulsky wanted this maniac taken alive, and I did everything in my power, even risked my own life, to make that happen. But there was absolutely no way I'd take the chance of letting a mass murderer escape to prey upon another victim. Another child. I thought back to the yellow windbreaker draped carelessly over a tombstone.

I lined the fae's lanky frame in my pistol's sights and fired three full metal jacket bullets encased in solid-iron shells, in rapid succession. The noise of discharging a firearm in the enclosed space was deafening. The shots echoed against the walls. My ears rang. The acrid scent of burnt gunpowder joined the medley of unpleasant odors around me.

The fae stumbled and fell face forward onto the ground, one of his long skeletal arms extending to within a few inches of the staircase. His body spasmed as though a jolt of electricity had passed through it, and then was still.

I approached warily, mindful of another trick. I put my gun back into the inner pocket where the fae couldn't grab at it and turn the tables on me. I needn't have worried. When I got close enough, I could see that two of the three bullets had found their target. One had entered at his left shoulder. The other had been a headshot; it entered at the top of the neck, just below the elongated skull.

The Mandible Killer was dead.

CHAPTER 2

I sat on the bottom stair and placed a call to the offices of the Watch. A cleanup crew would be on its way to deal with the, well, cleanup. If anything, the privacy of the place made their job a cakewalk. Far less stressful than mopping up chunks of exploded goblin in full view of the tourists in Midtown.

I caught a glimpse of movement from the corner of my eye and focused on the far end of the mausoleum. The would-be victim of the fae serial killer had finally escaped from inside the sack and was shambling unsteadily past the headstones, gaping at the evidence of the decedent's crimes.

I cursed under my breath and wondered what he must be thinking, what he must be *seeing* around him. Only a tiny percentage of humans have the gifted gene that allows them to perceive and perform magic. The rest are mundanes—regular people whose brains go into overdrive to prevent them from sensing anything unusual, anything beyond what's dreamed of in their philosophy. If a mundane meets a troll or a fae they'll perceive nothing more than a slightly unusual-looking human. Their brain will interpret a supernatural beast, no matter how exotic, as a wild dog/raccoon/

wolf/fill-in-the-blank based on the creature's general shape and size. Where mundanes are concerned, magic is something that happens to fictional characters.

This particular mundane appeared to be in his late thirties. He wore slacks, a short sleeved button-down shirt, and a bewildered expression.

I rose to meet him, projecting the maximum amount of confidence and authority I could manage to fake.

"Hey there. I'm Officer Brent. The threat has been neutralized." I waved toward the dead fae behind me. "You're safe. For now."

The mundane's eyes grew wider. "What do you mean, for now?"

"You see, Tall, Albino, and Dead over there"—I pointed at the fae again—"belongs to a cult of murderous maniacs responsible for a series of ritualistic killings. They pick victims at random, but once they choose someone, the entire gang is going to try their darndest to finish the job."

The man's face turned an interesting shade of white.

"The standard procedure would be to put you in a witness protection program. Relocate you to a small town somewhere in Idaho or North Dakota, where everyone knows each other and a cultist would have a difficult time sneaking up on you. But in this case, you seem to have caught a bit of a break."

I didn't enjoy watching fear and hope play out on the man's face like it was a movie screen, but I was doing this for his own good. There were magical means of removing the memory from his mind or making him keep silent, but those were so rough on one's mental health, the cure would be worse than the disease. Until someone invented a *Men in Black*-style neuralyzer and handed me a pair of shades, I preferred to rely on the noninvasive, holistic method. If you do it well, lying is every bit as effective as magic.

"Since you were just grabbed, randomly, off the street, there's no reason to suspect that his comrades know about you at all. So, if you want to continue living in the greatest city in the world instead of relocating to Sheboygan, Wisconsin, your best option is to get out of here before my colleagues arrive and to never tell a living soul you're linked to this case. That way you can just go on with your life like nothing ever happened. How does that sound?"

The man nodded vigorously and silently. What was it about the Necropolis that seemed to turn my would-be interlocutors into mimes today?

I patted him on the shoulder and pointed toward the stairs. "That way. And remember, don't tell anyone about this. Not your wife, not your therapist, not even Dear Abby via an anonymous letter. You don't want to put yourself or your loved ones in danger."

"Th … Th … Thank you!" stammered the mundane. He scrambled past me and up the stairs, steering as far away from the corpse as he could. In the short term, fear would keep him silent, and in the long term, whatever story he chose to tell would sound too fantastical for anyone to take seriously without supporting evidence—evidence which the cleanup crew would be disposing of any minute now.

I received an enthusiastic round of congratulations from seemingly everyone at the Watch—from the good folks on the cleanup crew to my fellow guardians, who were each responsible for one of New York City's five boroughs. When John Smith, acting chief of the New York Watch in absence of our longtime leader Mose, called me into his office, I expected more of the same.

Instead, John's congratulations came with a side order of guilt trip.

"Now that you've caught the Mandible Killer, I hope you will have more time to focus on all the other problems cropping up in Brooklyn." John squinted at the computer monitor on his desk. Wearing a bespoke suit and a fancy tie, he looked out of place in our less-than-glamorous office. The dark skin of his shaved head and his smooth, perfectly groomed face looked like it benefited from ointments and creams and whatever it is people who know about such things call "product." If I didn't know any better, I would've assumed I was talking to an attorney from some white-shoe law firm and not a guardian like myself who used to protect Manhattan, before the promotion he never wanted left him riding the desk in the Watchtower. To be fair, he dressed the same back then, busting ghosts and cracking cursed skulls in style.

11

John looked up from the screen and fixed me with his best frown. "I've got reports of a vampire nest in the Coney Island Train Yard, and of the Kwan brothers running pixie dust out of a gas station in Clinton Hill. Supernatural activity has been on the rise across the city. We need our best people laser-focused right now, instead of dividing their attention between protecting the city and freelance work."

I bristled at the implication. I've done just fine protecting my borough for years. And yes, I'd always taken on an occasional freelance job or two in order to pay the bills. Magical artifacts were expensive, and it wasn't like the Watch actually paid any of us. It was a volunteer organization. When Mose ran things, he understood that and never tried to micromanage us in this manner.

On the other hand, John was merely trying to fill Mose's oversized shoes: an impossible and unenviable task. I could sympathize, especially since I was partly responsible for his predicament, having turned down the role of Fearless Leader myself and nominated John for the position when Mose had gone missing. We'd hoped Mose would come back after a few weeks, but he never had. All we could do was wait, and hope. Until then, someone had to be in charge. Better John than me, I say. So, instead of snapping back, I merely said, "Sure, boss. I'll look into those things."

Placated by my respectful response, John relented and showered me with the compliments I so richly deserved for expunging the lunatic murderer from the fae gene pool.

A little praise is good for the soul, or so I kept telling myself while I headed to Abaddon, Inc., where I fully expected to get a proper chewing out, thus balancing the karmic scales of the universe.

Located in downtown Manhattan within sight of the Charging Bull statue, the three-story building housing Abaddon, Inc. looked as respectable as any old-fashioned bank in the Financial District, with its marble columns and tall windows. But instead of a bunch of greedy hedge fund managers, it housed an organization at least as ancient and secretive as the Watch.

Several young people were passing out campaign flyers in front of the Abaddon building's grandiose façade. "Restore New York City to its former glory! Vote Holcomb for mayor!" they barked as they shoved the glossy advertisements upon the passersby. One of the youngsters was gifted, as evidenced by an unmistakable presence of an aura around him. He noticed my aura just as I noticed his, and he zeroed in on me like a guided missile.

I picked up the pace and gave him a wide berth. Having once butted heads with the real estate developer who was now running for office, I'd found Holcomb wanting. The tycoon was clever in his own way, but he was no statesman. New Yorkers were more likely to elect the Mr. Met mascot as our mayor than to put Bradley Holcomb in charge.

"Hey, mister!" The persistent campaign volunteer caught up with me. "Did you know that Bradley Holcomb will be the first New York mayor to directly reach out to the gifted community?" he got out breathlessly.

I chortled at the naiveté of that statement. Mayors and other high-ranking officials were read in on the supernatural; how else could they be expected to govern properly? They were also taught enough history, and sometimes threatened outright, to leave their gifted constituents alone.

The volunteer misinterpreted my reaction. "He really is! Mr. Holcomb will breach the divide between the gifted and the mundanes, and ensure both groups are working together to restore New York City to its former glory!" He touched the rim of his baseball cap, which bore the same message.

I was uncertain of what kind of divide might exist between the two groups since the latter wasn't aware of the existence of the former, but I also didn't have time to argue with a zealot nor the desire to be unnecessarily rude. I took the flyer he was proffering.

"I'll give your candidate the consideration he deserves," I promised truthfully. When the volunteer headed back toward the gaggle of his mundane co-barkers, I dropped the leaflet into the nearest trash bin.

Having bypassed the front entrance in favor of a relatively humble side door, I entered a short vestibule.

13

"Papers," grumbled Tiny the doortroll from behind his massive desk, which took up much of the length of the guardroom.

Tiny was a smidgen under eight feet tall, which happens to be somewhat diminutive for a troll, a fact I never hesitated to underscore in my taunting of this curmudgeonly upstart security guard.

"Really? You're going to hassle me for an ID like I'm a stranger? Even now that I'm freelancing for Chulsky, which makes us practically co-workers? You wound me, sir. Does our mutual history mean nothing to you?"

The troll glared at me, a large drop of saliva pooling at his left tusk. Our mutual history included multiple instances of my tricking him to gain unauthorized entrance to Abaddon portals, and one instance of my temporary associate Moira punching him in his trollhood. Which was exactly why I'd brought it up.

"You always act like the rules don't apply to you, Brent," said Tiny. "But they do."

This was abstract thinking on levels Tiny was rarely capable of. I was almost tempted to let him have this one. Almost.

"Aha! So you *do* know who I am. In which case asking for papers is a waste of everybody's time, isn't it?"

I didn't wait for Tiny to formulate a response. I marched right past him, feeling the heat of his seething glare on my back every step of the way.

I took the ordinary if upscale elevator to the top floor. The sliding door opened directly into the spacious office of Abaddon's CEO, Daniel Chulsky.

The office contained only a desk and a single chair with no seat for visitors, which was an interesting choice. Chulsky must not have entertained many guests there, but he seemed to make an exception in my case. Three of the room's walls were enormous glass panes displaying stunning bird's-eye views of New York, London, and Tokyo. Although the building stood only three floors tall, the tiny taxicabs below suggested the window was located at least fifty stories above ground. Chulsky was fond of saying that the building was bigger on the inside. He rarely cracked a joke, but something about Time Lord lore must've appealed to him.

I often found Chulsky gazing out one of the windows lost in thought, but not this time. His lean, marathon-runner frame was folded into the chair and hunched over his laptop. From this vantage point, I could see a touch of gray at the temples, contrasting with his short black hair and his immaculate suit and tie. He looked up at me with tired eyes.

"Mr. Brent, I expected better of you," he said in lieu of a greeting, confirming my suspicion that he already knew about what had gone down at the cemetery.

"I did my best. In the end, it was either let a serial killer escape or take him out permanently. That wasn't much of a choice."

"If we're to work together, it is imperative you trust the information I provide," said Chulsky. "I had excellent reasons to require that the individual in question be captured alive, and I made my wishes in this regard very clear. You thought you knew better, relying on your moral compass instead of my instructions. You were wrong."

I looked past him at the beautiful sunrise in Tokyo. "I work with what I've got. Since you never bothered to tell me *why* you wanted him brought in alive, I had to weigh your wishes against the danger to the public. No more innocent people getting murdered won that contest in a landslide. If your reason for wanting the fae alive was so pertinent, you could've shared it."

Chulsky pushed his chair backward and stretched. He looked like he might have been hunched over that laptop for hours.

"I'm sorry, but that's not how an employer and employee relationship works. I can't always share all the information with my subordinates. If we're to work together, I have to feel confident that my instructions are followed."

"Then we're at an impasse," I said. "Let's not forget, I'm not your employee. I'm a freelance contractor who undertook a mission from you to repay a favor. You helped me out with that middling affliction business, and I appreciate it. I also respect you and hope we can pool resources and work together whenever our goals align. But I'm not some mindless flunky like that troll you keep downstairs who's going to follow marching orders without question. If you want to work with me, you have to be a little more forthcoming or expect me to use my brain—or my moral compass, as you put it—to fill in the blanks."

"You're indeed a freelancer, but when I'm paying you to do a job for me, I expect that job done to my specifications," said Chulsky.

"Is this about money, then? If so, I'm willing to forgo the payment; I would have pursued the Mandible Killer as part of my responsibility to the Watch, and—"

"Peace, Conrad," Chulsky waved me off. "It's not about the money. It's about managing expectations. I recognize that you aren't some landscaper whom I can hire and replace if he's underperforming. You have a unique skill set, and I'm willing to adjust somewhat to your style, if you'll do me the courtesy of at least trying to adjust to mine."

"Sure. What say we usher in this new era of cooperation and transparency by finally telling me what your interest is in the Mandible Killer? As much as I appreciate your help in getting my borough rid of this maniac, this sort of thing doesn't appear to fit within Abaddon's purview."

I spoke the words as though I knew what I was talking about, which I didn't. For all its influence, power, and prominence, I had no idea what it was Abaddon, Inc. actually *did*. They weren't actively a thorn in the Watch's side. In fact, they had a long-standing arrangement with the Watch, allowing our operatives to use their convenient portals. But then, I'd discovered they had a similar arrangement with the Cabal, an organization that was almost cartoonishly evil. Yet, Mose liked and respected Chulsky, which was enough for me to count him in the good-guys ledger. Beyond that, Abaddon's purview was entirely opaque to me.

"Yes, well, it seems you've left me no choice, seeing how you will need this information to help mitigate the damage you've caused." Chulsky's frown deepened. "Chad wasn't just a run-of-the-mill murderer. He was a fairly senior member of the sidhe royal family. He was high enough in their hierarchy for certain fae factions to possibly use his death to justify an all-out invasion of our realm."

"Hold up," I said. "The Mandible Killer, a fae prince whose primary hobbies were abducting random people, living in a cemetery, and scrimshaw on jawbones, was named *Chad*?"

Chulsky nodded. "Different spelling, as I understand it, but yes. You may find this amusing but, as the Bard put it, what's in a name? A murderer by any other name is just as vile."

"Chad," I repeated, shaking my head. "This will take some getting used to."

"As I was saying, the political climate at the sidhe high court is tense. There's a faction that's been advocating open war on humanity for quite some time, and they've been getting more vociferous and more aggressive by the century. Our analysts believe the warmongers nudged Chad—ever the black sheep of the royal family—to travel across the in-between into the mortal realm for this very purpose. If and when Chad's abhorrent activities would lead to his death by mortal hand, they could use that as a rallying cry and launch their invasion."

Ludicrous as Chad's name was, the situation was anything but funny. A single unhinged fae had managed to kill over a hundred people and cause endless trouble. What might a war band of *sane* sidhe warriors—sane by the fae standards, anyhow—be capable of? The resources of the Watch would not be enough to stop them, especially not without Mose at the helm.

"Wait." My mind was racing. "You said 'death by mortal hand,' right? But that doesn't entirely apply in my case, does it?"

Chulsky's frown gave way to a crooked grin. "This is one of the many reasons I like you, Mr. Brent. You're as efficient at evaluating a problem as you're pragmatic at resolving it."

"So, all we need to do is send my résumé to the fae?"

"Not quite." The frown reclaimed its rightful place on Chulsky's face. "You have to personally deliver the corpse of the slain prince to the high court of the sidhe, then participate in a ritual trial and prove that you killed him in honorable combat."

"You want me to take Chad's corpse to fairyland and tell his extremely dangerous royal relatives that I was the one who offed him?"

"I won't sugarcoat it," said Chulsky. "It's every bit as fraught with danger as it sounds. We can help improve the odds somewhat by preparing you for the trial, and we can furnish you with a guide who's traveled to the Land Under the Mound several times before, yet you will still be putting your life on the line. What you must understand is that if you refuse to go, that would place all of humanity in great peril."

My personal philosophy says, when life hands you a watermelon-sized lemon like this, it's okay to be scared witless while you make lemonade, but you better mix in a ten-pound bag of sugary bravado before you drink it.

"I risk my life on a regular basis at the Watch. Sometimes twice before lunch. Sometimes *during* lunch, when I dare order my food from a street cart. So why don't you introduce me to this guide, and we'll get started on returning Chad back to sender."

"You already know her. The freelancer who'll guide you is Moira O'Leary."

Well, crap. Did I say watermelon-sized lemon? This lemon was turning out to be the size of one of those fair-winning pumpkins, and it tasted of treachery and dark magic.

Nothing to do but roll up my sleeves and make lemonade.

CHAPTER 3

I leaned against the wooden coffin and drank coffee while I waited for Moira to show up. The coffin swayed gently like a boat in calm waters, as it levitated three feet above the ground. If I had to deliver Chad back to his people, at least I wouldn't have to carry his lanky, murderous ass. The coffee was pretty good, ground and brewed in front of me by a fancy Italian machine. Abaddon, Inc. didn't skimp on the amenities.

I scrolled through the local news feed on my phone. The breaking news was that Holcomb held a press conference to announce that he'd secured the endorsement of the MTA commissioner. Advertising this factoid made little sense to me. New Yorkers like the bureaucrats in charge of their subway system about as much as they like the rats that infest it.

My second cup was brewing when the door swung open and Moira walked in. The petite redhead wore green pants and a mauve traveling cloak over a silk shirt. A cutlass she called Kindness was sheathed at her hip. She might've looked like she just stepped off the *Lord of the Rings* movie set had her ensemble not been completed by a Red Sox baseball cap.

Moira O'Leary had been a Cabal agent and a necromancer, a one-time enemy and a one-time reluctant ally. She was an unstoppable force of nature in a diminutive red-headed frame and, in all honesty, I would've taken Tiny the doortroll as my guide over her, given half a choice.

"Hello, Conrad," she said, with a hint of a British accent. "You're looking pretty good for someone who was about to become dragon chow the last time I saw you."

"Yeah, thanks very much for that. You cut out and ran as soon as you saw that oversized snake. We had to twist it into a pretzel without you."

"A gaggle of mudlarks fought off a dragon?" Moira scratched her chin. "Not a gaggle. There must be a better collective noun for you lot. A *uselessness* of mudlarks? Someday you must tell me how you pulled that off."

"Must I, though?" I plucked the miniature porcelain cup from the bowels of the coffee machine and took a sip.

"Either way, you seem to have gotten on fine. I hear you regained your position at the Watch, too. Living the easy life while some of us travail and get in trouble." Moira pursed her lips and sniffed theatrically.

I breathed in the heavenly aroma of coffee and leaned against the coffin again. It gave a little and supported my back comfortably, like a fine office chair. "All right, I'll bite. *How are you doing*, Moira?"

Moira produced an exaggerated sigh like a starlet on a soap opera. "Oh, you know, the usual. After I returned from Chernobyl empty-handed, the Cabal put a bounty on my head. And it wasn't even a *sizable* bounty!" She bristled at the indignity. "Not enough to interest any of the people who could actually take me. When I got tired of fending off second-rate brigands and cutthroats and some of the dumber upstarts, I left Europe for the colonies, where no one seems to know of my predicament. Now, I have to take odd jobs for Abaddon and the like just to make ends meet."

It seemed Moira wanted someone—anyone—to take responsibility for her fall from dubious grace, but I wasn't about to volunteer. I said, "Yeah, well, when you hang with villains, you better spring for backstab insurance."

Moira was about to counter with something snide, but instead, she squinted at me. "Your aura has changed," she said out of the blue. She edged a few steps closer, and it took a bit of self-control for me not to visibly tense up. She examined my aura up close, sniffed at me like a trained dog at an airport searching for contraband. "You're not the same as I remember. No longer a mudlark, and certainly not a mundane, but not exactly a gifted, either. Fascinating."

Moira's ability to suss out my unique condition so quickly was unsettling. A gifted could recognize another gifted by their aura, and not a single one of them appeared to have noticed the change in mine since the events of what had become known as the middling affliction in the collective zeitgeist of the gifted community. I could reveal my new, much fancier aura at will, sort of like a peacock. It was the one useful trait that remained after my brief and temporary apotheosis, but Moira had recognized the change without my conscious effort to display it.

I tried to change the subject. "You've changed, too. Have you developed a passion for baseball since we last met?"

"Oh, this?" She touched the cap's visor. "Certainly not. Baseball is hardly even a sport. Rather fitting for a nation of sedentary lardbags. No, I simply enjoy raising the locals' blood pressure. I have a Yankee cap for when I'm in Boston, and a Liverpool jersey for when I'm in Manchester. Mundanes get worked up so easily about such nonsense things."

"Charming." I took another sip. "I think your winning personality should be enough to aggravate the average person, and it doesn't even require a localized wardrobe."

Moira looked me up and down. "And is *this* what you're wearing to the high court of the sidhe?"

My fingers brushed against the light trench coat I wore year-round. It may not have been much of a fashion statement, and it wasn't fun to wear during the summer, but it contained many inner pockets filled with amulets, charms, and other curios helpful in my line of work. Being able to quickly reach for the right item had saved my life—and the lives of others—multiple times.

"I didn't realize dressing like a Tolkien character was a requirement. I'd call dibs on Gandalf, but my robe and staff are in the wash."

"You haven't got the beard for it, anyway," said Moira. "But hey, wear what you want. It's your funeral. Well, mostly it's that guy's funeral." She pointed at the coffin. "But also yours."

"I thought the whole point of you was to get me there and back in one piece?"

Moira shrugged. "I cannot guarantee anyone's survival in the realm of the fae. Much less someone who likes speaking nonsense to power as much as you do. Abaddon pays me well, but not well enough to be an active participant. I'm just a guide. And as such, I'll guide you there, and bring what's left of you back. If the fae let me."

"Lovely," I said. "It's good to know that you do not have my back. Not that I suspected otherwise."

"There's only one back I care about," said Moira. "But at least I'm honest about it. Enlightened self-interest is one of the two most important factors that differentiate freelancers like me from goody two-shoes like you."

I couldn't help but ask, "And what's the second factor?"

"We tend to live longer," said Moira.

The ritual we used to cross between dimensions was a bit underwhelming for my taste. There was no cool portal akin to the ones generated by the basic teleportation spells, nor did we enter through a wardrobe or dive down a rabbit hole. Instead, Moira muttered her incantation, and the room began to fill with a dense, cold fog. Condensation formed on the Italian coffee maker and the cup of java in my hand cooled instantly. I gulped the rest of it down anyway, because I figured they probably didn't have good coffee on the other side. I wrapped my trench coat more tightly around my shoulders and wondered whether this damp, chilly soup felt like home to the British necromancer.

"Follow me," said Moira. She stepped deeper into the fog. A single step and she almost disappeared, with only a shadow discernible up ahead. I set the cup down and gave the coffin a gentle push. It glided into the fog, and I followed. For a few moments I walked through the gray mess with zero visibility. Unpleasantly cool moisture clung to my face and exposed skin. I rested my damp palm on the levitating coffin for even at such a short distance I could barely make out its shape. I thought it'd be silly to misplace the corpse five seconds into the trip, but before the idea fully formed, the fog began to lift. The temperature climbed back up to temperate, and very soon afterward the moisture dissipated entirely.

This was my first interdimensional trip. I twisted my head to-and-fro, taking in my surroundings like a small-town tourist who found himself in the center of Times Square.

"Dorothy," I declared, "we might still be in Kansas, for all I know."

I'm not sure what I actually expected. An alien landscape with two suns up in the sky? Drakes soaring over a medieval castle? At the very least, the lush foliage and green hues only found on New Zealand movie sets. Instead, we stood on a patch of forested land that was so ordinary, it could have well been Pennsylvania or North Jersey. Or maybe Kansas, if they have any forests.

Moira watched me with an amused expression on her face. "Something wrong?" she asked.

"As alternate dimensions go, this one seems rather milquetoast," I said. "I'm inclined to send a strongly worded email to my travel agent."

"Good luck with that. I don't think we're anywhere near a cell tower. And also, would you form such a quick opinion of New York City if you teleported into the heart of Central Park?"

"Point taken," I said. "Which way to the tourist traps?"

Moira pointed toward more trees. "That way. We couldn't just appear at the high court of the sidhe. First, it would be rude. Second, they would likely kill us on sight. The intelligent way to go about things is to use a spot that's a short leisurely walk away from our destination, and here we are." She headed in the direction she'd pointed out.

And so we walked. Leisurely. A sword-wielding Cabal necromancer, Dead Chad floating in his wooden coffin, and me. I thanked my lucky stars that Chulsky had had the foresight to enchant the coffin. Dragging it across unpaved terrain wouldn't have been fun.

"I'm not much of an outdoorsman, but I could swear this is the Poconos," I said. "The smells, the sounds." I slapped my neck. "The mosquitos."

"The sidhe occupy the continent geographically equivalent to North America in their realm," said Moira. "The flora of this place is bound to be analogous."

"American fae? I thought the sidhe come from Irish mythology?"

"The *aes sídhe* of Celtic mythology live across the western sea in an invisible world that coexists with the human world. And what's across the water to the west of Ireland, I wonder?" said Moira.

" 'Murica. Home of the free and the Whopper," I said.

"Indeed. The sidhe are as American as Apple iPhone," said Moira.

We traversed the forest and onto the fields, with a handful of fae working the land. They looked like Chad's slightly shorter, even more malnourished, covered-in-grime cousins who showed no great enthusiasm for their work. As a city boy, I couldn't name the gardening implements they used to lethargically poke at the dirt or tell you what crop they were growing.

"They don't seem to have any modern tools," I observed.

"They're serfs," said Moira. "The fae are a rigid feudal society, too set in their ways for any sort of innovation. They're head and shoulders ahead of us when it comes to magic, and we should consider ourselves fortunate that they're otherwise stuck in the dark ages, or humanity would be toiling in similar fields on Earth under the fae heel by now."

The serfs ceased their halfhearted efforts and stared as we passed by but said and did nothing to stop us. It wasn't until we reached the edge of a settlement—a handful of one-story buildings that were only a small step up from a TV version of a medieval village—that a band of armed fae warriors confronted us. They looked like they benefited from a better diet, still thin and freakishly tall, but not skeletal. Each one was armed with a pike and a short sword and, unlike the serfs, we couldn't smell them before we saw them coming. The warriors seemed no more pleased at our approach than we were to be accosted by them.

"State your business," one of them said gruffly. My translation amulet had no trouble converting his words into English.

I stated our business, using the formal terminology Chulsky had taught me. More or less.

"You have killed the prince?" the warrior asked. I didn't need the amulet to hear the incredulity in his voice and see it in his body language.

"Yes. But he started it."

The warrior glanced at Dead Chad's coffin, as though expecting the prince's vengeful ghost to rise and dispute my version of events, but the enchanted casket made no response beyond floating silently by my side.

"The high court shall be informed," the warrior declared with enough theatrical pomp that it felt like I was talking to a video game character. "You will wait there." He pointed toward a fenced-in area that was presently empty but looked a lot like it was where the fae kept whatever passed for cattle around these parts. We headed there under guard, while one of the warriors ran off, presumably to do the informing.

We waited for about an hour which, in all fairness, didn't seem like an excessive amount of time to inform and subsequently summon the entire sidhe high court.

The warriors escorted us into town. The streets grew cleaner, wider, and more prosperous as we went. Hovels made way for neat wooden houses, then brick houses, then two- and three-story buildings. The spacious structure at the center of town, which I understood to be their seat of power, was certainly no palace, more like a town hall of some impoverished third-world settlement. The entire setup here wasn't especially impressive. One could easily make the mistake of discounting the fae as worthy adversaries, until one saw their fighters perform their interdimensional assassin routine. In any case, Chulsky was concerned and that was something I knew to take seriously.

A bunch of fae milled about the hall. Most of them were dressed similarly to what Moira had chosen to wear. Mercifully, she'd left the baseball cap in our dimension. The fae wore elaborate brooches and sported decorated sword hilts.

"That's a lot of nobles for a small settlement," I whispered to Moira as flocks of fancy fae parted before us.

"Their realm is vast," she replied. "What need do beings that can teleport at will have of large cities?"

Chulsky's concern felt a lot more valid to me then. All these nobles showed up here within an hour, just to watch me bring back the body of their prince. How many warriors could they gather just as quickly should they decide to attack our world? Tens of thousands? Hundreds of thousands? More? It would be best not to find out.

We made our way across the hall, past dozens of very tall, albino beings dressed in fantasy movie garb and sporting scabbards, to where seven high-backed thrones were set up against the wall, spaced about eight feet apart. They were oversized high-backed chairs, each set up on a dais with a pair of steps leading up to it. Other than that, they were simple wooden jobs with no carvings or decorations. I realized that similar disused furniture must've been set up in every town hall across the fae realm.

A sidhe royal sat upon each throne, arranged in order of their age. The first four were occupied by wizened geriatrics stooped down to average human size by the weight of their years. Despite their advanced ages each of them appeared sharp as they scowled and looked down their noses at everyone else.

On the fifth throne sat a fearsome warrior who looked to be in his thirties. From Chulsky's description, I knew this to be Kallan, the de facto leader of the faction that wanted to wage war upon our world. He was the one to watch out for, the one who would go out of his way to cause trouble. A muscular, lean mountain of a fae, he looked like a healthier, more vigorous copy of his dead relative, whose coffin floated by my side.

The Lady Rhoswen occupied the sixth throne. It was Chulsky's hope that her voice of reason would counter Kallan's warmongering. She looked to be barely out of her teens, but looks were deceiving with the fae. Each of these royals was centuries old, regardless of their appearance.

The seventh throne should have been empty. It was the one previously occupied by the dearly departed Chad, the black sheep of this lovely family. The psychopath's royal lineage had earned his posterior this small bit of highly desirable real estate. Chulsky believed at least some of these royals would be secretly pleased to see him gone. A plump toddler of about four was ensconced upon a soft cushion placed on the last throne. The child looked as regal as the rest, but perhaps a tad less sure of himself. Was that just my imagination? Or was he someone who was never expected to occupy one of the seven thrones, thrust into the big leagues by the sudden and violent chain of events that had created this unexpected vacancy? Were his parents somewhere in this hall, or were they among those seated upon the other six thrones?

I mulled over all of that while I made my way toward the front. The other fae moved about the hall like this was a party and they had to network with anyone important, but everyone kept a respectful distance from their leaders. When we approached this invisible boundary that they all seemed to respect, Moira deftly stepped aside. For a blustery, bombastic rogue, she was quite good at blending into the background and keeping attention off herself when it suited her. I stepped forward, coffin in tow, leaving behind what little anonymity and false sense of safety being a part of the crowd had afforded me.

All eyes settled on me, but no one spoke. So, I launched into the ritualistic speech Chulsky had forced me to memorize.

"My name is Conrad Brent, and I am here to discharge a warrior's duty. I've come to return the body of a fellow warrior with whom I crossed blades, and who fought me honorably and well." I thought back to our encounter in the crypt but managed to keep on telling the story they wanted to hear. "As fortune smiled upon me and not him on the battlefield, it falls to me to return him to the mound and to beg all those gathered to consider the matter resolved between my clan and his." In other words, I'd like to trade in this corpse in exchange for you not initiating some sort of a vendetta against my clan. Or, in my case, against all of humanity. Chulsky seemed to think this could work. Standing there and reciting those hollow words from memory, I wasn't so sure.

While the rest of the royals regarded me in stone-faced silence, Kallan rose to his feet and took several steps forward until he loomed over me, muscles bulging under his shirt. He was taller and bulkier than Chad. Next to him I looked like a small child in need of an adult.

He looked me up and down with an expression of a homeowner examining a pile of droppings that a stray cat had left on their lawn. "You claim to have faced a prince of the royal blood in battle and emerged not only victorious, but also unscathed?"

Just like the guards we met earlier, this brute couldn't wrap his meaty head around the idea that I was capable of taking down Chad one-on-one. Being underestimated was generally a good thing, a small advantage in most situations. But it still stung the ego, a little bit.

"I wouldn't say unscathed," I replied. "Pretty sure I needed a Band-Aid or three."

Kallan snarled at me, murder in his eyes. I'm not sure what he might've done, but the second oldest of the royals raised her wrinkled hand weighed down with an assortment of bracelets and rings, staying his action. "We wish to see the body," she said in a hoarse but imperious voice.

It was clear who wore the pants in the royal family, because the meathead stepped away from me and opened the coffin. Dead Chad rested peacefully within, his face a mask of tranquility. I recalled the horrors he had done and wished I could kill him all over again.

"The wound," said another elder. "We would see the death blow."

Kallan pulled Chad's corpse out without showing any excessive reverence for the dead and stripped off the clean linen shirt with which someone at Abaddon had dressed the body. He twisted Chad around, exposing the bullet wounds in his neck and shoulder.

"This weakling lies about honorable combat!" Kallan roared as he held up the stiff's shirtless body. "The human weapon was discharged into the prince's back."

The hall erupted in angry shouting. I thought the gathered fae mob might surge forward and tear me to bits. Lady Rhoswen raised her slender hand, and they quieted down in short order. These rulers seemed to enjoy a tremendous amount of control over their subjects. Must be pretty sweet not being overly prone to any possible revolution and all that.

"Explain yourself, Conrad of Brent," said Rhoswen in a silvery voice.

"The only reason I shot him from behind is that he ran from a fight," I said. There was a murmur of indignation, but Rhoswen raised her hand again and it died down even more quickly. I pointed to the body. "Look, Chad here was not a good guy. He came to our world to hunt innocent people for sport. He killed *children*, and there was nothing honorable about the way he did it. I hunted him for months, and when I finally cornered him, he tried to run away, so I had to shoot him. I don't regret it."

"Our cousin's indiscretions against your inferior race do not matter," said Kallan. He placed Chad's body back in the coffin in a manner that seemed gentle and almost tender. "He was slain dishonorably by human hand, and it is, therefore, our sworn duty to exact vengeance upon humankind." He held up his right fist in a motion that, I recently had to learn, indicated a "yes" vote for whatever it is he was proposing.

One by one, three of the elders raised their fists in assent.

"My husband has been advocating for this war since long before the passing of Chaedde," said Rhoswen.

Husband? I thought back to the way the two of them looked at each other and noticed a pair of matching woven armbands on their wrists. Chulsky's information must've been out of date. Sometime recently, these leaders of opposing factions had gotten hitched. The implications of this weren't good at all.

"Even so, he is right," Rhoswen continued. "The death of a royal prince cannot be ignored." She raised her fist, as well.

Five of the seven royals voted for vendetta. Only one of the elders and the toddler on the seventh throne didn't raise their fists, but neither attempted to argue the point, either. Still, there was a reason Chulsky had sent me here. I had a card left to play.

"Your beef is with me, but it cannot be with humanity," I said with as much gravitas and conviction as I could muster. "Because Chad was not offed by human hand."

I used the trick I had learned from the trickster god Dolus to reveal my true aura in all its glory. It sparkled with otherworldly colors. This time the hall fell silent even without Rhoswen's orders. I could hear Moira mutter "holy shit" from where she stood, far enough behind me to avoid blood splatter, should it come to that.

29

All the sidhe royals, including the toddler, looked at me with an entirely different level of interest. It was as though a mildly annoying frog that kept croaking loudly in their garden was miraculously transformed into a prince. A prince who, unlike the frog, was definitively an intelligent life form.

"You are a celestial," said one of the geriatric royals. It was more of a statement than a question, but that's not how I chose to interpret it.

"There are many names for what I am." What I *was*, really. But they didn't need to know that. "A wise man from my realm once proclaimed that one should never deny it when asked if one is a god. So, yes. I'm a celestial."

Although the aura had already made the fact abundantly clear, my words set off another round of murmurs in the hall. Even this assemblage of ruthless killers was impressed by the sort of power being a celestial implied.

"You cannot hold mortals responsible for my actions," I said, raising my voice to be clearly heard over the background noise.

Kallan stepped toward me once again, and we studied each other for a long moment. A range of emotions played out on Kallan's face. The war he so badly wanted seemed out of his grasp, and the enemy he thought he could bully with impunity had bared sharp, deadly claws. The wise course of action would be to agree with my interpretation of things and to save face, but when was I ever lucky enough to square off against beings who chose wisdom over valor?

"Yes," Kallan said slowly. "Humans are not to blame." He stared me in the eye. "But you are!" He untied what looked like a narrow silk handkerchief from around his right bicep and tossed it at my feet. The crimson cloth fluttered in the air. "I challenge you to the Kra'Ga!"

The fae behind me roared in support of their champion. Even the royals were agitated, leaning forward and grasping the arms of their unadorned thrones. Rhoswen was on her feet, all her past composure gone, looking like a concerned wife of a drunken husband who'd challenged a superior brawler at a bar. Except I wasn't the superior brawler in this analogy. I was just bluffing.

Middlings were the ugly ducklings of the gifted society. They could perceive magic, but had no power of their own, forced to rely on artifacts powered by the gifted. I'd recently learned that an upside of being a middling was that they were god larvae—capable of ascending to godhood under special and extreme circumstances. I had ascended briefly but had to give up all that power and become a middling once more in order to save my city and the life of a dear friend.

"Well?" Kallan prodded me.

Chulsky had warned they would ask me to participate in a ritual where various forms of payment would be extracted for daring to best Chad in combat. To my knowledge, no part of that ritual involved any sort of a challenge. Uncertain of what was expected of me, I muttered, "I was told there would be Contrition Rites."

This elicited another round of ugly murmurs. Before things got out of hand, Moira approached, careful not to step between me and the angry sidhe royal.

"Please forgive this visitor's actions, for he's ignorant of your ways," said Moira. "May I request a brief respite to explain to this, ah, person what is being asked of him?"

Kallan's frown deepened further and the veins on his neck bulged even more, two events which a moment ago I would've sworn were physically impossible. Still, he took half a step back. "You may educate him," he told Moira. "Quickly."

Moira leaned toward my ear and whispered, "A god? Seriously?"

"This is really not the time," I said. "Explain this Krav Maga thing. I'm not much of a martial artist."

Moira sneered. "It's Kra'Ga, you dolt." My godhood was clearly not going to get her to treat me with any additional respect. "You'll be fighting in a special trance state using swords but also memories. The power of your memories and experiences can be used like a psychic attack during a Kra'Ga. Whatever the creepy elf shows you, you have to show an even more impressive memory, and you keep going until one of you can't top the other's life experience."

"I see. So it's a rap battle but with memories?"

Moira thought for a moment. "This comparison is crude, but not inaccurate."

"So what are the swords for, then?"

If looks could kill, the one Moira gave me would do the job better than any sword. "For murdering your opponent while your psychic dream attacks keep them off balance," she said.

31

"This is a duel to the death then?"

Moira nodded.

"And if I decline?"

"Then your god powers better have enough juice to take out the lot of them, because the entire sidhe court will judge you dishonorable and try to kill you."

"About that." I lowered my voice to a barely audible whisper. "I left my god powers in the human dimension."

"Of course you did." Moira sighed. "I think I liked you better when I thought you were a mudlark. At least then your ineptitude made logical sense."

I was a middling—a mudlark—once again. A souped-up aura and the ability to conceal or reveal it at will was my only fabulous parting gift from the stint on the godhood game show. But I wasn't about to reveal that, and not to Moira of all people. My new aura was a fabulous tool for bluffing and avoiding the fight, but it was the kind of bluff that could only work until somebody called it. Kallan had done just that. At least my handwavium about my powers only working on Earth had seemed to convince Moira. After all, how would she or most anybody else know the rules of celestials?

"I'll have to fight him man to man," I said. "Or man to fae. Whatever. Unless you can think of a better solution?"

Moira shook her head. "You have to win to survive. And without special powers of some kind, I wouldn't bet on you to do that."

"I'm used to being underestimated," I said with a bravado I didn't feel. "How do I accept the terms and conditions of this duel?"

"Stomp your foot on his armband and declare that you're ready," said Moira. "I wish I could say it was nice knowing you. You should've never volunteered to come here. You so-called good guys are lemmings. Your need to do what you deem to be the right thing despite all rhyme or reason will be the death of you every time."

"Aww, it's gratifying to realize you care. But before I go gently into that good night, I'm going to need one more favor."

"What is it?" asked Moira.

"It's a swordfight, and I seem to have only brought a pen." I glanced meaningfully at the scabbard hanging at her side.

Moira's hand landed protectively on the hilt of her cutlass. She had named the curved sword Kindness and carried it everywhere. I could tell that she hated the idea of lending it to me so much more than she hated the idea of watching me get chopped to pieces.

She exhaled, drew Kindness from its scabbard, and gave it a loving look. "If you chip the blade, I will reanimate your corpse so I can kill you all over again," Moira said as she handed me her most prized possession.

I hated to admit it even to myself, but as necromancers went, Moira O'Leary was all right.

CHAPTER 4

I was no great swordsman, but I'd had cause to fight with every manner of weapon and random item that I could get my hands on over the years. Never did manage to take down a monster or a bad guy with a sharpened pencil, John Wick style, but this just gave me something to strive toward in the future. I could handle a cutlass well enough. I hefted Kindness to get a better feel for its weight and balance, then stepped forward.

There was an ugly susurration from the crowd. Bringing a steel blade to a fae fight was probably a grave insult in and of itself, but I didn't have anything else I could stab Kallan with that he wasn't allergic to, and I didn't especially care anymore. The time to avoid an indelicate social *faux pas* had passed the moment I was challenged to a duel to the death. I stepped onto the silk armband and made a grinding motion with the toe of my shoe.

"I accept your challenge. Moreover, I'm going to use only mortal powers to fight you. To do otherwise would be dishonorable."

I was laying it on thick, but I figured there was no reason to make others question why I didn't squash the princeling with my celestial powers. Plan for what will happen if I survive, not for a horrid impending death, I always say.

"Then I will defeat you sooner." Kallan sounded unimpressed by my generosity. "But I will still kill you slowly."

"Lovely sentiment. I'll be sure to mention your hospitality when I review this trip on my travel blog," I said.

Kallan was not in the mood to trade barbs. He sneered, brooded, and generally looked like an extra-tall Prince of Denmark who'd spent years pumping iron in the gym. Well, maybe not iron, him being a fae and all, but you get the idea.

While my opponent channeled his inner goth, a trio of other fae prepared the dueling grounds. Their incantations made the floor of the hall glow faintly. Sigils appeared on the surface of the smooth floor as if they'd always been there, creating a circle roughly the size of a boxing ring. A shimmering barrier extended upward and enclosed the battleground within a fishbowl, its edges clearly visible but translucent enough for the audience to enjoy the unobstructed view of the violence.

"Within the sphere of Kra'Ga your memories have the power to hurt," said one of the trio. "Do you understand?"

"I think you mean to say 'the power to hurt *other people.*' Other than that, yeah, I get the gist of it."

The fae didn't so much as crack a smile. None of them appreciated my wisecracking ways. Note to self: never try performing stand-up at a sidhe comedy club.

The trio retreated, and the sigils flared brightly before growing dim again. I took that for the equivalent of a microwave ding, indicating that the Hot Pocket of memory combat inside was cooked to perfection. I gripped Kindness tighter and stepped into the fishbowl.

Kallan grinned savagely as he entered from the opposite side. His sword appeared to be carved from a huge chunk of obsidian. Volcanic glass is razor sharp but too brittle to make a good blade, a problem I was certain the fae had solved using enchantments.

The sidhe prince focused without preamble and a memory appeared in my mind's eye. Kallan was in a clearing, surrounded by three opponents. He held his obsidian blade in one hand and a serrated bone dagger in another, wielding them with incredible speed and agility. Although his enemies appeared equally adept with their weapons, he not only held his ground but advanced on them, inflicting wound after wound. He dodged a thrust of a short, wicked-looking blade and buried his dagger in the heart of the nearest combatant. I realized that his memory was not only playing out in my mind; it was projected onto the outer surface of the dome, for all of Kallan's bloodthirsty buddies to enjoy.

I felt like I'd been kicked by a horse. The militant memory blew right past the protections my plethora of amulets and charms afforded me. Perhaps it was the wrong kind of magic, or perhaps the dome nullified any such protections. Either way, I had no idea how to stop the onslaught, or if it could be stopped at all, so I did the only thing I could under the circumstances and counterattacked.

I focused on the memory of the patchwork monster I once fought in the lair of a mad alchemist in Cypress Hills. A misshapen creature made from the flesh and body parts of several humans and animals howled and clawed at me while I stabbed and stabbed with a tiny scalpel. I focused on the stink of formaldehyde and the howling sounds the monster made with its several mouths. The alchemist had used the scalpel to create the monster and it was the only tool that could hurt it without its body magically healing itself as quickly as I could inflict the damage. The memory superimposed itself onto Kallan's, though some of the faded images of his memory could still be seen through it.

The disturbing way the monster looked, sounded, and smelled would've shocked most people, but it barely served to ease Kallan's own attack. He had clearly seen and fought worse, which meant I'd have to do better.

As we traded memory blows, I quickly realized I was outmatched. Kallan was a warrior who had lived and fought for hundreds if not thousands of years. The memories of his victories were like a movie montage of blood and gore, featuring battlefields under alien suns and dueling grounds in caverns lit only by malignant magic. How could my years at the Watch match up against that?

I tried my best anyway because upping the ante on past adventures seemed to be the only way to lessen the pain inflicted by those memories. The layer cake of gore and destruction projected itself onto the dome.

I knew that I'd have to change tactics to survive, so I advanced on Kallan, who until then had remained stationary at the other edge of the dome, and swung Kindness at his neck.

Kallan parried and dodged, but his concentration faltered briefly. The waves of pain I was feeling abated somewhat. We traded blows and memories both. Kallan was not as good a multitasker as me, but his centuries of combat experience partially made up for that shortfall. I still wouldn't have said we were evenly matched, only that I was now losing a little more slowly.

I ached all over and bled from several shallow cuts. Kindness had only connected once, and the small wound on Kallan's forearm didn't slow my opponent at all. I should have been terrified, and I was, but I was also angry. Is this how I was to die? In gladiatorial combat against a fae, with only a rogue necromancer possibly rooting for me? Anger and desperation welled up within me, and it fueled the memory of the first time I died, back on that ship in the Mediterranean, and the memory of a newly minted goddess of death bringing me back to life.

Kallan staggered and retreated, his face twisted in pain. The memory projection was vivid, powerful enough to supersede all previous images. The psychic pain inflicted by his memories receded and gave me a chance to recover. I rejoiced. It seemed memories of impressive deeds that extended beyond combat could also be wielded as weapons in this ritual. This gave me a fighting chance.

Kallan wasn't out for the count. Another memory washed over me, hitting harder and more painfully than any that preceded it. In it, Kallan tamed and rode a tentacled sea beast the size of a half dozen blue whales.

I struggled to focus and conjured up the memory of floating over Brooklyn in armor made of Atlantean crystal, squaring off against Willodean, with both of us discharging amounts of magical energy inconceivable to a regular gifted.

The power of this memory brought Kallan to his knees. After all, he couldn't possibly compete with battling a goddess of death to a draw.

He proved me wrong.

As I stepped toward him, he parried Kindness with his obsidian blade and unleashed an equally powerful memory. In it, his younger self led an army of fae warriors and sorcerers against a god of war.

The god was naked from the waist up, save for a pair of gauntlets on his wrists engraved with an intricate design. There was both something familiar and something alien about the god's appearance. His posture was arrogant and regal, and I fought against the impulse to drop to my knees at the very sight of him, even through the prism of Kallan's memory. Muscles bulged on his perfect body that looked like a Greek marble statue. Long, wavy red hair and a thick beard framed a tanned face that looked Persian or perhaps Assyrian. The god stood atop a verdant hill tossing lightning bolts and fireballs at his fae assailants. If a projectile connected—and in many cases, it did—the unfortunate mortal burned to a crisp. And yet, the fae kept coming. Heedless of personal survival they swarmed the god from all sides, attacking him with all manner of weapons and magic.

Kallan had been fast enough to dodge several fiery attacks, getting ever closer to the god until he was within striking distance. He swung a pair of glowing scythes at the god's back, but they only scraped uselessly against a force shield. The god turned toward him, but before he could complete the turn, Kallan tossed the scythes aside and drew what might have been a gem or perhaps a miniature star from his pouch. It burned so brightly with pure heavenly light that I squinted at the mere memory of it.

Young Kallan thrust the star toward the god. Surprise registered on the deity's regal face and then he blinked out of existence. It was abrupt, leaving Kallan alone at the top of that hill holding the shining star. Somehow, he knew—and through his memory so did I—that the god wasn't slain; he'd merely chosen to cede the battlefield. But Kallan also knew the great enemy wouldn't be back, at least not any time soon. The star had banished the god of fire and lightning and war from the fae realm.

Kallan held the star up higher and roared in triumph.

The memory, detailed and sharp as it was, lasted only a fraction of a second in real time. Yet it hit me with such incredible force that I nearly lost consciousness. Like my opponent, I staggered to my knees. There was no impressive fight, no life experience I could conjure up to upstage that. Kallan seemed to be in the same boat. We'd reached the apex of our past experiences, and each suffered the pain of the opposing memories, while our beaten-up physical bodies staggered to their feet, interlocked blades and pressed them against one another, relying on what remained of our respective strengths.

The images of our greatest battles also seemed to fight one another projected onto the outer surface of the Kra'Ga dome. They flickered and interposed as though they were in fact parts of the same memory, as though somehow the battle up in the skies above Brooklyn was taking place concurrently with the fae onslaught against the god of war on the ground below.

The fae prince was physically stronger than me. Ever so slowly the cutlass blade he'd blocked so near to his neck was being pushed away. Obsidian scraped against steel and, little by little, edged toward me.

I was too stubborn to give up. Through the psychic pain and the fire in my muscles, I pressed back, making the fae pay with effort and pain for every hard-won inch.

And then a melodious voice rang out through the hall. "Stop! I invoke the síocháin!"

The memory projections vanished along with the dome. The sigils on the ground faded out of existence. The psychic pain was gone. Now, it was just me and Kallan, locking regular, physical swords.

We looked each other in the eye, neither daring to disengage. Finally, I gave in. I didn't know who'd stopped the duel or why, but I knew that if we persisted, Kallan's superior strength and experience would eventually win out, and I'd be surely dead anyway. I had to trust that he would abide by whatever crazy tradition or rite was now being invoked.

I slowly eased up pressure and then lowered Kindness. The obsidian blade was now at my throat, its edge biting deep enough into the skin to draw a trickle of blood. There was murder in Kallan's eyes, but he held back. Slowly, reluctantly, he lowered his blade as well.

Kallan groaned in pain. It took visible effort for him to walk away from me. I slid to the ground, panting and bleeding onto the formerly immaculately clean floor of the hall.

Moira rushed over and cast a healing spell on me. I immediately felt better, though not quite well enough to try standing up. Instead, I handed Kindness to her, hilt first. "Good as new," I said.

An edge of her lip curled ever so slightly upward. She was about to say something but was preempted by an argument.

Kallan stomped over to the seventh throne and confronted the toddler. "What is the meaning of this interruption?" he demanded. He still bled from the wound on his arm but didn't seem to care.

"You're both worthy," said the toddler in that melodious voice that sounded childlike and yet far older than his physical appearance. "It isn't right for a pair of warriors who have defeated gods to engage in a Kra'Ga against one another."

"This is not for you to decide, Aelfric," said Kallan. "The seat of power you occupy is still warm from Chaedde's lifeblood. He deserves vengeance."

"And yet I occupy the seat now," Aelfric replied with the serene patience of a tiny Buddha. "I speak for my clain, and I say the warrior from the human realm came to us respectful of our ways. As Chaedde was one of us, it is the prerogative of my clan to see the visitor perform the Contrition Rite—and nothing more."

"Offense has been caused and blood has been spilled," said Kallan. "Your clan is entitled to the Rite, but my business with the godling is to be concluded afterward."

The toddler considered this, and for a moment I thought I was screwed. I didn't expect round two to go any better for me. Then the littlest royal took off his own armband, this one plum purple. For a moment there, I thought he was about to challenge the big strong warrior to another duel.

"In that case, I shall offer our guest protection and hospitality," said Aelfric. "Surely the friendship of my clan is more important to you than petty vengeance, Cousin?" The toddler then looked at me. "Approach, Conrad of Brent."

I stood up with Moira's help and leaned on her as we made our way toward the seventh throne.

Aelfric offered me his armband. "Put this on. So long as you wear this, you shall remain safe."

I nodded gratefully. It felt odd to be indebted to someone who looked like he might not have been potty-trained yet.

"May the blessings of light be upon you," Aelfric recited as I donned the armband. "Light without and light within. And in all your comings and goings, may you ever have a kindly greeting from them you meet along the road."

Kallan watched this, his expression sour. "The moment you remove this, godling, my cousin's generous offer of protection will expire. Whatever realm you are in, wherever you might hide, my clan will come for you and finish what we started today."

"It's a date then." I grinned at the sidhe warrior through the pain.

"The Contrition Rite must still be completed," said Aelfric. "You must offer reparations to our clan for the death of Chaedde. A payment in treasure, pride, time, and blood is expected from you."

I was about to ask the kid if he accepted Mastercard when Moira inserted herself between us.

"We humbly offer this payment in treasure." She fished out a diamond the size of her fist from the satchel she wore and offered it to Aelfric.

The toddler looked sideways at the inhabitants of the other thrones, and they nodded.

"We find the payment in treasure acceptable."

Personally, I wouldn't have appraised Chad's life as being worth much more than a six-pack of warm domestic beer, but there was something about being surrounded by a bunch of murderous dimension-hopping blade masters that, on occasion, made even me keep my thoughts to myself.

Moira nudged me. "Get on your knees and beg forgiveness."

I groaned. I considered myself to be a prideful guy and bending the knee in front of anyone wasn't fun for me, but I supposed that was the point. I lowered myself to my knees.

"I humbly beg the court's forgiveness," I said.

"He's not repentant," croaked one of the elders.

"He's not humble," said another.

They were both right.

"Humility comes in many forms," said Rhoswen. "It is especially difficult for a celestial to let go of their pride. And yet, this one has traversed the in-between to honor our traditions. He accepted my husband's challenge without hesitation and was honorable in offering to fight him on equal terms. Is that not a sufficient example of his pride being cast aside when it mattered most?"

The royals looked to each other, considering her words. After a pause, Aelfric said, "We find your payment of pride acceptable."

Moira reached into her satchel again and produced a tiny plastic hourglass. "We humbly offer the payment of time, with the two of us sharing the burden as traveling companions through the in-between."

Again, the sidhe lords shared a look, deciding. I had no idea what was special about that hourglass, which looked like it came from a dollar store shelf, but I didn't especially care. If Chulsky's trinket was going to satisfy their ritual, all the better.

"We find your payment of time acceptable," said Aelfric, as he took the proffered hourglass. The tiny device looked just right in his small hands.

Blood was up next, and I sure hoped Moira had a vial of pig blood in that satchel.

Aelfric said, "As to the payment of blood, Conrad of Brent has already bled for us during the Kra'Ga. With a promise of more to come." He glanced meaningfully at Kallan. The others made no protest. "We find your payment of blood acceptable," he added.

"The Contrition Rite is complete," said Kallan. "It is best you leave our realm promptly and never return."

"Fine by me." I was happy to get the hell out of there, even if I didn't relish the upcoming trek back to the sylvan area we'd initially arrived at.

Aelfric flicked his little hand and a portal opened in front of me. "Fare thee well, Conrad of Brent and Moira the Multifaced," he said. "Go home."

"Moira the … . Did he just call you two-faced?" I asked Moira.

She made no reply as she stepped through the portal.

I followed.

CHAPTER 5

THE portal dumped us in midtown. I was able to orient myself quickly, because the Empire State Building loomed only a few blocks away. I was freezing. Also, light snow was falling.

"What in the world?" I looked around for signs of magic being used. It doesn't snow in New York in September. Not via natural means. September is still T-shirt and shorts and air conditioner on full blast weather.

There were no signs of magical tampering. Pedestrians hurried past us—no one but a tourist walks leisurely in midtown—all wearing winter clothes.

"Excuse me," I hailed a businessman in an expensive wool top-coat and Italian shoes who was power walking down the street a tad less rapidly than the rest. "Could you tell me today's date?"

The man looked at me like I was crazy. Thankfully I was wearing my all-seasons trench coat and not the T-shirt and shorts. And I wasn't asking him for money. But Moira stood next to me, with her sheathed cutlass, wearing her medieval getup.

"I'm trying to write a check," I explained lamely, feeling every bit like a cliché from a time travel movie.

"It's February 19," he told me without stopping and picked up his pace.

How could that be? Over five months appeared to have passed since we traveled to the fae realm. Unless …

"What year?" I shouted after the pedestrian, successfully completing the time traveler cliché, but he kept on walking.

"Relax, Conrad," said Moira. "It's been months, not years."

I took in her calm demeanor, and the fact that she was a bit tense behind that swagger, and it all clicked.

"The payment of time. That was literal, wasn't it? You knew they would steal time from us from the get-go, didn't you?"

"I knew that would happen if they didn't choose to kill you instead," said Moira. "I charged Daniel an appropriate fee to have split the burden with you; otherwise, you'd have ended up returning in midsummer."

The portal Aelfric had so conveniently opened for us back in the Land Under the Mound must've been what did it. I should've paid better attention to those public service announcements, admonishing one not to get into strange portals ….

I shivered, and not just because of the cold. I'd been gone five months, my responsibilities to the Watch once again abandoned, no notice given. Just the other day I'd promised John that I would be there for him, to protect my borough and help normalize things in the absence of Mose. Just the other day, for me. As far as any of my friends knew, I had run off on Abaddon business, again.

"Why didn't you warn me?" I asked, exasperated. "I should've known. I could've made arrangements—"

"That's between you and Chulsky." Moira looked me in the eye with a smirk, as though daring me to try to blame her. "I performed the job I was hired for. Flawlessly, if I do say so myself." If the cold bothered her, she showed no sign of it. "Besides, are you saying you had something better to do than saving the entire world from a fae invasion?"

As angry and disappointed as I was, I had to admit that she had a point. Had I known about this price, I would've grumbled and complained, but I would've ultimately gone anyway. But I was still angry. I wanted to lash out against the injustice of the situation. I glowered at Moira bitterly as she stood there, looking comfortable in her own skin.

"I could've warned the few people in this world that care about me. But you wouldn't know anything about that, would you?"

Moira looked like she had just been slapped. The unflappable, fearless rogue, oozing bravado and swagger, always so self-assured and confident, dropped the façade. Her eyes widened, her expression soured. Suddenly she looked gaunt and haunted rather than like a card sharp in a poker game, perpetually hiding a pair of extra aces up her sleeve. She crossed and uncrossed her arms.

"For a long time I've always thought you and I were the same," she said, her voice even and soft, without the usual drop of poison in the mix. "We both walk through the world alone. But I had my magic, and you were a pathetic mudlark forced to rely on trinkets, and that made me feel better about myself. Then you dropped the ruse and revealed that you were a god. I'm still having a difficult time with that, but in that moment I found a way to make myself feel superior, too. After all, if someone with so much power chose to slum it at the Watch and *his* life was so empty and unfulfilled, then surely I was doing all right for a mere gifted." Moira absent-mindedly brushed snowflakes out of her hair. "But then came the Kra'Ga. I watched memory after memory of battles where others came to your aid even if it meant risking their lives, and memories where you did the same for them, and I kept thinking, of all the associates and co-conspirators in my line of work, none would even consider taking those kinds of risks for me. Not now, not recently, not as far back as I can remember." The moisture on her cheeks was melted snow. I was pretty sure. "So now, I'm envious of you, Conrad, and I hate myself for it. I'm envious of the fact that you have friends. And knowing what I know now, understanding what I understand now, I'm sorry for not having warned you in advance about the time jump."

This outpouring of hers was so unexpected, I didn't quite know what to say. I thought about the people she'd seen in my memories. Terrie Winter and John Smith, my counterparts from Queens and Manhattan at the Watch who frequently found me mercurial and unreliable. Hercules Mulligan of New Jersey, who had been a close friend once but felt so betrayed by my keeping him in the dark about my being a middling, it had demolished our friendship. Mose, the leader of the Watch who'd done what he could to protect me as a middling and then given up his godhood and possibly his life in a bid to help me stop Willodean. And then there was Willodean herself, a one-time goddess of death whom I had loved enough to let go. Willodean had no memories left of me. They had been erased, wiped away as a kindness, to protect her from any danger, but mostly from the guilt of knowing what she had done. As to the others … . Not only was the list short enough to count on the fingers of a single hand, but did any of them still consider me a friend at all?

I did my best to shake off those doubts. For all the deplorable things she had done in the past, Moira was hurting, and I had no appetite for adding to her pain. Instead, I asked, "Sympathy or advice?"

"What?" asked Moira.

"It's a very wise thing Terrie Winter once taught me," I said. "When someone is going through a difficult time, they usually need one of two things from the people who are close to them, she would say. It's either sympathy—for someone to comfort and empathize with them—or advice, for someone to brainstorm with them and figure out possible solutions. The latter is also often something that can be difficult to hear. You offer the wrong of the two options and you stand an excellent chance of making the problem worse. So the thing to do in these situations is to straight up ask which it is the person would prefer."

I was feeling a little foolish, and my explanation was not nearly as smooth or convincing as the way Terrie had once explained the concept to me. Besides, it wasn't like Moira and I were close. But then, if I were to take her at her word, I might be as close to a friend as she had in the world.

Moira seemed to consider my words. We stood in the snow, together yet alone, with crowds of passersby moving around us like ocean currents past the shores of two uninhabited islands. When she finally spoke, it was barely audible.

"Advice," said Moira.

"All right," I said. Shrink to a rogue necromancer wasn't the job I was in any way qualified for, but it was the job I needed to do at the moment. "The way I see it, you find yourself in this situation because you're on the wrong side of things."

"Come again?" Moira blinked in confusion.

"Bad guys don't make good friends. Would you really expect someone from the Cabal to watch your back? Could you trust them to do it even if they offered? If you wanted to build any sort of bond with worthwhile people, you would have to be on the same side as those people, working toward similar goals. Which means, you would have to do good."

"What you call the good guys tend to be idiots who stick their heads out and subsequently get them chopped off." Moira was rapidly recovering her usual composure and acerbic speech pattern. "You're trying to do this *good* you speak of"—she made air quotes around the word—"and in the past few days you nearly got yourself slaughtered by Chaedde and killed in a duel by Kallan, got robbed of five months of life, and earned yourself a suspended death sentence." She pointed toward where the armband was, under my trench coat.

I nodded. "And yet here you are, wanting to be my friend."

Moira was silent for a while, again. When she spoke, it was in a soft, vulnerable tone. "And yet here I am, wanting to be your friend."

"We've got history," I told her. "Most of it bad. But you can make an effort, have a redemption arc. You can start doing good. It won't be easy, and it may not be fun, and you will have to choose to stick your head out for other people, but that's about the only way you can get anybody else to come around to the idea of sticking their head out for you."

"What you describe sounds a lot like karma," said Moira.

I thought about it. "I suppose it does. But perhaps it's more like Alcoholics Anonymous. It's neither easy nor quick, and you have to work on yourself every single day. No one is going to give you a medal for not having kicked a puppy that day. But your life can slowly come around, if you don't fall off the wagon. Just do the right thing, one day at a time."

"I'm not even sure I know what the right thing is," said Moira.

"I think you do. You just don't like yourself enough to believe you can do it. The self-absorbed, in-it-for-myself persona is easier to pull off when you convince yourself you're that kind of person."

Moira frowned. "Perhaps I should've gone with sympathy."

"Too late," I said. "I warned you that advice can be difficult to hear, but it's the truth."

"I might give it a go, for a spell," Moira declared. "See how I like it. I mean, why not. I've tried being evil and it was fun for a while but not especially fulfilling. Perhaps being good will suit me better. If not, I can always write it off as a *very* early midlife crisis." She grinned, the armor of bravado and self-assurance already reasserting itself around her. "Besides, what can possibly go wrong? I'm on the side of an actual god, even if he's slumming it as a mudlark."

I could've told her the truth. Keeping secrets hadn't exactly done wonders for my friendships in the past. If I truly wanted to set her on a path to becoming a good person, then perhaps sharing my secret would be a good start. But I still didn't trust her. For all I knew, she would change her mind the moment being a good guy turned out to be inconvenient or dangerous. So, I held my tongue, while also wondering what I should do to ensure that I still had any friends left of my own.

We had a difference of opinion next. I wanted to visit the Watch headquarters while Moira was keen on checking in at Abaddon.

"Even the good guys have to eat," she reasoned. "And they have the second half of my fee."

I gave in because I figured Moira wasn't anyone's favorite person at the Watch regardless of her newfound desire to rehabilitate. And—I had to be honest with myself—I didn't relish the verbal dressing down I was sure to receive from John as opposed to the praise Chulsky would surely lavish upon me. Finally, it was a short walk between the two locations. So I hailed a cab, thankful that I'd brought my wallet with me to fairyland.

Our driver was a lanky older man from Senegal, who didn't bat an eye at Moira's outfit or the sword dangling at her hip. To an average New York City cabbie, that wouldn't have made the top three of the strangest things he encountered on his shift. He nodded at the address, turned up the radio, and focused on the business of cutting off one's fellow man and getting cut off by them; the live-action video game of driving in midtown Manhattan.

The screen mounted on the plexiglass divider between the front seats and the back lit up, and played clips from the local news station, commercials, and other infotainment.

"The mayor held a press conference today, defending the wide range of sweeping changes his administration has been introducing to every aspect of city government," said the anchor's voice while the screen displayed the larger-than-life grinning mug of Bradley Holcomb.

"No way!" I leaned closer to the screen, staring gormlessly at the visage of one of the city's most prominent real estate tycoons. "This walking hairpiece commercial managed to get himself elected mayor?"

The anchor droned on about Mayor Holcomb's policies, but I was still too shocked to pay close attention.

"Are you sure we got back to the right timeline?" I asked Moira.

Moira appeared as dumbfounded by the news as I was. We'd first met when she was working for Holcomb on behalf of the Cabal, an experience none of us had found pleasant for a variety of reasons.

"Having spent enough time at his side, there are two things I will tell you about Bradley Holcomb with absolute certainty," said Moira. "First, he's a brilliant populist who can rile up the crowds and get himself elected to whatever position he wants, from rat catcher to prime minister. Second"—Moira frowned at the screen—"once elected he wouldn't be able to govern his way out of a paper bag."

The anchor finished his list of grievances and the image changed, showing Holcomb at a podium, facing a dozen microphones.

Moira beat me to the touchscreen, raising the volume on the display from tinny to relatively audible.

"Fake news media is falling all over themselves to report on the so-called controversies and cast my administration's reforms in the worst possible light," Holcomb complained. "They're still sore about the fact that I defeated the establishment candidates and for the first time in many decades our city is on a path toward complete recovery. They seem to forget that I'm one of the greatest business minds of all time, with many years' experience at the helm of a multibillion-dollar corporation. A job more challenging and more demanding than any public office position. The entrenched bureaucrats are not ready to deal with the likes of me! I will cut the rotten pieces out of the Big Apple, so that it may become unblemished again!"

Then the cab's infotainment show moved on to a segment about whichever Kardashian was inexplicably considered newsworthy that week.

"That was … something," I said. For once, I was at a loss for words. "Also, that's not how apples work."

Moira shrugged. "I don't suppose politicians are expected to make sense. No matter whether they utter the wisdom of the ages or speak utter nonsense, half the people will disagree with it, while the other half will cheer them on."

The cab cut off one of its brethren and double-parked on the corner of Broadway and Morris, a two-minute walk from the Abaddon building. Call me paranoid, but I pretty much never reveal my ultimate destination to cabbies or rideshare service drivers when I can help it. Makes it that much more difficult for anybody to trace my steps.

I paid, leaving a generous tip as one should any time a cabbie spares them unnecessary chatter en route. We climbed out and headed toward Bowling Green.

Alongside the Charging Bull statue, right in broad daylight, a pair of young men were harassing an older woman.

I would have thought this a mugging, but all three were gifted—their auras clearly visible to us as we approached. The taller youth was leaning toward the woman, invading her personal space. She shrank back, her winter jacket nearly pressing against the bull's bronze flank.

Moira and I glanced at each other, and we picked up our pace. She had this look of anticipation in her eye. It was easy to guess what she was thinking: she could chase off a pair of delinquents as her first act as one of the good guys.

The youth were intimidating their quarry, pointing at the ring she wore on her pinkie. White as the falling snow, the woman was struggling to take the ring off. Was this really something as banal as a mugging after all? With the gifted being relatively rare, the odds of such an event were low but—in New York—never zero. Could it be that the young delinquents knew the Watch wouldn't interfere in the affairs of the gifted and chose their victim accordingly? That seemed like way too much foresight on the part of petty criminals. Regardless and unfortunately for them, I wasn't exactly known for toeing the Watch orthodoxy, and Moira was under no such obligations at all.

The muggers were so intent on their victim, that they didn't realize we were there until we arrived within arm's reach and Moira spoke.

"Bugger off, louts," she declared in her best menacing voice.

The youths whirled to face us. The taller one sized us up while the shorter one gaped at us for a moment before reaching deep within his vocabulary reservoir and responding with, "Huh?"

"That's British for 'step away from the nice lady if you know what's good for you,'" I explained helpfully.

"Threatening an officer of the law is a serious offense," said the taller youth. He pulled on a chain around his neck and fished a badge out from under his jacket. He held the badge up in his right hand. "Move along, citizen."

I squinted at the unfamiliar logo and read the inscription. "What the devil is the Office of Preternatural Solutions?"

Both youths and the older lady all seemed confounded by this, as though I'd just asked them how many moons hung in the sky, or whether Chicago deep-dish counted as pizza.

"Tourists, eh?" said the shorter youth.

The taller one straightened up, overflowing with self-importance. "We're an enforcement organization established by the order of Mayor Holcomb. We oversee all matters pertaining to gifted activity in this city. We protect the city from any wrongdoing by the gifted."

"You don't say." I glanced at the elderly gifted woman who still looked terrified. She appeared neither protected, nor engaged in any manner of wrongdoing. "I thought the Watch handled that sort of thing."

Blood rushed to the shorter one's cheeks. "The Watch are a bunch of vigilantes and borderline criminals," he blurted out. "We'll carve their corruption out of the Big Apple so that it may become unblemished again!"

Was that some sort of code, or did this kid drink out of Holcomb's Kool-Aid fountain a little too much?

Moira stifled a giggle. Then she laughed, and went on laughing uproariously.

The shorter one's face turned a deeper shade of red. "What's so funny?"

"Oops," Moira managed through the laughter.

"What?"

She made an effort to pull herself together. "Office of Preternatural Solutions abbreviates as OOPS. Whoever named you lot is either incredibly dumb or exceedingly clever, and I can't figure out which."

"That's enough," said the tall one with the badge. "Go back to England or wherever you came from and leave us to our business."

The elderly woman's pleading eyes met mine.

"I don't think so," I said. "Not until we know why you're pestering this lady."

"She's in possession of an illegal artifact," said the tall one. "We must confiscate it."

"It's only a small charm that makes the temperature around me a few degrees warmer," said the woman. "It's harmless. Please, this is my grandmother's ring, and it has sentimental value to me." Her voice sounded as brittle as she looked.

"Ma'am, any artifacts that store and discharge magic are now strictly prohibited in New York City," said the wannabe magical cop.

I felt like I'd landed in the mirror universe version of the city, and the goateed evil Spock was bound to pop up at any moment. There was no way any mayor had the authority to do this. I didn't think there was anyone who had the authority to do this, any more than to tell the regular folks they'd have to give up indoor plumbing. While middlings like me were forced to rely on artifacts to perform any sort of magic, most of the gifted used them on a regular basis for all sorts of reasons.

"Now hand it over, or I'm going to have to bring you in." The youth held his hand out toward the terrified woman.

"I've heard enough," said Moira. She touched the side of the statue and effortlessly imbued it with more magical power than the two idiots together could muster in a week. "I'm a battle sorceress of the Cabal, and I command you to *bugger off, louts.*"

Animated by Moira's magic, the bronze bull lowered its head, pointed its horns at the wannabe cops, and bellowed a challenge.

The two looked like a pair of jackals who'd had their would-be feast interrupted by a lioness. The taller one let go of his badge. It hung crooked around his neck.

"Now. While you can still bugger off in one piece," said Moira. As if to underscore her point, the bull scraped a hoof against the cobblestones and flared its nostrils.

The two backed off rapidly. The taller one muttered something under his breath as they retreated. Whether it was curses or threats, he had a strong enough sense of self-preservation to mutter quietly and at a sufficient distance from Moira so she couldn't hear them.

"Battle sorceress of the Cabal?" I asked, once they disappeared around the corner.

She shrugged. "In case there's any actual muscle backing their despicable little club, let them direct their vitriol toward the equally nasty Cabal."

"Thank you," said the woman. "Those selfies have become insufferable!"

"Selfies?" I asked. The word sounded wrong, coming from a lady who predated smart phones by quite a few decades.

"It's an unflattering nickname for the Emersonians," said the woman.

I'd heard of language changing over time, but surely it couldn't have changed enough in five months for the New York slang to become so completely incomprehensible to me, could it? I stared at her in confusion.

"At first those no-goodniks tried to regulate or even shut down all the magic shops around the city, then persecute the better-known practitioners. Now they're invading homes of the gifted and stopping us in the street! Don't get me started on their so-called volunteer program! And to think, Holcomb and his commissioner of preternatural affairs condone this." The elderly woman sighed. "I can't believe I voted for him."

"Why don't you head on home and maybe hide that ring, lady?" said Moira.

She thanked us again, profusely. I half-listened as I tried to process all these changes happening in so short a time. I recalled the volunteer telling me about how the would-be mayor was going to reach out to the gifted. From where I stood, the hand he offered seemed encased in a war gauntlet. Holcomb wasn't gifted himself, which meant he had to rely on others to institute and oversee these enormous changes affecting the lives of the gifted community.

The woman we'd rescued was already on her way when I called after her. "Excuse me. Who's this new department's commissioner?"

She turned back. "Oh, let me think. He's not a flashy fellow." She furrowed her brow, struggling to recall the answer to my query. "Ah yes," she said. "Vaughn. I think his name is Vaughn."

CHAPTER 6

EVERYTHING seems smaller when your vantage point is at the top of the world. Everything, that is, except problems.

Abaddon's headquarters existed in many cities throughout the world, and all of them seemed to be the same building once you entered. They also contained a series of inner doors that let you step through into any of the other city 'branches' across the globe. No one I knew of claimed to understand what manner of sorcery or quantum physics—if the two could be reasonably distinguished between—made something like this not only work, but run like clockwork in perpetuity. Even during the brief time I'd spent being a god, that sort of thing was beyond my understanding, let alone ability.

Chulsky and I stood side by side in front of the enormous three-pane window that covered three of the four walls of his office and watched the major cities across three continents sprawled beneath our feet.

The pane on the left revealed a stunning view of nighttime Tokyo, lit up like a Christmas tree decorated in flashing and glowing neon. The pane on the right showed the London skyline painted orange and red by the diminishing rays of a setting sun. Before us lay New York City in all its glory, skyscrapers reaching toward the cloud-laden sky. Snowflakes danced in the air on their way down, swaddling the streets below in a white blanket.

I took another sip of the outrageously expensive scotch the CEO of Abaddon Inc. had poured for me. We had loads to talk about, but events and revelations had been coming at me so rapidly that I needed a quiet moment of reflection, and Chulsky seemed to intuitively understand this.

Moira was off somewhere on the second floor, collecting the balance of her fee from accounting. I had gone straight up to Chulsky. Spacious as his office was, it seemed far smaller than the spaces that occupied the floors below it, and it had no obvious egresses other than the elevator. This place had to have been designed by the spiritual ancestor of M.C. Escher.

I had been furious with Chulsky for sending me off in the manner he did without a warning, but in my heart of hearts, I knew I would've done the same in his shoes. As would Mose, or John, or Herc—anyone burdened with the responsibility of making unpleasant decisions in service of a greater good. So, instead of accusations and recriminations, I merely recounted the events of what—for me—had been the past few hours.

"Do not underestimate the gravity of what the armband you wear represents," Chulsky told me when I was finished. "You've been marked for death by beings who are as dangerous as they are capricious. I'm going to have some of my best people look into ways to break the curse, but I must caution you that, as of yet, I'm not aware of any means to circumvent it."

I took another sip. "So, what then? At some point I'm going to need a shower, and I feel as though I've passed that point hours ago."

"You must shower, sleep, even fornicate with the armband on," said Chulsky. "You can remove it for a few moments so that you may readjust or tighten it around your upper arm, but if the material is cut or if it remains separated from your arm for much longer than a ten-heartbeat span, its magic will call forth the avenging sidhe." Chulsky frowned into his scotch glass. "The material is more resilient than it looks, but given the lifestyle you lead, I'm concerned that you may damage or lose it by accident. In fact, I believe Kallan may be counting on this."

"I shall add this to my rapidly expanding list of problems," I said.

"I promise, resolving this will be a priority for my research team," said Chulsky.

"Speaking of promises." I downed the rest of the scotch and placed the empty glass next to the decanter. "You swore you'd tell me what it was Abaddon, Inc. did, for real. And as much as I need that shower, I want my payment in information as badly as Moira wants her payment in gold, or bitcoin, or whatever it is you use to pay people like her."

"Of course." Chulsky also set down his glass. "Simply put, Abaddon was created to mediate conflicts between Heaven and Hell."

I gaped at Chulsky. "Literal Heaven and Hell?"

Cosmology is a tricky thing in a world where gods walk among mortals. Sure, demons existed, but it was a word one used for horrific and powerful monsters. To the best of my knowledge, they weren't tied to any particular belief system. As for angels, the only kind I knew appeared in the Victoria's Secret catalog.

"It's complicated," said Chulsky. "We actually prefer the terms On High and Down Below but the idea is the same. You've got forces that are generally considered to represent light, and those who stand for darkness. There are celestials that are far more powerful than those who ascend from middlings. Those celestials create beings of immense power, who in turn serve their interests and follow their philosophies. The lowest forms of such beings manifest on our plane of existence. Angels and demons are a simplistic vernacular, but it gets to the crux of the situation."

"Let's say for the moment that I get it. And, believe me, saying so is a considerable stretch. How does one mediate between beings that are the polar opposites of each other? I thought their idea of conflict resolution was for the two teams to eventually meet at the base of Mount Megiddo and duke it out until one side or the other wins the coveted Armageddon Cup?"

Chulsky's lip curled up into an almost-smile. "*Eventually* is the key word here. Earth was originally created as the predestined battleground for this conflict. That had been the plan. But, over time, the archangels and the fallen lords have both come to feel that this place, and the species that populate it, is actually rather nice. It's got rainbows and volcanoes and such. Even snowflakes." Chulsky gestured toward the window. "You know how no two snowflakes are exactly alike? Humans are like that, too. Humans are frequently useful to both sides, and constantly fascinating. So, they keep delaying Judgment Day, and it is my learned opinion that they will continue to delay it indefinitely."

"That is … unexpectedly sweet, actually," I said.

Chulsky nodded. "Quite so. Having said that, you must understand that each side contains incalculable groups and factions. The nature of each group is as pugnacious and parochial as it has been since the beginning of time. Thus, someone had to ensure the lower-level entities in either camp wouldn't escalate their grievances into an all-out war and initiate the Armageddon no major player truly wants."

I rubbed at my temples. "In other words, you get to be the adult in the room and ensure the children don't break their toys or set the playground on fire?"

"Yes, there was a desperate need for such an arbiter, one respectful of both sides yet beholden to neither. Ultimately, the archangels and the fallen lords created me, and they imbued me with the necessary wisdom and power to maintain a careful balance between their rank and file."

I held up my hand. "Excuse me, do you mean to say they created Abaddon?"

Chulsky's lips stretched into a pretty fair approximation of the Mona Lisa. "That, too."

"You're telling me I've been drinking scotch with a being jointly created by Heaven and Hell thousands of years ago in order to play referee in their reindeer games?"

Chulsky shrugged. "You're a biological machine made of meat and stuffed with free will that operates on fuel made of calories, who has managed to ascend to a higher state of existence and voluntarily went back to meat form. Is that any less peculiar?"

"Touché, referee," I said.

"I'm more a barrister than a referee," said Chulsky. "I have no power over the factions. Rather, I mediate between them relying mostly on the fact that neither side wants for things to get out of hand, regardless of their posturing."

"I think the term you're looking for is 'marriage counselor.' But then, how do the fae fit into this? Last I checked, those tall brutes wear neither crosses nor pentagrams."

"Over time, my mandate has been gradually expanded. Since the goal is to prevent the destruction of this planet, which my joint creators so enjoy, it seemed only reasonable that I would try to forestall *any* possible apocalypses, regardless of whether the root cause happened to be the demons, the fae, or the upstart humans thinking it might be a good idea to split the atom." Chulsky pointed to the window again, each pane teeming with life. "All this is a long way from a few thousand uplifted monkeys hunting mammoth and painting graffiti on cave walls. The apocalypses are increasing in frequency. It's frankly become a handful. I need qualified, resourceful, fearless people to help thwart the disasters to come." Chulsky leveled an earnest gaze at me. "People like you, Conrad."

All that sounded flattering, but I couldn't shake the feeling of being the poor schmuck on the precipice of a hero's journey. Like Chulsky was about to hand me a cursed ring, or a magic sword, or some other pain-in-the-ass token that would send me tumbling down the rabbit hole of a dangerous epic quest at great personal inconvenience and discomfort. A fate I'd very much like to avoid, and to also unsubscribe from all future offers, please and thank you.

"Let me get this straight," I said. "You need the guy who's been helping you out for nearly a year now, even without knowing those pesky little details? That seems like an overly dramatic pitch given our already amicable working relationship, doesn't it?"

"I'd like for you to come work at Abaddon full time. Leave your position at the Watch. Quit chasing after the petty criminals in your borough and focus on the big-picture problems instead."

I looked at the panorama of New York City spread out before me. It was out there, in the streets, where I felt the most myself. Tracking down rogue sorcerers and shape-shifting monsters, rather than negotiating with fae royals or placating angels.

"I'm no diplomat," I said. "My place—"

Chulsky held up his hand. "Do not give me an answer now. What I ask is that you absorb the information I've given you and consider it. Protecting the people of this city, of your borough, is a noble endeavor. But you can't make the sort of difference in a lifetime of service at the Watch that you could in a year of working here." Chulsky straightened his tie and tilted his head slightly as he gauged my reaction. "As to diplomacy, you say you're not sufficiently subtle, and you're right."

Not quite what I'd said, but sure, I could live with that assessment.

He went on, "Different situations require different approaches, varying degrees of finesse. My job is to assign the right agent to each task. In fact, would you consent to handling the sort of assignment I had in mind for you next, as a freelancer again?"

I frowned. This was the time to batten down the hatches and refuse the call to adventure. To return the messenger owl back to sender. To turn the geriatric pipe-smoking wizard away from my front door. But, I couldn't help wanting to *know*. Curiosity would be the end of me. If I were a cat, even nine lives wouldn't have been enough to make up for all the times I stuck my nose where it didn't belong. So, true to my nature, I answered a question with several more questions.

"Another assignment already? Does this involve pursuing fae serial killers? Or throwing myself at the mercy of fae royals? Or anything whatsoever to do with the damn fae? Because if so, then there's the matter of five months' worth of accumulated weekends I'd like to use up."

"I assure you, it does not," said Chulsky. "This is much more along the lines of Abaddon's primary focus and, in fact, will be of a special interest to you. A faction of On High and a faction of Down Below have both laid claim to the estate of a recently deceased human, and are highly intent on being the first and only group to collect it. Each faction appears quite willing to escalate if they don't get their way. As both groups are located in your city, a direct conflict between them would turn the streets into their battleground. We very much want to prevent that."

No big deal, just get in-between angels and demons, and make them play nice with each other. Delivering a cursed ring to a faraway volcano sounded like a way safer quest than that.

"I'm all for preventing carnage in the streets. But I take it that's not what you meant when you mentioned the special interest part?" I asked.

"The estate in question is a house in South Brooklyn. The house is so well-warded that neither side has been able to break through. Yet."

Chulsky had piqued my interest, and he knew it. A house located practically in my own backyard so well protected that neither angels nor demons could get inside? I definitely wanted to poke around and see those wards for myself.

"All right," I said, shoving the feeling of impending doom deep into a far corner of my psyche. "I'll consider taking that on. But I do have to check in at the Watch first. Say hi, let them know I'm alive, warn them about the evil lurking in City Hall, that sort of thing."

"An evil?" Chulsky asked. "I take it you aren't a fan of our new mayor and his clumsy attempts to interfere in the affairs of the gifted?"

"I'm not, but he's also not who I meant. Are you familiar with his head of the Preternatural Affairs department? A man called Vaughn?"

"I've heard the name in relation to that newly formed organization, but nothing further. He appears to maintain a low profile," said Chulsky.

"That's his thing," I said. "Vaughn used to be Marko Hanson's right-hand man at Nascent Anodynes International."

"Ahh. The biotech firm responsible for unleashing the middling plague last year," said Chulsky.

"The very same. We defeated Hanson, but Vaughn managed to slink away, only to re-emerge within the Holcomb administration."

Chulsky shrugged. "It appears he's a bureaucrat who is good at sidling up to those in positions of power. So what?"

"I don't think he's merely some pencil pusher with a penchant for landing himself cushy gigs. Nascent Anodynes grew from obscure to powerful and wreaked havoc on New York City before we managed to stop Hanson. And now Holcomb's administration and especially its OOPS goons are terrorizing the gifted community of this city, even if they're going about it in a different way. Could it be a coincidence that Vaughn is at the center of both webs? I think not."

Vaughn had also killed people in the process of escaping from the NAi compound. I supposed Chulsky would see this as a small problem, one for the Watch to deal with and beneath his notice. The thought didn't sit well with me.

Chulsky took a slow sip of scotch as he mulled over my words. "The trait NAi and the new city leadership seem to share is kakistocracy," he declared.

"The what now?"

"Kakistocracy is a system of government where the least capable and least competent individuals rise to the positions of power," Chulsky explained. "It is as common a problem in human societies as it is counterintuitive, and those governments and organizations led by the gifted aren't immune from it. Marko Hanson developed a powerful bioweapon against the gifted, and he deployed it in a foolish and crude manner that ultimately accelerated his downfall. Likewise, the Holcomb administration is attempting to control and manipulate the gifted in ways that are sweeping but also unsubtle and heavy-handed. It's not worth the effort to focus on opposing such regimes. They will inevitably cause their own destruction through ruinous incompetence."

"Except," I countered, "these empires of stupidity will also cause endless grief and suffering to countless people on their slow march toward collapse. Isn't it better to oppose them, to help accelerate the advent of their ruin, so as to spare people additional suffering?"

"It's a noble thought, but who will replace the kakistocracy you topple?" asked Chulsky. "What makes you think that the next mayor or governor or CEO will be better? That the next batch of leaders won't surround themselves with parasites like Vaughn, who have existed and thrived in all social structures since the dawn of civilization? This is where the Abaddon philosophy diverges from that of the Watch. Instead of slapping a Band-Aid on each of a thousand different wounds inflicted by small-minded villains, we stop the one villain who aims to chop off the head."

I shook my head, frustrated at Chulsky's aloofness and literal inhumanity.

"Those are not mere wounds. Those are human lives we're saving at the Watch. They may seem really small from your perch up here at the top of the world, but they're no less important to the people who live them."

"In time you will come to understand the importance of the big picture," said Chulsky.

In time. He was a being who had lived for millennia, who had been created for a purpose, who was perhaps more a complex magical artifact than a person. How could I expect him to think about time, about the value of individual lives in the same way as a human being? Did he expect me to be of like mind about such things, since I'd experienced a higher state of existence? Was that why Chulsky wanted me on his team so badly, because he saw a sort of kinship between us, both almost but not quite human? Both choosing to protect humanity, each on our own scale? Those questions deserved serious consideration, preferably in a comfortable armchair with a glass of something strong and well-aged. Definitely not while exhausted after having the crap beaten out of me in a fae version of a cage match.

"Get me the details of this case you want me to undertake," I said. "I'll consider it. And the rest of what you said."

"That's all I ask," said Chulsky.

As fatigued and overwhelmed as I was, there was one more figurative beating I needed to endure before I could finally go home to lick my wounds.

I headed to the Watchtower.

The Watchtower is a misnomer, because the headquarters of the Watch are actually located deep in the bowels of the Manhattan Municipal Building. As if the layers of wards and protections conjured by powerful gifted over the course of a century weren't enough, the existential despair of a skyscraper full of bureaucrats, and the petitioners they annoyed, cast a psychic pall of misery nigh-impenetrable by most magics.

My key card got me into the building, and the Watchtower protections allowed me safe passage downstairs. Either my compatriots had held out hope I was still alive, or they believed me dead and hadn't thought it necessary to bother expunging my credentials.

Imagine all the secret organization bases as portrayed in the movies. Spacious and well lit, bustling with activity, lots of shiny bits of futuristic tech scattered about for effect.

The Watchtower was nothing like that.

A handful of folks slouched at their desks, typing on computers that were out of date, but not so out-of-date as to seem retro-cool. Heaps of printouts lay atop filing cabinets, marred with an occasional coffee stain. The drip coffee maker in the corner produced a vile brew that was hardly suitable for consumption. Like all Watchtower equipment, the coffee maker was tamper-proof and magic-resistant, thus thwarting any attempts to improve upon the dismal fruits of its labor through sorcery.

Those not powerful enough to conjure a perfect brew out of thin air were reduced to venturing outside in search of the nearest Starbucks.

I marched past the desks. Their denizens ignored me. They seemed more downtrodden than usual—perhaps the doom and gloom from the higher floors was getting to them. More of the desks were empty than usual. I headed for Mose's old office, now occupied by John Smith.

John was tall, but he couldn't hope to take Mose's place—literally or figuratively. Mose had been a giant of a man, four hundred pounds of muscle. John sitting behind Mose's massive desk looked like a toddler who'd climbed into his parents' computer chair.

Across from him sat Terrie Winter, my friend and closest ally in the Watch. They were deep in discussion, looking as somber as the office denizens I'd encountered on my way in.

They both turned as I entered. John's eyes widened. His mouth formed a silent "o." I couldn't tell whether he was happy to see me, or merely surprised.

Terrie visibly shed the weight of whatever concerns burdened her, and a relieved smile blossomed on her face. "Conrad! I knew you'd make it back. I knew it."

She rushed over, and there was so much genuine relief, warmth, and even exuberance in her expression, it melted all doubt about how my closest friends might feel about my return. She hugged me tight and I wanted that hug to last forever.

"You look terrible," said John once she had disengaged and returned to her seat.

I stifled a yawn. The exhaustion was really catching up with me. Perhaps the fear of my Watch compatriots rejecting me outright had kept the adrenaline pumping. With those concerns somewhat alleviated, even the insane changes New York City had undergone during my absence weren't enough to keep me going too much longer.

"Thanks. I feel worse."

He pointed to a chair next to Terrie's, and I eased myself into it with a grunt worthy of an octogenarian.

"He's right, you know. You look like you've been to hell and back," said Terrie.

"Close. It was actually fairyland." I launched into a recap of my field trip, and the small matter of a payment in time that had caused me to disappear for months.

When I got to the armband part, and the need to keep it safe and intact, Terrie interrupted.

"Gauze," she said.

"What?"

"You wrap the armband tight to the skin and then cover it with gauze as if it were a wound. That should keep it snug and well-protected against the sort of scrapes you get yourself into."

I nodded. My medicine cabinet at home was well-stocked with bandages, iodine, and other first-aid kit materials that I frequently needed in my line of work.

"I hope Mr. Chulsky follows through on his promise and finds a way to protect you from fae retaliation," said John. "I'm afraid our own resources are stretched thin at the moment."

"Let me guess, it's because of Holcomb and Vaughn, isn't it? Is that why the office is half-empty, and the people here look like they've just returned from a particularly unpleasant funeral?" I pointed toward the office door. "I've never seen a group of people more in need of a kitten poster that reads *Hang in There*."

"Got it in one." Terrie leaned forward in her chair, her expression hardening. "Those fascists have been making things difficult for us."

"They claim the Watch is a vigilante organization that has no right to operate within the city of New York," said John. "They do not recognize our authority or our mandate."

"What does that even mean?" I asked. "Since when does the mayor, or any civil authority for that matter, get to lord it over the Watch like that?"

"There is precedent." John sighed and pointed at the right side of his desk. Computer printouts, grimoires, and ancient scrolls were stacked in a precariously tall pile. "Over the centuries, the Watch has had to operate under circumstances where the civil government was aware of the gifted or were themselves gifted. Those precedents were the foundation of a considerable amount of case law, which I've recently had the displeasure to peruse."

"Please do not launch into a lecture about all that again," said Terrie. "Let me just bottom line it for the prodigal son." She waved toward me. "We cede priority to the local authorities if and when they happen to display sufficient wherewithal in understanding how the gifted community functions and offer a viable alternative in overseeing the areas covered by the Watch mandate. Or something like that. I'm paraphrasing the legalese."

"I've been back for all of five minutes, and I've already watched them *understand* the gifted community by attempting to rob an old woman of her family heirloom," I said. "How much more understanding are we expected to tolerate, exactly?"

"Oh, it gets way worse than that," said Terrie. "You've got a lot more catching up to do after you've availed yourself of a hearty meal and a warm bed."

"It comes down to an interaction between the gifted," said John. "We don't have to like it, but protecting gifted from one another was never part of the Watch mandate. Our goal is and always has been to ensure that the mundanes are protected from any gifted who might be tempted to use their powers to cause them harm. As best I can tell, the Holcomb administration has not neglected to carry out that responsibility." He sighed. "I've been keeping a very careful eye on their activities, hoping to prove that they're not capable of doing this properly, and that there is sufficient reason for the Watch to step in again. So far, they haven't given me the justification I need."

"We've been benched by Holcomb," summarized Terrie, "but that isn't the worst part of it. The exact same argument we're having has been ongoing for months throughout the Watch. Some of our people have quit in frustration. Others have moved out of New York to work in other Watch branches where the civil leaders are friendlier—or more clueless." She chewed her lip. "Others yet bought in to Holcomb's rhetoric wholesale and joined the OOPS and the Emersonians."

"Let me guess. Karl?"

Karl Mercado had been my one-time protégé who'd come to dislike me intensely. He was also no fan of middlings. I could see someone like him running, not walking, to sign up for the Vaughn goon squad.

Terrie nodded. "Karl, too. But also a surprising number of people we've worked with over the years who seemed nice and friendly and not at all like the type to endorse shaking down old ladies for their heirlooms."

She sounded hurt. Terrie always had a big heart. She genuinely liked the rest of us, believed in us, gave us second chances when we needed them, regardless of whether we deserved them. It would've been hardest on her to have some of those people run off and become bad guys.

"We've lost people to both sides," said John.

"Both sides?" I repeated.

"We can't fight the selfies, but the irregulars can," said Terrie.

"Herc's irregulars?"

This was a group of the gifted who'd coalesced around my friend Hercules Mulligan during the middling affliction. They weren't bound by the Watch orthodoxy. While Holcomb may have accused the Watch of being vigilantes, its leadership adhered strictly to the rules. The irregulars, however, fought the good fight like true vigilante superheroes.

"Herc is across the Hudson, organizing the resistance from New Jersey," said Terrie. "It got ugly really fast, with the irregulars and the selfies clashing in the streets. Preternatural Solutions went after the irregulars and their families. They've even been harassing the families of the folks who still come into work at the Watch despite John's neutral stance." She shot John a look that made it crystal-clear she disagreed with his policies, which had likely been the subject of their conversation when I entered.

"It's low-level harassment that never quite crosses the line for us to retaliate," John insisted. "We have to handle this carefully, not just for our own sake, but also for the sake of the Watch and its relationship with the people and leaderships of the cities we protect around the world."

"Mose would not sit idly by and—"

John slammed his fist against the desk. "Mose isn't here!" Usually so calm, cool, and collected, he looked trapped by the office, and so small in the enormous chair, figuratively and not just literally. "Someone has to make the difficult decisions, even when they're unpopular."

I'd also been thinking about unpopular decisions and the weight of command just recently. John took a deep breath and calmed himself. "You've turned down the heavy crown before, Conrad. Are you having second thoughts about that?"

"No," I said quickly. "The Watch doesn't need a hothead like me in charge. I'm not sure if you're right, John, but I'm certain I would impulsively follow where my heart leads, even if my brain knows better. The crown is where it belongs."

"At least you're back," said John. "Remember the promise you made to me the last time we talked?"

For John and Terrie it had been months. Tumultuous months, filled with challenges and heartbreak. For me, the promise I'd made to be there for him and the others, to take my Watch duties more seriously, was uttered only yesterday.

"I have to figure things out," I said. "So much has happened, and I don't know that I can stand on the sidelines and let Holcomb's goons terrorize the gifted. Perhaps my place is with the irregulars." I didn't even mention Chulsky's offer, or the new case he'd handed me. Even so, I watched disappointment play out on my friends' faces, and that hurt more than any damage Kallan had inflicted on me during the duel.

"There's only so many times you can walk out on us and still expect us to stand by you when you need it most," said Terrie after a long pause. Her voice was soft and imbued with sadness rather than anger.

"I promise, I'm not going anywhere. Either way, I will be here for both of you if you need me."

I intended to honor this promise this time.

Just as I had intended it yesterday.

CHAPTER 7

IT was dark outside by the time I finally made it to my Brooklyn apartment—not the one listed on my driver's license where I get my mail, but the secret one where I keep my various and expensive tools of the trade: an unassuming ground-floor two-bedroom in a private house, located on a sleepy residential block in Sheepshead Bay. Rows of nearly identical two-story brick houses built in the late 1940s dominated the neighborhood. It was always soothing to return here, to the normality of it all: people walking their dogs, kids playing in the snow, residents shoveling their driveways and dumping excess snow onto their postage stamp-sized front yards.

My home away from home was both well-warded and completely innocuous to the outside observer. And if I could pull that off, so could whoever warded the house that both the angels and demons wanted a piece of. Yet, they chose not to? But I digress.

I stumbled inside and breathed in warm, stale air. First, I checked my various protections to confirm no one—gifted or mundane—had messed with the place in my absence. Thankfully my landlord already believed that my job involved frequent and long-term travel. That and an up-front rent payment six months in advance kept him happy and his curiosity at bay. With all the upheaval going on around me, I was pleased that my safe haven remained safe for the moment.

I lay down atop my made-up bed to rest my eyes for a second—

—the persistent buzzing of a cell phone served as my wake-up call. Groggy, I turned and squinted at the grandfather clock across from the bed. The hands were roughly in the same position, and the heavy drapes cut off any light from outside, so I checked the phone. I had been asleep for over twelve hours.

The phone kept ringing, an unfamiliar number displayed on its screen.

I picked up and croaked, "Hello?"

A woman's voice I didn't recognize said, "Conrad?"

"Speaking," I managed.

"Oh, thank goodness you're back. Word got around that you popped in at the Watchtower yesterday, but we weren't certain."

Maybe I did know that voice. However, my brain cells appeared to have unionized and gone on strike overnight. At that moment, their demands included coffee, some breakfast, and more coffee, and I had to admit, I sympathized with their plight.

A few of the errant brain cells crossed the picket lines; enough to formulate the deep and meaningful response: "Who is this?"

"It's Aysha. Aysha Rehm."

I blamed my mutinous brain for failing to recognize her sooner. Aysha was a research librarian who specialized in studying ancient magic. She was also one of Herc's trusted lieutenants among the irregulars. Presumably, she was still working with him now that the irregulars had banded together again to oppose the new regime …. I blinked sleep out of my eyes. I really needed that coffee.

"Hi, Aysha." I continued to impress with my pre-caffeine conversational skills.

"We need to talk. Can we meet? I can be in Midwood in forty minutes."

Midwood was where I had my official residence. Even the irregulars did not know about the Sheepshead Bay apartment.

"Let's meet at the Bagel Beagle in forty-five?" I rattled off an address.

"See you there!" She ended the call.

70

I crawled out of bed and into a long, hot shower. It was a tad weird to keep the damn armband on, but what could I do? The thing soaked up water, and I had to gently squeeze it out afterward, careful not to rip the fabric. One wrong move would've resulted in the most pointless bathroom death since Elvis Presley.

I bandaged over the armband as Terrie had suggested, covering it in layers of gauze, snug and secure. Short of something with sharp, long fangs biting through my arm, the silk harbinger of doom wasn't going to be a problem for the moment.

I shaved and got dressed, feeling more of that sense of normality returning to my life. The power struggles and revelations around me were big and important to be sure, but I'd experienced all of that and more in the past, and I'd survived it all. In the aftermath of the middling affliction, I'd picked up the jagged, broken pieces of my life and somehow molded them together again into a semblance of what it had once been. My position at the Watch was something I had never expected to get back, but I had, and ultimately that made my life feel fulfilled and even happy at times. Despite the constant danger of patrolling the streets of my borough against deadly magical threats. Or, perhaps, because of it.

Why then would I even contemplate working for Abaddon full time? The idea wasn't something I was prepared to reject out of hand. Chulsky's cold equations were compelling: I could make a bigger difference, save so many more lives, operating at Abaddon's level and with full access to their resources. Was it merely the idea that dealing with fae from another dimension, angels, demons, and who knew what else, was a step out of my comfort zone? Was my desire to protect my native borough irrational when examined dispassionately?

I shook my head. These questions didn't have a clear-cut answer. At least, not without having downed an extra-large cup of java first.

A few minutes later, I drove to Midwood.

The Bagel Beagle serves the finest bagels in the world. It's the sort of an open-secret local spot that hasn't been discovered by the hordes of tourists the way Junior's or Katz's Deli have, but every bit as superb.

To the best of my knowledge, the good folks who operate the Beagle are mundanes. I say this because, barring magic, I have no explanation for why their bagels are so good, even by New York standards. Which are seriously high. If you haven't eaten a New York bagel, you haven't tried a bagel at all. What they serve in the rest of the country is just donut-shaped bread.

I wolfed down a bacon-and-cheese on a toasted everything bagel and was finishing my no-frills coffee when Aysha Rehm walked into the shop. She was a dark-skinned woman in her early fifties, smartly dressed in fashionable brand-name clothes that most librarians would find out of their price range. She wore the sort of distinct round glasses that people tend to associate with either John Lennon or Harry Potter, depending on their age.

"It's so good to see you're well," said Aysha. She slid onto the stool next to mine at the counter. "Bob and Zach send their regards."

Bob and Zach were among the irregulars I had fought beside, and there were few people in the world I genuinely liked more. It hadn't escaped my notice that Aysha failed to mention Herc—who had been one of my closest friends, as well as the fearless leader of their band of vigilantes. Our falling out stung all over again.

"It's great to see you too, Aysha. May I treat you to the best bagel ever?"

She cast a longing glance at the bins filled with delicious bagels of every variety. "Thanks, but I'm doing the gluten-free thing."

"Oh." I surveyed the offerings. We were on the wrong side of Brooklyn for a bagel shop to serve gluten-free anything.

"I could do with a coffee and a walk," she suggested.

I picked up a pair of coffees with milk and no sugar, and we left the steamy confines of the bagel shop for the wintry streets outside. The air was crisp and sunshine reflected off the snow. The snow had stopped falling overnight, and the residents were busy scraping the few inches of light accumulation from the sidewalks in front of their homes and businesses before foot traffic turned that fluffy powder into a flat sheet of ice hugging the ground with a death grip.

"I take it you've caught up on current events?" Aysha asked.

"More or less. I'm still processing some of what's happened." I pointed at the Holcomb campaign bumper sticker on a parked car we passed. "Can't leave you kids alone for a few months without everything going to hell and the handbasket falling apart halfway through the trip."

"It's hard to believe how quickly evil takes root," said Aysha. "In a span of less than two months, we went from a free modern society to internalized oppression and legalized forced labor."

"Wait." I didn't know what 'internalized oppression' meant, but it was hard not to focus on the other bit. "What do you mean, 'legalized forced labor'?"

Aysha sighed. "So, you're not fully caught up. The day after Holcomb took office, he rolled out this program where every gifted New Yorker is expected to *volunteer*"—she made air quotes—"four hours a week, using their magic to rebuild, improve, and otherwise service the city. When he talks about restoring New York to its former glory, it's on the backs of the gifted, whether they like it or not. Those who fail to volunteer are harassed and intimidated. But a surprising number of gifted are going along with this scheme of their own volition."

"There are gifted who find this palatable?" I asked, genuinely surprised.

"Consider this block." Aysha pointed ahead to a handful of miserable people shoveling snow. "A single moderately powerful gifted could use magic to melt all of this accumulation on sidewalks and roads and save dozens of mundanes the trouble. It wouldn't be hard labor, either. They'd barely work up a sweat. Is it more unethical to ask them to perform this service for the good of the many than to ask everyone to pay taxes so that the city can buy snowplows and pay drivers to operate them?"

I thought about that for a moment. "You can't force a gifted to use their magic, just like you can't force a really strong mundane to clear the sidewalk on account of them being more physically fit than their neighbor. They have to volunteer to do it."

Aysha adjusted her glasses. "That's right. Some buy into the idea of service and volunteer."

"Nothing wrong with that," I said. "I volunteer for the Watch. You volunteer as an irregular. The difference is, neither organization is pressuring anyone to join against their will."

"Precisely. They're getting away with it because they're strong enough to cow the unwilling into silence. This is what we're fighting against."

I took a sip of my coffee. It lubricated the path for my brain cells to slowly return to their workstations. "I always knew Holcomb was trouble."

"Holcomb is frustrating and boorish, but he's only the enabler. I have reason to suspect there's a far more devious and dangerous adversary who is manipulating the mayor and the entire system to wreak havoc upon the gifted."

"Yes, I believe you're right!" I thought back to my conversation with Daniel. Finally, here was someone who was not dismissing or underestimating Vaughn!

"We must do something about the Emersonians before things get any worse," she said with conviction.

Not what I'd had in mind, but I was willing to listen. "You mean selfies, right? I've had the displeasure of running into a couple of those already."

Aysha nodded.

"What's their deal? Who is this Emerson guy, and what does he want?"

"I think I better start from the beginning," she said, a puff of steam escaping into the cold air. "A few months ago, right after Holcomb was sworn in as mayor, he established the Office of Preternatural Solutions. In theory it was to help the city recover after the middling affliction business, to use magic and the resources of the gifted to the betterment of all citizens, gifted and mundane alike. The commissioner of this new office then recruited a fringe group of extremists to act as his department's personal Gestapo." Aysha was getting worked up. She squeezed the paper cup in her gloved hand hard enough that it was dangerously close to bursting. "They call themselves Emersonians, after Ralph Waldo Emerson and the foundational essay he wrote on self-reliance that became the basis for American transcendentalism. Except they interpret that as magical self-reliance. They're strictly opposed to the use of any trinkets or charms; any artifacts that store magic. Ludicrous as that position may be."

"You call them selfies because of the self-reliance thing and not because they like to snap photos of themselves?" I asked.

"Oh, yes, that's why that nickname has entered the vernacular. Thing is, their stated philosophy is utter nonsense. A gifted using a charm has about as little to do with self-reliance as a mundane heating their meal in a microwave instead of gathering wood and rubbing two sticks together. The lower echelons may buy into the ideology, but the puppet masters are definitely after something else."

"After what, exactly?"

"We don't know." Aysha kicked at the snow with the heel of her fancy boot in frustration. "They've been aggressively confiscating enchanted items from the gifted population of the city. Maybe they're looking for a very specific and important artifact, but what artifact and to what end? There could be any number of reasons for the bad guys to sow discord. What I do know"—she paused for dramatic effect—"is that there's historical precedent."

"Really?" I asked. I didn't doubt her conclusions, but she was clearly enjoying the chance to lay out whatever it was she had discovered, and that required an interlocutor who would occasionally nod, gasp, or ask a pointless question to assist in the exciting reveal.

"Most certainly. Groups have risen up throughout recorded history under different names and with different stated goals but exhibiting the same patterns of behavior." Aysha's eyes shone. Her only regret must've been not having slides and charts to go with the presentation. "Small, vicious groups of people, seemingly loyal to a regime that has recently acquired power, eager to confiscate wealth and possessions, with that serving as an excuse to round up magical items."

"For example?" I prodded.

"The most infamous such example is the bonfire of the vanities during the Renaissance," said Aysha. "Friar Girolama Savonarola wrested control of Florence from the Medici family and preached that most luxury items and works of art were immoral and led people toward sin. A group called the *Piagnoni*, or the Weepers, was nominally in charge of shaking down the wealthy for such items to be burned, but they really existed to do exactly what the Emersonians are doing now: gather magical items on behalf of the heretical priest."

I had no idea about any of this, but this sort of research was exactly Aysha's forte.

"Another such group was the *jeunesse dorée*," she went on. "The Gilded Youth, who operated during the reign of terror era that followed the French Revolution."

"Same MO?" I asked.

"Same MO. There are others, who can be traced as far back as the Roman Empire." Aysha paused to take a breath and sip her coffee.

"So, if we were to figure out what powerful and rare artifact was present in Rome and Florence and Paris, and may now be located in New York ..." I trailed off.

"We can thereby infer what the knaves are after, and how to stop them," Aysha finished the thought.

"I'm so glad we're on the same page. I was talking to someone else the other day," I said, recalling the conversation with Chulsky, "and they were dismissive of the threat Vaughn poses."

Aysha looked at me in surprise. "Vaughn?"

"Well, yes. Surely you don't think Holcomb is clever enough to have come up with all of these plans on his own?"

"I suppose not. But, so what? History is filled with examples of obtuse rulers who are guided—willingly or not—by clever advisers."

"The problem isn't the fact that Vaughn is the smarter of the two." I was getting worked up. First Chulsky, and now Aysha. Did no one see Vaughn for the threat he was? "The problem is the enormity of the intelligence gap between them. While Vaughn is playing chess, Holcomb is stuffing checker pieces up his nose. He's got Holcomb wrapped around his boring little finger and that's dangerous!"

Aysha thought this over. "He may be steering and nudging things in the direction he wants, but he isn't in direct control of the ruffians stealing the artifacts."

"How do you mean? He's in charge of OOPS and the Emersonians, right?"

"OOPS—yes. Emersonians, no. Of course, his position and his previous involvement with Nascent Anodynes put him right at the top of my suspect list," she said. "I've looked into him. He appears to be in it for the power. The Emersonians draw legitimacy from their affiliation with his department, but they don't seem to answer to him or coordinate with him in any way." Aysha finished her coffee and dropped the cup into somebody's brown recycling bin at the curb. "They're extremely unforthcoming about their organizational structure, and we've been unable to ascertain who is in charge, but it isn't Vaughn. I wanted to meet with you to bring you up to speed, and see if you possessed any information on the Emersonians or any contacts or leads worth pursuing. I'm at my wits' end."

"I'd never heard of them before yesterday," I admitted. "Nor am I overly familiar with what may or may not have been their past iterations. I could ask around, I suppose, but ..." An idea had been percolating in my head. "Do I have it right that Karl Mercado is with the Emersonians now?"

"Sadly, yes. But I doubt he'd help us," Aysha said. "And I doubt you'd be able to infiltrate them as a double agent. Your reputation is too closely tied to Herc and the rest of us."

"Oh, I have no intention of applying for membership in their club, but I have a pretty good idea who can." I grinned. "How do you think they'd react if a well-known agent of chaos banished by the Watch and with close ties to the Cabal decided to join their ranks?"

"I don't get it," said Moira O'Leary. "Just the other day you were waxing poetic about how hanging out with a bunch of do-gooders was going to turn my life around. You spouted all that nonsense about how performing good deeds together with them whilst singing kumbaya would get karma to give me a foot massage and make me a sandwich. How's joining those selfie losers going to improve my life?"

We were in Moira's expensive hotel room in midtown Manhattan. She lounged on the couch while Aysha perched on the arm of a leather armchair. The librarian wasn't really sold on Moira's participation, which she broadcasted clear as day with her body language and facial expressions. Truth be told, I wasn't completely sold on the idea either. I only hoped I was better at keeping my opinions to myself.

"If you wish to *hang* with the good guys as you so eloquently put it, don't you think you need to give the good guys a reason to want to *hang* with you?" asked Aysha. Each time she pronounced the word *hang*, it was with all the delight and enthusiasm of scooping a pile of dog poop into a plastic baggy. "We're not asking you to buy into the Emersonians' beliefs or make friends with the nut jobs. We need you to infiltrate the organization long enough to learn their goals and identify their leaders."

"I know how infiltration works." Moira scoffed. "I've been infiltrating places since before …" She glanced at Aysha, who had a good couple of decades on her. "Since before you started coloring your hair to cover gray roots instead of coloring it 'cause it's cool."

Aysha blanched and stared daggers at Moira. If looks could kill, Moira would probably need to reanimate herself.

"Forgive my rough-and-tumble demeanor." Moira backpedaled quickly after seeing the expressions on both our faces. "I'm sure you're a very nice lady, for an aging librarian. And I like your coat. Is that Burberry? Maybe we could go shopping together."

Aysha was decked out in designer clothing, as always. She looked Moira up and down, taking in her sweatpants and T-shirt that read *All the Best Things in Life Are Free* with a picture of a treasure chest filled with gold coins and jewels, signed *Level 20 rogue.*

"Sure," said Aysha. "We could discuss Sartre's take on existentialism while I show you the finest tourist gift shops in Times Square."

A smile spread across Moira's face. "Ah, the girl's got sarcasm once you push the right buttons." She sat up and leaned forward. "I happen to have read Sartre. And Nietzsche. And even Kierkegaard. Just because I don't go around bragging about that stuff, doesn't make me stupid. I happen to have a lot of layers. Like an onion."

"She smells like an onion," Aysha told me.

I wasn't certain as to whether Moira had showered since our trip to fairyland.

I raised my hands. "Peace, ladies. We all want the same thing here."

"That couldn't possibly be true, Conrad," said Moira. "You're way too young for her."

"Pig," said Aysha.

"Bookworm," replied Moira. "Conrad, are you blushing?"

"You see what I meant, Aysha?" I said, rushing to change the topic. "This is someone the bad guys will believe is on their side. I mean, how could they not?"

"I do believe it," said Aysha. "I'm having a harder time believing she's on our side."

"I am," said Moira. "I'm an open-minded person who is ready to try the goody two-shoes thing, even if those shoes aren't Jimmy Choos." She glanced meaningfully at Aysha's boots. "So long as you're willing to accept my gruff demeanor and onion scent. Willing to look past my past. Do you think you can do that?"

Aysha crossed her arms and studied the necromancer. "I'm willing to try. Besides, I'm rather curious to hear your thoughts on Sartre."

"In that case, consider the selfies as good as infiltrated." Moira reached for an open can of beer on the coffee table, downed the remaining contents, then tossed the can into one of those tiny hotel garbage pails, and belched loudly.

CHAPTER 8

HAD someone told me a year ago that I'd be called upon to broker a truce between angels and demons, I would've laughed them out of the room. Yet that was precisely the item on the day's agenda for me. With Moira presumably doing her thing as an expert infiltrator, I could dedicate my time and efforts to Abaddon's cause.

Chulsky had texted me the times and locations of my meetings with each faction, but he'd failed to provide any powerful weapons, impenetrable shields, or sage advice. When I'd asked for some, he claimed all I would need at those meetings was my "natural quick wit and an open mind." I vehemently disagreed. In my experience, one survived such encounters by backing their quick wit up with some heavy firepower. I wasn't about to bring a proverbial knife to a potential demon fight.

I went over my inventory looking for items that could save my bacon if the negotiations went sideways. My demon-fighting arsenal was quite sparse, on the perfectly reasonable assumption that if I ever had to fight a demon, I was thoroughly screwed regardless, so why commit my finite financial resources to such an unlikely eventuality?

My search yielded a few enchanted crosses, and holy water that I sprinkled onto my weapons, even if these items were meant for run-of-the-mill vampires at best. None of this was likely to slow down a demon, but it made me feel a little better, anyhow.

Angels were a different story.

There's plenty of literature and research dedicated to the art of fighting or banishing demons. It's been a thing for millennia, even if most of the strategies and items described in such texts were no more effective than what I already had in my possession. No one, however, seems to have given proper consideration to the methods of fighting against angels. Even the most dedicated devil worshippers focus on fighting against humans (and especially fellow devil worshippers, which is less surprising than it first sounds, when you think about it) but they simply assume the nice angels would leave them alone.

Wishful thinking never pulled anyone's feet out of the fire. Also, it should be obvious to anybody who has read the source material that angels are *terrifying*. Humorless bad-asses with flaming swords, wrath, general disdain of humanity … the list goes on and on.

I was woefully underprepared to face either faction. Still, I got up bright and early and started my day the way I had done so many times in the past, by making the rounds of Brooklyn's finest purveyors of magical artifacts.

This proved a lot more difficult than I'd expected, thanks to Holcomb and those dastardly Emersonians.

When I called the shop in Boerum Hill, a prerecorded message informed me that it had shuttered its doors temporarily, "by the order of the mayor's office." At Mordecai's Jewelers, I reached a live person, but an unfamiliar voice explained that the proprietor was on vacation and the store would reopen upon his return. He did not know when, nor could he provide any means of contacting Mordecai directly. No one picked up the phone at the Russian bookstore in Brighton Beach. It was a short enough trip, so I decided to drive there.

Along the way, I saw a group of several gifted tending to the trees. I pulled over and lingered as they worked their way down a residential block, pressing their palms against each tree trunk to strengthen its health and rejuvenate it. Each tree needed about a minute of effort before the gifted could move on to the next. Between them, the group could clear each block pretty fast. For some of the gifted who trafficked in sylvan magic, such as my druid friends, this healing labor should have been a joyous act. Instead, the gifted I watched seemed dejected and miserable, like convicts collecting garbage on the side of a highway as part of their court-ordered community service. A surly young man walked among them but did none of the work. Instead, he supervised the others—if his efforts to nudge them along and berate them could be called supervising.

This must've been one of the gifted "volunteer" brigades Aysha had told me about. They were set to a minor task, but the city would save a fortune on trimming or removing the dead trees, residents would be pleased to avoid any damage to their homes and cars caused by fallen branches, and the mayor's office would claim all the credit. It was a win for everyone, except the poor gifted, who'd been forcibly pressed into service.

I recalled a short story I'd once read about a city called Omelas, powered by the suffering of a child. Some citizens accepted this as a small price to pay for their prosperity, while others fled Omelas, unwilling to partake of the benefits gained by paying such an immoral price. In Bradley Holcomb's twisted vision for New York City, the gifted were that child. Except, the ordinary residents weren't even aware of the small minority being oppressed on their behalf.

How many would walk away, or speak out against this, if they knew?

When I reached my destination, I was briefly gladdened to see that the bookstore was open. Once inside, however, I found the door to the magic shop on the second floor had been boarded up with plywood. The bookstore's sole employee on duty, an old woman wearing a babushka headscarf, babbled something in Russian in response to my questions. When pantomimes and speaking slowly produced no results, I looked up the translation of "magic shop" on my phone, pointed at the boarded door, and did my best to enunciate *volshebnyy magazin*. The old lady nodded enthusiastically, browsed the dusty shelves, and produced a thin Soviet-era picture book of the same title.

When I exited the bookstore, another gifted was passing by. He was an old man in a ratty coat and an ushanka hat, carrying a bag of groceries, unremarkable except for his aura. Our eyes met.

"You searching for wizard store?" he asked in heavily accented English.

"Yes!" I said. Perhaps this old timer would have a lead for me. "Where did they move to?"

"They fled! Cowards!" He spat on the ground to underscore his displeasure. "Too scared of new wizard police." He looked up at me from under his oversized hat. "Wizard police, they bad people. If you give them one spoon of borscht, they will take entire borscht. Now they want magic items, but if we not fight back, soon we have gulag and wizard registration, like in my country."

The man had lived under a tyrannical regime and, on the most basic level, he seemed to understand the problem a lot better than Chulsky ever could.

"If you want to keep freedom, you must fight!" Fire burned in the old man's piercing, pale-blue eyes. "Yes?"

"Yes," I told him. "I intend to."

Placated, the old Russian frowned at the bookstore window display and walked on.

I'd struck out everywhere else so far, and that left only my neighborhood spot, a game store in Midwood a few blocks from the studio apartment that I kept as my official residence.

Kings Games, so named for its proximity to Kings Highway rather than any professed affiliation with royalty, was open for business. It was packed with bleary-eyed gamers blowing up aliens on computer screens or rolling weirdly shaped dice and moving miniature warriors across tabletop battlefields.

A mundane staff member led me upstairs, onto the third floor of the two-story building. Unlike Abaddon, Inc. there was no Dr. Who TARDIS-level weirdness involving non-Euclidian geometry with objects being larger on the inside going on here. A relatively simple but reliable concealment spell made the building appear shorter and hid the floor that housed its magical artifacts from mundane eyes. As with most magic-related things, a mundane could perceive and interact with it once they knew it was there—much like the young man who was leading me upstairs—but not otherwise.

My exuberance at the magic shop being open was short-lived. When we got to the third floor, the shelves and glass counters normally packed with artifacts were bare. Steve, the proprietor, was sorting Pokémon cards on the countertop. He glanced up when I walked in.

"Conrad! Welcome back, buddy. It's been a minute."

"I've been traveling." I made a show of looking at the empty shelves. "Fire sale?"

Steve chuckled. "I wish. We've been having a rat problem, is all."

"A rat problem?"

"Those rat-faced goons trying to confiscate our inventory." He slammed his fist against the countertop. It rattled, and a pile of cards came precariously close to toppling over. "It's a good thing the collectibles business downstairs is booming, or I don't know what I'd do."

"I'm sorry for your troubles, Steve."

I was resigning myself to rely on my meager inventory for the foreseeable future.

"It don't mean we ain't got the goods for our regulars," said Steve. "We had to move our inventory to a stash house nearby. I can send a runner and bring back whatever you need in a couple of minutes, no sweat." He shrugged. "It ain't the most convenient way of doin' things, but when needs must …"

"All right," I was cautiously feeling optimistic again. "I can work with that."

"What's your pleasure?" asked Steve.

"Do you have anything I can use against angels?" I asked.

"Angels?" He cocked his head.

"Yup."

Steve stared at me, probably trying to figure out whether I'd lost my marbles. In his business, both upstairs and downstairs, he was used to dealing with a lot stranger than that. "You mean like them folks playing harps on top of clouds wearing white bathrobes angels?"

"I was thinking more the Old Testament Heaven's warrior sort."

Steve scratched at the stubble on his chin. "That's a tough one, man. I've got a Sumerian clay tablet with a spell written on it that banishes god's spirit warriors. Supposedly. Except I don't think that's the right god, and you'd have to read Sumerian to use it. Also, it ain't been tested, at least not in the recent centuries."

"I skipped the Sumerian alphabet day in grade school. Got anything else?"

"There's a gramophone that repels all manner of spirits and otherworldly creatures while you play it," said Steve. "Bit bulky, though."

I liked Steve fine and he offered quality goods at fair prices, even if, on occasion, he pushed a little too hard to move his inventory. The items he suggested were long shots—but a good retailer wouldn't just admit to not stocking merchandise of use to a customer with money to spend.

"I don't think those are going to work," I said. "Got anything I can use against demons?"

He was visibly relieved, being that he stocked items that were actually useful toward this, or at least purported to be. He rattled off a list of suggestions, but none of them were much different from the assortment of trinkets that already filled my pockets.

I was preparing to politely disengage when I heard a commotion downstairs. There were muffled sounds of an argument, followed by the staccato creaking of the staircase being rapidly ascended by several sets of boots.

Four gifted in their early twenties stomped into Steve's showroom. They had the cookie-cutter look of presumed righteousness about them. They were the sort of angry young men Billy Joel sang about: men who lacked intellectual depth or a moral compass but eagerly fell in with whatever cult or ideology that allowed them to bully and harass others and still feel morally superior. No generation or society had managed to purge itself of such men, gifted and mundane alike. These men flocked to the banners of tyrants and terrorists, and even well-meaning agents of change who can't resist the Faustian bargain of unleashing such pliable, ruthless foot soldiers upon their ideological enemies.

The four men glared at Steve and me with the passionate conviction of youth, and I knew without having to be told that they were Emersonians.

Steve glared back at them with equal distaste. "What do you want?"

85

"You're engaging in the illegal sale of magical artifacts," declared one of the men breathlessly. "You're to cease such activity immediately and to relinquish any and all illicit items to our care."

"Ain't no artifacts here." Steve pointed at the empty shelves. "Just showing some high-end collectibles to a private client." He nodded to the stacks of cards in front of him. "He's in the market for a foil Charizard. I trust it's still legal to sell trading cards in this city?"

"Don't bother with the theatrics," said another Emersonian. "We know exactly who this man is." He sneered at me. "You shouldn't have come back to New York, Brent."

"I go where I please," I said in a low, even tone.

Steve put a protective hand on my shoulder. "Don't worry about it, Conrad. Nothing illegal is happenin' here. These mooks are just fishing for trouble, but they ain't gonna find it."

"We'll see," said the Emersonian who'd bloviated the legalese earlier. He nodded to the others, and they spread out like bloodhounds seeking the scent of a hare. They peeked behind shelves and opened the boxes piled in the corner, but found only ordinary shipping supplies stored within. One of them unceremoniously walked behind the counter and checked back there, brushing past Steve.

The shopkeeper watched them with a smirk, though I was certain his merriment was an act. The increasingly exasperated look on the faces of the wannabe gendarmes was only a small trade-off for the indignity he was being forced to suffer.

"Like I said, I got nothin'," Steve reiterated.

The lead Emersonian looked like he had eaten an especially unpalatable crow.

"Search him!" he pointed at me.

"I think not," I said, still keeping my voice calm.

"Yeah," said another Emersonian. "He always carries a bucketful of gadgets like some sort of a dirty middling."

If you only knew how right you were, random cold-eyed thug.

"You can't hassle my customers like that!" Steve shouted.

The bloodhounds surrounded me.

I hesitated. I didn't want to make trouble for Steve. He'd gone to great lengths to avoid a confrontation, but I wasn't about to fork over the items I carried. My pockets were extra heavy with my usual charms and talismans, as well as a number of additional trinkets that I'd judged to be possibly useful against demons.

"Why don't we step outside?" I told the Emersonians. This time, my voice most definitely wasn't calm.

"You aren't going anywhere." The head thug made a fist. It glowed with a greenish hue. The air around us crackled and smelled of ozone.

I hesitated still. I kept my arms in plain sight, resisting the urge to reach for one of my many toys. It would be so easy to unload on these idiots and annihilate them. After facing fae assassins, dragons, and gods, four-to-one odds against a gaggle of overconfident punks barely even registered as a threat. My concern was for Steve and his shop. What sort of retaliation would he face from the Emersonians and their bosses after I mopped the floor with the selfies? I couldn't always be around to protect him and his staff from the fallout of such a fight, as much as I wanted to. What if I got stuck in fairyland again, or looked at an angel funny and got smited for my trouble?

I was already calculating how much it would cost me to surrender a few of my trinkets. The idea made my teeth ache.

Steve made the decision for me.

He unleashed a bolt of energy that threw the lead Emersonian halfway across the room. The thug's body slammed into the wall, leaving an indentation in the Sheetrock, and slid to the floor like a rag doll. The arcane energy Steve had mustered up hissed and fizzled, then dimmed around his unclenched fist.

"I said no one hassles my customers," Steve repeated.

Steve knew what his decision meant. He realized the situation I was in, and the choice I'd been forced to contemplate. He knew that the only way to rein in those angry young men was to push back. So he stepped up and pushed, heedless of the risk to his person and to his business.

One of the remaining goons shot an energy bolt at Steve. I blocked it with my bare palm. The bolt fizzled against my skin. The Emersonian stared at my unharmed hand, mouth agape. I made a fist, and punched that mouth.

The problem with subscribing to the bullshit self-reliance philosophy of only using one's own magical powers is that you're stuck using whatever power you were born with, which, in most cases, isn't all that much. Sure, you can throw a bolt of energy or a fireball, but it has no chance whatsoever of penetrating a defensive shield put up by an amulet crafted by an experienced and vastly more powerful mage.

The man I punched staggered back, clutching at his teeth, blood trickling between his fingers. His two remaining compatriots attacked me with spells of their own, launching such mediocre and sluggish energy bolts, I hardly felt I needed arcane protections and could've just shifted slightly to get out of their way. I didn't bother to move, and my shield absorbed or deflected the bolts with little effort.

Only a small percentage of humans are born with the necessary gene to become gifted. The gene seems to awaken at different times, most often at puberty but in some cases in early childhood, and on occasion even in one's sunset years. Just because someone is capable of perceiving magic, however, doesn't make them into a fireball-flinging wizard straight out of the pages of a fantasy novel any more than having fingers guarantees one's proficiency with a gun.

An average person isn't a great fighter when using their bare hands. They need a tool: a gun, a knife, even a rock to fling at that wooly mammoth. Likewise, an average gifted isn't a very effective magician when relying solely on their inner power. They stand to benefit greatly from using artifacts the same as a middling would. To my mind, any paramilitary group consciously choosing to disadvantage themselves in a fight is little more than a bunch of dumb lemmings.

I didn't bother with magical means. Unlike the lemmings I faced, I was a fighter. I may not have had their innate magic, but I was Conrad Brent of the Watch, and I'd spent decades battling all manner of bad guys. My bare hands would do fine.

I walked straight into the weak arcane flame cast by one Emersonian, closed the distance, and punched him in the solar plexus. He doubled over, and I turned to the remaining thug who was the largest of the bunch. He'd seen his magic and that of his compatriots have no effect on me, so he switched tactics, meeting me head on and throwing a punch.

He was half a head taller than me, had a longer reach, and knew how to handle himself in a fight. I slipped his first punch, but it still landed on the side of my head. My ear stung. The amulet did nothing to protect me from an ordinary, kinetic attack.

My opponent's superior size was no substitute for experience. I ducked under his next punch and kneed him in the groin. He doubled over, and I punched him in the temple, sending him crashing to the ground where he brayed like an aggrieved donkey.

The four Emersonians were all down. None were hurt worse than they might've been in a bar fight, even if I couldn't say the same about the state of their collective wounded pride. Some of them looked like they might've been contemplating a second round against all common sense, so I addressed Steve.

"How many of them do you think I should kill? It'll only take one to carry back the message."

This was the final straw. The four thugs, disheveled and humiliated, beat a hasty retreat down the staircase. They cursed and issued threats, all of which became less and less audible as they went.

Steve walked to the windows facing the street and peered down. I joined him. Together we watched the four selfies exit the store and book it down the street.

"Just makin' sure," said Steve. He looked at me. "You good?"

"Peachy. I'm more concerned about you. The Emersonians will come back. And, to quote a wise Jedi: in greater numbers."

Steve grinned. Despite the circumstances, he was visibly pleased at a well-placed Star Wars reference. "Had to be done," he said. "They're bullies, and bullies ain't gonna stop 'til you bloody their nose."

"Couldn't have said it better myself." I rubbed my throbbing ear. "Even so, would you mind if I asked some friends to hang around for a while, keep an eye on the place?"

Steve's eyes narrowed. "Your friends at the Watch?"

I shook my head. "The Watch is busy pretending to be Switzerland for the moment. I was thinking more along the lines of my friends, the irregulars."

Tension drained from the shopkeeper. "Oh, sure. Those folks are always welcome to chill with us." He leaned in and added conspiratorially, "Some of them are good customers."

CHAPTER 9

I headed to see the angels, armed no better against them than the Emersonians had been against me.

Like most sane New Yorkers, I avoid driving in Manhattan at all costs. Even on a good day it is slower and more frustrating than taking the subway. And don't get me started on looking for parking. This time, however, I opted to drive.

My '84 Oldsmobile was stuffed with more wards, protections, and magical abilities than I could possibly carry on my person. It may not have looked like much, but in a situation where I was definitely biting off more than I could chew, it offered a slightly improved chance of survival, compared to a MetroCard.

In addition, my destination was in Morningside Heights, uptown. This meant a trip up the West Side Highway and onto Riverside Drive, and the latter happens to be one of the most scenic and pleasant boulevards in New York City. The Hudson River in all its glory was to my left, a succession of stately nineteenth-century mansions interspersed with parks and statues to my right. Manhattan may have been my least-favorite borough: the colder, more dangerous place with darker secrets and more terrifying threats lurking among its skyscrapers than any of the outer boroughs surrounding it, but I could almost forgive its flaws when cruising along this route.

I turned onto West 114th Street, and the car stalled a few hundred feet short of its destination. To be clear, my car doesn't stall. It doesn't get engine trouble, its battery doesn't die, and its tires don't deflate. Those problems are for lesser vehicles, and beneath its dignity. The problem wasn't mechanical. It refused to move forward, like a horse sensing a pack of wolves lying in wait.

This didn't bode well, but I wasn't about to let my skittish mechanical steed deter me from doing something stupid and dangerous. I leaned on the gas.

The car wheezed in protest but didn't move. A Lexus pulled away from the curb up ahead, and the Oldsmobile pounced, claiming the precious parking spot. This was a good-enough compromise for me. I slammed the door shut and walked toward Broadway.

Halfway down the block laid one of the more peculiar New York City landmarks. Rat Rock is a thirty-foot-tall boulder nestled between what looked like a pair of apartment buildings. They say when the area was developed and the city block erected in the late nineteenth century, the cost of demolishing this enormous schist formation would have been astronomical. It was left undisturbed to occupy an outrageously valuable plot of real estate on the Upper West Side. Even at today's rates and with modern technology, removing it would be prohibitively expensive. And so there it remains, a literal huge piece of schist. It attracts various kinds of vermin: rat packs congregate at its base, flocks of pigeons cover its top with droppings, and tourists snap photos of it from behind a metal fence.

One of the structures it bordered was an apartment building. The other one was merely pretending to be.

The building in question was enveloped in a low-level aversion spell. The spell wasn't strong enough to prevent a determined gifted from getting through, but it would turn away door-to-door salesmen, flyer distributors, or anyone else in the habit of poking their noses into other people's business. Although an average gifted could navigate past the spell, most wouldn't choose to. It was a tricky and difficult spell to set up and maintain, broadcasting to the world that whoever wanted their privacy was also tricky and difficult, and therefore best left alone.

I made it through the spell and to the front door of the proverbial Dread Gazebo in apartment building's clothing. A pair of signs written with arcane paint visible only to the gifted hung by the entrance and spelled things out for the especially dense visitors. The first read Keep Out. The second, Beware Of God.

Against my better instincts, I walked inside.

Three women of indeterminable age sat behind a sizable white quartz reception desk situated along the back wall of the lobby. They looked nearly identical and reminded me of Tilda Swinton. Each wore a pristine white lab coat. They had auras, but unlike the shimmering warm glow of the gifted auras, theirs emitted a colder, pale turquoise light. Their auras resembled body-length halos. The brushed silver sign above the trio's heads read Department Of Natural Philosophy in two-foot-tall letters. There were no directories, other signage, or decorations in sight. Three pairs of unnaturally blue eyes zeroed in on me in silent disapproval.

"Hi there, ladies." I strutted over to the counter with counterfeit bravado. "I'm here on behalf of Abaddon, Inc. and would like to see whoever's in charge, please?"

"You don't have an appointment," said the one on the left.

"We don't take walk-ins," said the one on the right.

"The Archdocent is very busy," said the one in the middle.

"I'm certain he'll want to see me," I said. "It's regarding a dispute your fine organization is presently having with a certain faction of Down Below, and—"

All three women rose from their seats and leaned forward as one. Their eyes flashed with the cold blue turquoise of their auras.

"Do not speak of the unclean within these walls," said the one on the left.

"Such affairs are beyond your understanding," said the one on the right.

"Only the voice of the worthy may be heard in matters celestial," said the one in the middle.

I'm not easily intimidated, but the trio were creeping me out. I felt like a Catholic school kid who'd forgotten to do his homework, confronted by ruler-wielding nuns.

"I'm worthy," I said quickly, backing up a step. "Definitely worthy, and I can prove it. Do you have a hammer that needs lifting, or a sword stuck in that big rock outside?"

The glow in their eyes dimmed somewhat but didn't disappear entirely.

"You may prove your worth," said the one in the middle.

"What doctorates do you hold?" asked the one on the right.

"Which journals have published your research?" asked the one on the left.

"I'm not a scientist," I told them. "But I did once stop a warlock from mind-controlling the faculty of Brooklyn College. Oh, and another time I cleared the zombie infestation on the campus of Kingsborough Community College. The hardest part was telling the zombies apart from the students—"

"Not worthy!" screeched all three in unison. They stepped toward me, right through the solid desk as if it weren't there. They encircled me, their eyes aflame. I stood perfectly still. The trio got closer and closer until one of them grasped my neck with her long, slender fingers. Her touch felt ice cold.

She yanked her hand away and hissed. All three took a step back, maintaining the disquieting unison.

"He has the divine spark," said the one who had touched me.

"Guilty," I said, and forced a smile. Having been a god for a brief time kept paying dividends in that, on occasion, powerful beings voluntarily chose not to kill me. "Told you I was worthy."

They hissed again. A trickle of cold sweat rolled down the back of my neck.

"Not worthy," said one of them.

"You're merely a higher being, not an academic," said another.

I straightened my coat. "I thought I've seen it all, but … angels who dig academia? Does that make you Christian Scientists?"

The three appeared none too pleased by the pun. They hissed louder, and their eyes flared up again. I fought against the instinct to curl into a ball.

"It's not wise to antagonize them," came a voice from behind me. I turned to find a gray-haired elderly man with a severe, sharp nose, bushy eyebrows, and a long beard. Given a pair of slippers, a toga, and a fluffy cloud to stand upon, he could've cosplayed the Abrahamic God. Instead, he wore a tweed jacket with elbow patches and a striped bow tie. The sleeves of his jacket were marred by chalk.

"They're Heaven's warriors, and they do not venerate idle merriment," the man admonished.

"Sorry," I said. "I will keep merriment to a minimum."

The trio bowed to the newcomer.

"The interloper has the spark, Archdocent," said one.

"He's not worthy," said another.

"He claims to speak for Abaddon," said the third.

The Archdocent nodded sagely. "Leave us," he ordered.

The Archdocent's angels retreated to their original positions behind the visitor's desk without a word.

"Come," he told me with equal authority. He turned and walked up the wide marble staircase without waiting to see if I'd follow.

I rushed after him.

"You know, I met a three-headed dragon once that reminds me of those ladies," I told the Archdocent once I managed to catch up.

The old academic waved me off. "Kindly spare me the small talk. We're much too busy here for shenanigans."

We reached the top of the staircase and walked through a spacious workshop. Here and there scientists in lab coats congregated in front of blackboards covered with formulas, peered into microscopes, and scribbled on notepads, both paper and electronic. Their equipment was eclectic to say the least, ranging from medieval-looking contraptions to Victorian steam-powered machines, to sleek modern gadgets. Each scientist, including the Archdocent, emitted the same pale turquoise aura as the angels I'd encountered downstairs.

His office was rather modest for a person in charge of whatever this was. It resembled a typical tenured professor's tiny, cramped domain at some run-of-the-mill university. An L-shaped desk buried under stacks of printouts, an overfilled bookshelf, a filing cabinet, a well-used office chair, and a smaller folding visitor's chair left little room for anything else. A glass wall separated his office from the rest of the workshop, offering a panoramic view but no privacy.

The Archdocent motioned for me to sit and watched in amusement as I took it all in. "Not what you expected?"

"To be honest, I'm having a difficult time reconciling angels with doing science," I admitted.

"Who better to study the Almighty's creation than his firstborn and most perfect servants?" countered the Archdocent. "What better way to exalt Him than to try to understand the effulgence and intricacy of His creation? Those of us from On High pioneered natural philosophy, and we remain on the cutting edge of it still."

On the other side of the glass, a scientist was hyper-focused as he calculated something using an abacus. I didn't suppose *cutting edge* meant what the Archdocent thought it meant. Not that I wished to argue the point. I broached the subject I'd come there to discuss.

"My name is Conrad Brent. I've been asked by Abaddon to mediate the dispute you appear to be having at the moment. Would that be all right?" Given the ladies' reaction downstairs, I was careful not to specify who the dispute was with.

"Abaddon serves the Almighty in its own way," said the Archdocent. "It would be impolitic of me to refuse any potential help." He radiated the expression of an indulgent grandfather putting up with the antics of overexuberant babies.

I smiled. "Excellent, Archdocent … . What may I call you, sir?"

"The title will suffice. Names have power, and I'd rather not insult you by proffering an alias."

I winced inwardly, for that was precisely what I had done. Conrad Brent was not my birth name, but it was the only name anyone knew me by, for the exact reasons the angel had stated. I hastened to change the subject.

"Of course, Archdocent. Forgive me, but as a research facility, what possible interest does your department have in the estate of the late Benicio Rojas?"

I'd learned the name from Chulsky, and it had been the only useful lead he provided.

"Mr. Rojas bequeathed his estate to us in exchange for an indulgence," said the Archdocent.

"An indulgence?" I repeated, surprised.

"A way to save his immortal soul," said the Archdocent. "Those among the On High may occasionally offer such an … unorthodox manner of salvation to a worthwhile and repentant human."

I nodded. During the Middle Ages, the Catholic Church had sold indulgences in much the same manner. Why lead a righteous life when the clergy will forgive any sin for the right fee? It appeared angels were no different, and funding whatever research they engaged in must've been expensive.

"The … other party"—I proceeded with caution here—"laid a counterclaim to the estate, as I understand it."

"They lie!" The Archdocent's bushy eyebrows formed a V, and he slapped his palm against a stack of papers on the desk. "It's what they do!" In a calmer tone, he added, "Our claim supersedes theirs, in any case."

"Is there some room for negotiation? Perhaps a dollar amount you would care to place on the value of the estate so the property could be sold and split between your organizations?"

The Archdocent's frown deepened. He appeared hesitant to reply.

"Come on, surely you're open to some sort of discussion, since you were willing to hear me out," I prodded.

He was silent for a time. I waited patiently. This dispute about a single house in South Brooklyn seemed petty and small, given the players. Could it be a simple matter of selling the property so each faction could earn a few hundred thousand dollars? It didn't track.

"We want the wine collection," said the Archdocent. "They," he added with distaste, as if a mere mention of the other party was something one didn't do in polite company, "can have the rest."

"Wine? This is about wine?" I'd hoped this conversation was going to help me make sense of the problem, not make it even weirder.

"The collection is of interest to us," the Archdocent said in a tone that didn't brook further inquiry.

"This is something I can work with," I said. "Thank you. One last question: what is the address of the property?"

The Archdocent appeared at least a little surprised. "You don't know?"

"I have only the most basic of details," I admitted. "I figured if Chulsky hadn't told me, it was for a good reason."

"He didn't tell you because he doesn't know, either. The house is well protected, even from the likes of us. We could break through the wards, but it would be messy and time-consuming, and it would certainly agitate the other claimants ..." He trailed off, then picked up a quill, dipped it in an inkwell, and scribbled something on a Post-it note. He handed the pink square to me. "The address. Perhaps someone like you can investigate more surreptitiously."

I thanked him and got up. As I was about to leave the office, he called after me by name. Not Conrad, but my *real* name. The name I hadn't heard uttered in decades.

"I expect you to look after our interests," the Archdocent told me. "If you fail to do so, I shall be extremely disappointed."

The threat in those words wasn't veiled at all.

I left the building without incident and got back into the car, my heart racing. It was only within the relative safety of the Oldsmobile that I looked up the address I was given. Any place housing a valuable wine collection in South Brooklyn was likely to be located in Manhattan Beach, or perhaps Sea Gate, or along Ocean Parkway—all local enclaves of wealth and privilege. Instead, the address was in the blue-collar neighborhood of Gravesend. I pulled up a map on my phone and confirmed my suspicion: it was right next to the Old Gravesend Cemetery.

Cemeteries. Why did it always have to be cemeteries?

I was sure the house's location was no mere coincidence, and I wasn't looking forward to finding out why. But first, I had another appointment to keep.

My next stop was in Greenwood, Brooklyn, only a short hop from where I'd confronted the Mandible Killer, but thankfully outside the confines of any place decedents are interred.

Having survived rush hour traffic, I pulled up to a two-story warehouse that had been converted to office space. My car didn't stall this time, and allowed me to park it a stone's throw away from the entrance. I wondered if the Oldsmobile considered the demons a lesser threat, or had it simply gotten used to the idea of encroaching upon the home turf of powerful beings? The optimist in me hoped for the former. The realist in me shuddered; the angels were cold and threatening, and they were supposed to be the good guys. How much worse would the demons be?

There were no protective wards around the building, or placards admonishing me to go away. A modest but tasteful sign above the entrance read MAMMON, IS, & GOODE: ANGEL INVESTORS.

The receptionist was a human girl who looked barely old enough to hold a job. She listened politely to my request and then led me across an open office that featured wooden benches, lots of potted plants, and soft Muzak playing in the background. A few individuals dressed in T-shirts and slacks lounged on the benches, staring into their laptops. Some were gifted humans, others possessed the same aura as the angel academics. Angels and demons were supposed to be cut from the same cloth, after all. Regardless, there was not a single horn or hoof in sight.

The Oldsmobile may have been right. These folks didn't appear hostile, even though I was certain they were dangerous.

The receptionist led me to a pudgy individual who appeared to be in his early fifties. A Hawaiian shirt struggled to contain his rotund belly, its buttons straining against the outward pressure. He sported a goatee, which was the most demon-like thing about him, and a ponytail which was the least.

"Welcome, welcome, Mr. Brent," he said as he vigorously shook my hand once I introduced myself. "It's an absolute pleasure to meet you. May I call you Conrad? Wonderful. As they say, any friend of Daniel, and all that ..."

He spoke quickly, without letting me get a word in edgewise. More importantly, he hadn't yet threatened me even once, a courtesy which I happened to appreciate.

"I'm the fund manager and chief executive officer here at Mammon, Is, & Goode," he said. "Name's Beelzebub. Oh, not *that* Beelzebub, oh no." He chuckled. "It's just a really common name, like Chris or Mohamed or Ivan in human cultures. In fact," he leaned in conspiratorially, "you can call me Bub."

I tried to speak again, but he was still going a mile a minute. "May I offer you a beverage? We have kombucha, cold brew, and bottled water. Or perhaps you'd like something stronger? It's five o'clock somewhere," he added, heedless of the fact that it was around five o'clock right there in Brooklyn.

Sensing that he wouldn't take no for an answer, I went with the simplest option. "That's very kind of you. A water will do fine."

"Tina, would you please?" Bub sent the receptionist to get the water. "Now, what is it that I can do for you?"

Once again, I explained my desire to mediate the conflict on behalf of Abaddon, Inc.

"That is a most gracious and welcome offer," said Bub. "Especially in light of the fact that we have the legal claim on this estate, and those folks' counterclaim is simply egregious. They act like pigeons, squatting atop any landmark and property they fancy and leaving their droppings all over it. Do you know why they chose their location? Flocks of them like to circle that big rock and land on it, just like the pigeons! Those rigid know-it-alls never evolved enough to suppress their pseudo-avian urges."

Tina returned with two little bottles of water and placed them in front of us. She rolled her eyes surreptitiously at her boss's verbal diarrhea, smiled when I nodded thanks, and disappeared again.

"Anyway, as you must've already gathered, we're an investment firm."

"Angel investors," I managed to interject.

"Oh, yes." He laughed. "The irony is very much on-brand for us. Anyhow, we're in the business of funding promising individuals in exchange for a financial return and ... certain other considerations. Mr. Rojas managed to leverage our investment into building a considerable fortune, and now that he is—how shall I put this delicately—done with it, the contract stipulates that his assets come into our possession."

"Assets and 'certain other considerations'?" I asked.

"His soul, Conrad." Bub smiled warmly. "We get his soul. We do represent the interests of Down Below, after all. So yes, that is of course a key component of any investment we make. But!" He raised his index finger. "We also get all his stuff. There's paperwork, in triplicate, signed in blood and witnessed by a notary public. It's ours, fair and square, Conrad, no matter what those feathered egg-heads may claim."

I was getting a clearer view of the situation now. It seemed one Mr. Benicio Rojas had sold his soul in exchange for oodles of money, success, the works. In addition to collecting his priceless but financially irrelevant soul, the crafty demon investors also had themselves written into his will. Why let the accumulated wealth go to waste when they could use it to fund the next batch of suckers, and so on and so forth, for generations to come?

Except that Rojas hadn't relished the idea of eternal damnation and had decided to leave his earthly possessions to the angels in exchange for a get-out-of-hell-free card.

"You seem like a surprisingly reasonable fellow, Bub," I said, doing my best to imitate his speech patterns. "And one who won't let needless pride stand in the way of good business. This Rojas, he tried to get out of the deal, and in the process, he created a headache for you and for your counterparts, and even for Abaddon, Inc. Surely there's a compromise to be made, some deal that will let you get this particular investment off your books and focus on more important things? Throw the On High a bone, let them have a token piece of the pie, so they too can declare it a win. Everyone happy, everyone moves on. What do you say?"

I tried to be as verbose and talk as fast as him, in an effort to ingratiate myself to my interlocutor. It seemed to work. Bub was nodding along.

"What do you have in mind?" he asked.

"Oh, I don't know …" I pretended to think. "What about his wine collection? I understand it's impressive, and something our avian friends might like?"

Bub tilted his head. "You think they'd settle for that?"

"No promises, but I might be able to talk them into it," I replied. "I'm certain they're eager to resolve the situation in a manner that lets them save face."

"Hmmm …" Bub sat there, hesitant, his chubby index finger twirling his goatee. "I realize this is incredibly selfish of me, but there's a bottle of Bordeaux in Rojas's cellar I've personally had my eye on for years. It's not the most valuable item in the collection, hardly a standout at all, but …" He closed his eyes and smacked his lips. "1961 Chateau Latour, perhaps the greatest Bordeaux of the past century. Benicio has a top shoulder bottle, perfectly preserved. I'm eager to taste that vintage again."

"If it's not so expensive, then perhaps our pal the Archdocent would let you have it?" I asked.

"Oh, no," said Bub. "The Archdocent isn't fond of me. I'm certain if I were to ask, they'd make a big stink of it, out of spite. No." He looked me in the eye. "If you were to retrieve this bottle and bring it to me, I'd be extremely grateful. Grateful enough to see that the negotiations proceed smoothly and the On High get what they want. And, of course, I'd owe you a personal favor."

I pretended to consider it. "I understand the house is heavily warded."

"Surely, someone of your substantial skill and reputation can find a way in," said Bub. "I'd owe you a *big* personal favor." His tone remained friendly, almost saccharine, but something of his demonic nature bled through the amenable veneer. "A copacetic relationship with my organization can come in handy in so many ways."

"I bet it could," I told him. "Let me look into this further. See what I can do."

"Wonderful." The demon rubbed his hands together. "1961 Chateau Latour. Let me write that down for you."

CHAPTER 10

I wasn't buying the story Bub was peddling, not by a long shot. As soon as I got back to the car, I researched the vintage he was after on my phone. It was indeed a highly rated Bordeaux, and a "top shoulder" referred to an old bottle that had been properly stored, which meant the wine would likely still be drinkable. But my search also showed that a handful of bottles were readily available for purchase, and ones in top shoulder condition cost about ten thousand dollars each.

That meant someone like Bub could order a bottle or ten off the internet any time he wanted. An outrageous price tag wouldn't deter him in the slightest. Which meant he didn't just want an old expensive bottle of wine; he wanted the specific bottle from Rojas's house. And, given the Archdocent's willingness to settle for the wine collection, it was a good bet the angels wanted it, too. Why? Short of asking pointed questions of dangerous beings, there was only one way to find out.

I drove to Gravesend. Contrary to popular belief, the grim-sounding name has nothing to do with graves, let alone sending anybody to them. It was what the early Dutch colonists named the area, and it meant either Count's Beach or Grove's End, depending on who you ask. The excommunicated British Puritans subsequently founded a colony there, in the mid-seventeenth century. The colony welcomed heretics of all stripes, from Anabaptists to Quakers, under the relatively tolerant Dutch rule. Soon after the town was founded, so was its cemetery. It remains the oldest intact cemetery in Brooklyn, with all the arcane weight such a distinction provides.

The house in question was in a sleepy cul-de-sac off Van Sicklen Street, which had once been part of the common square of the Town of Gravesend. The back of each house on the south side of the cul-de-sac bordered the Old Gravesend Cemetery. Hidden behind the above-ground F train line that runs along McDonald Avenue, the unassuming and dilapidated Z-shaped patch filled with headstones weaved its way among houses and businesses across two city blocks.

I approached the house, which seemed like an ordinary home on an ordinary street. Warm light emanated from the windows of the surrounding houses. Snowmen built by children earlier in the day watched me with their coal eyes from along the sidewalk. Where did kids even get coals in this day and age? Rojas's house was quiet and dark, but once I approached, I felt an aversion spell stronger than the one protecting the angels' nest uptown.

It took considerable effort to overcome the aversion spell, and once I'd managed to wade through its invisible barrier, some of the wards and protections guarding the house revealed themselves to me.

Enchantments swirled like angry storm clouds above the house, and an intricate combination of wards, sigils, runes, and hexes covered the outer walls in an arcane quilt. Some of the protections I recognized, and some were unfamiliar to me. Among those I knew, most were aggressive, even lethal. Meant to lash out at the intruder rather than merely deter them. The Rojas house was the magical equivalent of a tank with a multitude of turrets tracking my every move, ready to fire its payload at the first sign of a provocation.

By my estimation, it would take half a dozen powerful gifted to stand a chance of breaking through something like that, and not all of them would walk away from the experience. Even armed with my choice of artifacts, I couldn't hope to do this on my own.

Maintaining protections like these required an enormous amount of power, and there was an obvious reservoir that could be tapped for such a steady supply.

The cemetery.

If I could somehow sever the connection between the house and the pent-up arcane energies it was drawing upon, it would alter the difficulty level of getting inside from insuperable to merely difficult. Or so I hoped. There had to be a reason neither claimant had attempted such a clear-cut solution, so I proceeded with caution.

I walked around the block until I reached the cemetery fence. Its metal gates were locked. The small graveyard had been closed for nearly a century, and held a reputation among the gifted as a spot to keep away from. Troublemakers who liked to practice the dark arts, summon the dead, or otherwise do the sort of mischief one might get up to in a shuttered cemetery, avoided the place, because it—supposedly—ate them. That was the rumor, anyway. I'd never tested it, but in all my years I'd never had cause to tread upon its grounds, which meant someone or something else guarded its serenity.

It was easy enough to climb the fence. I'd observed mundane children from the nearby school do so more than once, and I had lingered each time, ready to lend a hand, given the place's reputation. Curious kids gaped at the weather-beaten gravestones, and giggled as they raced through overgrown grass. Whatever ghosts or spirits resided within left them alone, and the children would quickly lose interest and move on to other adventures.

I took one more look at the empty snow-covered graveyard illuminated only by the ambient light from nearby streets and homes, and hopped over the fence.

I landed in summer.

Overly bright light made me squint, and it took my eyes some time to adjust. The cemetery was bathed in sunlight, with grass and wildflowers reaching toward the clear blue sky. Insects buzzed all around me, and taller grave markers gleamed in the distance.

In the middle of it all, a tuxedo cat sat atop an old crumbling gravestone that protruded barely high enough to be noticeable among the grass.

The cat looked old, its black fur speckled with gray, its amber eyes cloudy. It sat upright and still, head tilted slightly toward the ground, as though it was contemplating some deeper truth beyond human understanding.

Outside the gates, winter evening persisted. I could see the gloomy streets illuminated by artificial light, a sparrow pecking at a frozen piece of bread by the curb. I hadn't traveled in time again. Something willed for summer to linger within the boundaries of this place, and summer obeyed.

It was quiet. I couldn't hear the distant sirens, the F train passing, or any of the other greatest hits of the city's perpetual soundtrack. The only sound came from the insects and the leaves caressed by a gentle breeze. The place was peaceful. It made me want to simply stand there and enjoy its tranquility.

A jolt of adrenaline coursed through me. Was this a trap? The sort of enchantment that convinced a careless visitor to stand there feeling at peace until he died of thirst or exhaustion? But no, nothing seemed to hold me in place. I could think clearly and move at will. I took a tentative step forward.

The cat looked up. Its eyes focused upon mine. We stared at each other for only a moment, and then I was flung over the fence by a violent force.

There was no time to react, nor did any of my amulets and charms activate quickly enough to counter the invisible giant hand that grabbed and tossed me over an eight-foot-tall fence. I barely had time to wrap my hands around my head before I landed in the street and rolled through a thin layer of dirty slush.

I earned a fresh assortment of scrapes and bruises, but I was lucky; nothing was broken. I groaned as I got up onto my feet and approached the fence with extreme caution. On the other side, winter ruled over the cemetery. I found the crumbling grave marker at the center of the field, but it was unoccupied. There were no paw tracks in the pristine field of white snow.

Getting inside that house wasn't going to be easy. Wet, bruised, and humbled, I opted to quit while I was behind, and headed home.

My phone buzzed as I was driving. John Smith's name appeared on Caller ID.

I was exhausted, sore, and minutes away from a soft bed and a hot shower, so I considered ignoring the call. I thought back on all the times I'd ducked calls from Mose. I always operated on the philosophy that it was easier to ask forgiveness than permission, that the victor was not to be judged, presumably because they'd be too busy writing history. But events had been in flux, John was not Mose, and I was at least somewhat responsible for getting him stuck on the hot seat, running the Watch in this most tumultuous of times. I picked up the call.

"What have you done, Conrad?" John sounded disappointed rather than angry. He also sounded deeply, deeply exhausted.

"How much time have you got?" I replied. "Seriously though, what do you mean?"

"Did you or did you not get into an altercation with the Emersonians this morning?"

The fight at Kings Games had taken place something like ten hours earlier, but after the day I'd had, it seemed more like a week. It was also the only time I hadn't felt outmatched, wasn't a minnow navigating its way through shark-infested waters. The mental image of those thugs fleeing down the block made me smile. "I may have had a disagreement with them. Yes."

"They claim you attacked them, Conrad." John sighed. "They claim you used artifacts against them."

I replayed the fight in my mind. The only artifact I'd used was a defensive amulet, and there was no way for them to tell whether I was relying on one or drawing on powers of my own. "They accosted me. And I didn't need artifacts to take care of a few upstarts."

"In the complaint they filed, they claim you used a shard of Atlantean crystal to defeat them. They have witnesses who attest to you chasing them down the street as you clutched it in your hand," said John.

"That's utter nonsense! I never chased after them at all. And if I had an Atlantean shard—which I don't anymore!—using it against those punks would be akin to trying to eradicate a cockroach infestation with a machine gun."

"I realize their version of events is embellished and twisted," said John. "But the fact is you confronted them. The mayor's office has been looking for an excuse to move against the Watch. Your reckless actions have provided them with one."

I squeezed the wheel hard with my right hand. "Move against us how? They already have us paralyzed, doing zilch, while their goon squads terrorize the gifted. Do you know what I've seen since I got back? Fear! The sort of fear among the gifted that an oppressed people experience under the rule of a tyrant. The—"

"Holcomb is evicting us," John cut me off.

"What?" I pulled over and stopped the car.

"Our headquarters are in a municipal building, and technically the city has the right to kick us out," said John.

"Technically?" I roared. "Technically?! We've been protecting this city for generations. That building wouldn't be standing today if it wasn't for us! Someone who clawed their way into power five minutes ago shouldn't have the right to so thoroughly wreck things!"

"Calm down," said John. "Think of what you're saying. Do you believe we're above the law? We're not vigilantes. We're the Watch. We have to preserve our way, our principles. And that means working for the people of this city, not against them, or their elected officials."

"You mean the officials that want to kick us out on our ass? What's going to be left to preserve?" I asked.

"You don't get to claim the moral high ground in this," said John. "Your actions are what gave them the opening."

"They were always going to do it. It's easy to manufacture an excuse."

"I'm exploring our legal options," said John. "To that end, I need you to come in and give a sworn statement, first thing tomorrow morning."

"You're going to fight them in court? You do realize they're already willing to lie about what happened. This isn't a fight you're going to win playing by their rules, like in some sort of an insipid after-school special."

"If you have a better plan, I'm open to suggestions. In the meantime, be here first thing tomorrow morning. If you're still a guardian of the Watch, then consider this an order."

"I'll be there," I said through gritted teeth, and dropped the call.

The following morning I showed up at the Watch as promised and gave my statement, at length, to a graybeard in a three-piece suit who nodded at everything I said, scribbled something in his notepad, and asked the next question. I stuck to my story: I used no artifacts in defending myself against the Emersonians. I was at the game store on personal business. The rest was true: I didn't pursue them down the street, and I didn't possess anything as powerful as an Atlantean shard.

I wasn't sure what the point of this was. It wasn't like the evidence could be presented in a regular courthouse. The only civil authority that intersected City Hall and the gifted community was the Office of Preternatural Solutions, and I didn't need two guesses to figure out what their solution to this preternatural problem would be. I did what John had asked of me regardless, but I wasn't happy about it.

Terrie Winter was waiting for me outside. The sight of her made my frustration melt away. I don't know how she did it; it seemed to be a magical power unique to Terrie, and one she may not have even realized she possessed.

"Let's take a walk," she suggested.

Once we left the building, she said, "John's a good guy, one of the best. But he's screwing this up. Big time."

I nodded. "Tell me about it."

"The shoes he has to fill are way too big," Terrie said. "Metaphorically, also. He's so concerned with preserving the legacy of the Watch that he doesn't take chances, won't do anything risky. And we're dying a slow death through inaction."

"We have to take the fight to Holcomb, Vaughn, and the Emersonians," I said.

"Yes," said Terrie. "We do. Maybe your necromancer friend will uncover something useful, maybe not, but at some point soon we're going to have to act. Thing is, it can't be a couple of us lashing out. The Watch needs to speak with a unified voice. John is being Chamberlain. He goes out of his way to appease the bad guys instead of standing up to them. We need a Churchill."

"I don't want the job," I said quickly. "Didn't want it last year, and sure as hell don't want it now."

"Sweetie, don't take it the wrong way, but you're no Churchill." Terrie's smile disarmed me as usual.

"Who, then? Do you want the big chair?"

She outright laughed. "I'm no Churchill, either. No, what we need is Mose back in his own chair, his steady, oversized hand at the reins."

"Mose is gone," I said.

I remembered watching him fall to his knees, the last of his divine spark consumed in the celestial battle. That was the last time any of us had seen him.

"Gone," said Terrie. "But not dead."

"Mose is alive!?" A flood of conflicting emotions coursed through me. The last time I'd seen him, up on that rooftop, he saved my life, and countless others. He didn't hesitate to fight by my side, even though his abilities were relatively insignificant by comparison. But they were enough to tip the scales, at the last possible moment. He'd burned all of his celestial power, the same way I had. Draining my powers like that had turned me back into a middling. It stood to reason that the same could have happened to him. After all, his body was never found. But why would he walk away? Why would Mose disappear when we needed him so badly, and he knew it? It was contrary to all I knew of the determined, implacable leader of the Watch.

"We've been looking for him," said Terrie. "The Watch, the irregulars, and many other friends and allies. He disappeared, but there is a very rare and difficult spell some of us risked our lives to perform. I can tell you with absolute certainty that as of a few weeks ago he was alive and present in our world."

Despite his disappearance now seeming more like a parent walking out to buy a pack of cigarettes and never coming back, mostly I felt an immense relief. It was as though the death of a friend and ally had just been erased from the ledger of the many mistakes and unpleasant decisions I've had to make in my life, and will one day answer for. I wiped moisture from the corner of my eye.

"Truly, this is the best news I've heard since returning to New York," I said.

Terrie noticed me tear up, and offered her best, reassuring smile. "That's how those of us who know about this felt as well."

A realization hit me. "John doesn't know, does he?"

"It would break him," said Terrie. "It's bad enough that he's trying so hard to maintain a status quo on behalf of a dead mentor. If he knew Mose was out there, somewhere, impossible to reach, perhaps in need of our help this entire time .... He wouldn't be able to function, let alone lead."

"I ... I think I know how that feels," I admitted.

"Yes, I wasn't keen on telling you, either," said Terrie.

This surprised me. I wasn't nearly as close to our absconded leader as John was, and Terrie couldn't possibly have known how much I blamed myself for him being gone. Or could she? Terrie had always been the most perceptive and empathetic of us.

"I tell you now because we've hit a wall. We need him back, Conrad. It's the only way I can think of to restore the Watch. We've tried every spell, followed every lead. I'm hoping that you might think of something else. Perhaps ask your friends at Abaddon." She looked around to make sure she wasn't overheard. "Or perhaps your own abilities could be helpful in such a case?"

Terrie was the only one at the Watch who knew the truth. She knew I had been a middling who ascended to godhood and burned off his power to stop Willodean. She knew Mose had been a minor godling as well, the god of the nexus of power located under the Manhattan Municipal Building. She'd never once asked me to tap into whatever vestiges of divine abilities or knowledge I may have retained after my brief apotheosis. She was asking now.

"I will do everything I can to find him," I told her. "Count on it."

I headed straight for the Abaddon building and called Chulsky as I walked.

"I never assumed Mose was dead, but I have no idea as to his whereabouts," the CEO told me. "I appreciate your desire to find him, but I must remind you that your assignment resolving the issue between the factions of On High and Down Below is of far greater consequence."

"I'm working on that, but I never promised you one hundred percent of my time. I have other goals and responsibilities as well.

Finding Mose is at the top of that list, just so we understand each other. If that's not good enough, somebody else can take over the Rojas case and I can focus my attention on something easier, like negotiating peace in the Middle East." I was getting progressively louder as I walked and ranted. Passersby turned their heads.

"There's no need to lash out at me," said Chulsky. "I'm not preventing you from pursuing your other goals. I'm merely advising you regarding priorities. I hope my counsel hasn't become unwelcome."

I forced myself to consider things rationally. Chulsky wasn't responsible for my role in Mose's disappearance, nor was he out of line in what he had said. Like any paying client I ever had, he was merely following up on his interests when I had to tell him I was simultaneously pursuing something else. And in this case, he might've been right. It didn't matter whether Emersonians controlled the city or if the Watch kept its headquarters if New York got obliterated in a localized armageddon. My nerves were getting the better of me. I needed to get a grip if I hoped to achieve any of my goals, whether they involved Abaddon or not.

"I'm sorry," I told Chulsky. "The news about Mose hit me hard, and I haven't sorted out my emotions yet. I shouldn't have taken it out on you."

"I stand by what I said about priorities," he said. "But for what it's worth, Mose is my friend, too. I hope you find him."

"I'm glad you feel that way, because I'm going to need a quick ride on the Abaddon express."

CHAPTER 11

TINY the doortroll sized me up when I entered the Abaddon building.

"You look like crap, annoying loudmouth," he said. "I mean, more than usual."

I said, "Not in the mood," and marched toward the door on the other end of the guardroom, straight at the eight feet of looming, toothy troll.

Tiny took a good look at my grim expression and stepped aside. He appeared almost disappointed at the missed opportunity to exchange barbs with me.

The vestibule beyond the guardroom contained a corridor with a row of identical doors. Each door had a sign on it, with the name of a city. An instance of Abaddon, Inc. existed in most of the major financial and political centers around the world.

I found the Paris door and stepped through.

On the other side lay an identical Abaddon building. The same building, in fact, though thinking about that made my head hurt. I was in Paris, and that's what mattered. A very short cab ride later I arrived at the residence of Dolus, the trickster god.

When Dolus didn't answer the doorbell, I tried the handle and found the front door of his fancy Parisian flat unlocked. I knew this

112

wasn't actually the case; the door merely recognized me and allowed me entry. This method sure beat leaving a key under the doormat, and it boded well for me overall, since I didn't know what kind of reception to expect. Dolus had helped out Willodean and me at one point but ghosted us once things went sideways.

"Dolus?" I walked through the opulent apartment. It was filled with paintings and statues, furniture and books, and none of that stuff appeared to be less than two hundred years old. "Where are you?"

The creaking of parquet floorboards was the only response. The apartment was empty.

I returned to the study where Dolus had first explained his true nature to us.

We'd met him in our travels through Europe, and he'd pretended to be Dale—a down-on-his-luck middling—while secretly observing and evaluating me all along. It was Dolus who'd revealed to me that middlings were god larvae—gods-in-waiting, capable of ascending to become powerful celestials.

The decanter we'd drunk from was there, filled with something undoubtedly fine and expensive. The fruit in the bowl standing next to the decanter was fresh.

I didn't have time for Dolus's usual games. "Come now," I reproached the empty room. "Show yourself. We're long overdue for a talk."

"You believe we have something left to talk about, after what you've done?"

It took me a second to focus on Dolus, who appeared out of nowhere and was now lounging in the same armchair he'd occupied after teleporting us to this room from Ukraine.

"What *I've* done?" I repeated in a rather gormless manner.

"I took you under my wing. Taught you things you needed to know. Offered you a place by my side among the gods." Dolus picked an apple from the bowl and bit into it. "You threw that gift in my face, burning off your powers to stop your lady friend, who I also warned you about, by the way. As a result, I'm down one useful underling *and* a vial of ambrosia."

"The vial wasn't yours in the first place," I pointed out.

"Please." He took another bite of the apple. "You managed to steal it. It would've been a piece of cake for me."

"Yet you sent me to get it. And I died! If it weren't for Willodean bringing me back, we wouldn't be having this conversation at all."

"What? You wanted me to hand you godhood on a silver platter? That's not how it works." Dolus tossed the half-eaten apple without looking, and it landed in an antique trash pail. "You could've gone after it with a more competent crew. You could've stopped Willodean before her powers blossomed and she lost her mind. But no, you waited and waited, and as a result, I got nothing for my troubles. And now you show up at my home uninvited, like we're old pals, and you demand an audience? I'm rather cross with you."

"I don't think so," I said.

Dolus arched his eyebrow. "You don't think I'm upset?"

"No. I think you got exactly what you wanted, Willodean took care of the Nascent Anodynes International problem for you, and I took care of a dangerous goddess of death, whom you needed to mop up the mess in New York but couldn't count upon to play for your team long-term."

Dolus stared at me with an amused expression on his face. "Ah, so you believe I gave you the illusion of free will while manipulating events surreptitiously. How very … godlike of me."

"It's exactly what a trickster god would do. The only missing piece of the puzzle is your motive. Would you care to enlighten me?" I asked.

"Not at all," said Dolus. "It's a nice theory, but it stinks of human desperation, doesn't it? The drought killed the crops? Blame the rain god. Some king got his army mired in a land war in Asia over an infatuation? Blame the god of love. Things didn't go well for Conrad Brent? Why, it must be the trickster god's fault, because Conrad is infallible, you see. If you've come here to blame me for your troubles, you've wasted a trip."

"If you don't want to admit it, fine. But there's something you might not know." I dropped into the armchair opposite him and looked him straight in the eye. "I wasn't the only one who burned off his powers to stop Willodean. Mose had to help me, and he depleted his powers, too. New York City is down not one, but two good-guy gods in the aftermath of these events—be they my fault or yours."

"You think I don't know this?" Dolus leaned forward, somber. "Mose was a young, weak god, but he was a force for good indeed. His sacrifice is another casualty of your poor decisions."

He was so convincing, the ancient trickster god looking at me with an oh-so-sincere expression. But there was something in his eyes that made me even more certain that my version of events was correct. But, why such a gambit? Was Marko Hanson of Nascent Anodynes even more dangerous than I'd known? Was this an over-complicated ploy to remove Willodean from the game? Then again, he could've simply left her, or even both of us, in Ukraine and let the dragon eat us. There was something I was missing, some crucial piece of the puzzle. Dolus didn't seem interested in offering me clues at the moment.

"I can't make you tell me the truth if you don't want to," I said. "I came seeking a favor, and—"

"Of course you did," Dolus interrupted. "I'm only surprised it took you this long. You could've come and had this heart-to-heart at any point, but you only showed up when you needed something from me."

"Same as you never showing up to help us take Willodean down," I countered. "I figured you could see me any time you wanted. After all, only one of us can teleport anywhere at will, right? But you never drop by, you never call—"

"What do you want?" asked Dolus brusquely.

"I want you to help me find Mose," I said.

Something akin to surprise flashed in Dolus's eyes. "Is that all? You don't want me to take care of your fae problem, dethrone Holcomb, or loan you twenty euros for cab fare?"

"I don't expect you to do any of those things, Dolus. Besides, I don't want to owe you any favors. I want us to be even, after this," I said.

Dolus contemplated my words. We sat in silence, which was an atypical thing for either of us. When the silence stretched to the point of discomfort, he spoke.

"I will grant you this favor," he said. "But, no more. I'm not your personal wishing well. The next time you show up here, the door of this dwelling will not open to you. Do you understand?"

"Thank you," I said, and I meant it.

"I'm not doing this for you as much as for Mose," said Dolus.

I frowned. "What do you mean? Is he in some sort of trouble?"

"You'll see."

Dolus waved his hand and everything around me disappeared.

I was teleported into a desert. It was dark. I assumed I was somewhere in Asia because it was the middle of the night. It was cool but not especially cold, so it might have been close to the equator or somewhere in the Southern hemisphere, where it was summer. Australia, then? Or New Zealand? Did New Zealand have any deserts? The sky was full of stars, but I wasn't one of those people who could identify the constellations. I only knew that the majesty and multitude of lights in the night sky meant we were far from major population centers and their light pollution.

My eyes adjusted to the dim light. Unless Dolus had played a practical joke on me, and I really didn't think he would, Mose was around here somewhere. I saw the outline of a small and dilapidated single-story house nearby. More of a hovel, really. There were no power lines leading to it, so the place was literally off the grid. A phone booth-sized structure next to it must've been an outhouse, so it also lacked indoor plumbing.

I was a city slicker. Even a cozy cabin in the Poconos was firmly outside of my comfort zone. Mose was a lifelong New Yorker, too. What was he doing in a place like this?

I approached the house and knocked, calling Mose's name. The front door creaked, slightly ajar. There was no response, and no light emanated from the dirty windows. I pushed the door open, and it squealed in protest. It was dark inside. I heard the low growl of a wild animal within. I fumbled for my phone and turned on the flashlight, also noting the lack of cell service.

The flashlight revealed a room littered with fast food wrappers, cans, and empty bottles. There was a table piled high with trash, a wardrobe, and a bed that would've been too small for me, let alone Mose.

On the floor next to the bed, Mose slept atop a pile of dirty blankets. He was still a very large man, but he was thinner than I remembered and appeared haggard. A thick, unkempt beard covered his face. There were crumbs in it. Mose looked like he stank, though I couldn't really tell as the overbearing aroma of stale French fries and beer permeated the room. Mose snored, and that solved the mystery of the animal growling sounds.

"Mose," I said. When he didn't react, I called out his name louder. Eventually, I took hold of his immense shoulder and shook it.

Mose groaned, tried and failed to shift his weight like a beached whale struggling on dry land. Finally, he blinked several times and rubbed at his eyes.

"Mose," I repeated. "It's me, Conrad."

He sat up slowly, brushed strands of dirty hair away from his face, and focused on me.

"Turn that flashlight off, will you?" Mose's voice sounded rough, as though he had grown disused to speaking.

I pointed the flashlight away from the big guy and aimed it at the ceiling, creating a small makeshift lamp. "What happened to you, Mose?"

"You know damn well." Mose plucked a beer bottle off the floor. It had a little liquid still sloshing at the bottom, and he downed it.

I looked around for a place to sit, but there wasn't a single chair in the room and Mose's rags blocked the bed, so I remained on my feet.

"I suppose I do," I said. "I'm sorry about that."

Mose grunted something incomprehensible in response.

"Why did you leave?" I blurted out. When Mose didn't respond, I added, "We needed you. We still need you."

Mose made a chortling sound that grew louder until his belly-deep laughter rang across the cabin. He sat up.

"No one needs *this*," said Mose. He gestured toward himself with the empty bottle and tossed it to the side. It rolled and clinked against one of many identical bottles on the floor.

"You're wrong." I thought back to my years at the Watch, the implacable Mose in his office as much a fixture of New York City as the Chrysler Building or the Brooklyn Bridge. "You're so much more than the powers you've lost. You're a leader, an inspiration, a symbol. You unite people and get them to do the right thing."

"I have none of that left to give," said Mose. He climbed to his feet, his head inches away from the ceiling, and stretched. "I

117

protected my city for two hundred years. I've put out fires in the Bowery and fought sea serpents in Lower New York Bay. I've been a leader, a symbol, whatever the hell I needed to be for the sake of my city and its people. Hasn't it been enough? How much more can anyone expect me to give?"

"Being a protector isn't something you owe us. It isn't something we demand of you," I said, looking up at him. "It's who you are. Those fires you put out in the Bowery, that was back in the early 1800s when you were called Mose the Fireboy?"

Mose nodded, a fraction of an inch.

"You were a middling then, weren't you? All those feats, all those acts of courage; you were a middling the entire time. It was many years later, after you recruited others into the Watch, that you disappeared for several decades. That must've been when you ascended to godhood. Do I have that right?"

Mose heaved a deep sigh and nodded again.

"You became a legend without any powers. And that was before you had loyal followers, an organization to lead, before you'd accumulated centuries of knowledge and wisdom. You're the best of us, even if you're no longer the god of the nexus."

"You don't understand," said Mose. "You don't know how it feels."

"I'm a middling who ascended to godhood and burned my powers, same as you. Who would understand what you're going through better than me?"

"You were a god for a very short time. You never became ..." Mose paused, searching for the right word. "Addicted to it."

"Addicted to power?" I asked.

"What better, more euphoric a thing is there?" said Mose.

I recalled learning that after Mose came back to the Watch, he curbed his infamous appetites. A notorious glutton and bon vivant, Mose became practically a monk after he returned to New York City during the Reconstruction era. Was power a stand-in for his past vices, one so potent and pure that all others paled by comparison?

"Imagine your limbs cut off, your eyes gouged out, your nose broken," Mose said. "You can still hear and taste, but you can no longer see, touch, or smell. That's the equivalent to how I feel every waking moment." Mose ran his hand through his tangled hair. "You had the power for a brief time, too brief to become reliant upon it. Believe me, that is a blessing. I've tried to dull my remaining senses with alcohol and drugs, but the relief they offer is fleeting at best."

"What about companionship?" I asked. "Have you tried being among the people who love and respect you instead of this self-imposed existence as a hermit? Come back to New York with me. We'll get you cleaned up, ply you with good food, and most importantly, distract you from what you've lost."

"No," Mose said firmly. "This is my detox. If I'm to survive the change in my circumstances, I must have this solitude. My only chance to reconcile myself to life as a middling again is to stay here. It may take years, perhaps decades …" He trailed off, lost in thought, then refocused on me. "I don't know how you managed to find me, but if you truly care about me, you will leave me be, and never tell anyone where I am."

I considered pressing my case. Surely, Mose would choose to help if he knew the threats his organization and his city were facing. Surely, the needs of millions outweighed one person's mental health and well-being. But those were only rationalizations; cold equations that permitted logic to rule over emotion. I thought of Omelas again, of Mose suffering at the heart of New York City. There were people willing to shove him into that torture chamber. Leaders of men who steeled their hearts and found it within themselves to accept that the ends justify the means.

I was not one of those people. Perhaps that was ultimately why I refused to become the next leader of the Watch, deferring to John. For all of his indecisiveness, I had little doubt he would've dragged Mose kicking and screaming back into the fold.

I nodded reluctantly. "I won't tell anyone how to find you. I will say you're indisposed. But I will lie to them, and tell them you're well."

Mose's lips split into a bitter smile. "Trickster gods do make the best liars," he said.

"Is there anything you need? Anything at all? Money? Magical artifacts?" I wrinkled my nose. "Air freshener?"

"Solitude is all I require," said Mose. "This is literally the farthest and the loneliest place I could find."

"I'll respect your wishes," I promised. "One last question and I'm gone."

119

Mose waited impassively.

"Where are we, and how do I get back to New York?"

It turned out that Mose was hiding in the Australian outback. He made his home on the outskirts of a village called Little Topar, in New South Wales. I had no artifacts on me capable of opening a portal, so my only option was to rely on mundane transportation for a thousand-kilometer trip to Sydney where the nearest branch of Abaddon, Inc. was located.

It was late afternoon by the time I finally got there. After a twelve-hour ride and various annoying misadventures and delays along the way, the sight of those marble columns was most welcome. The front doors had been locked, so I headed for the guardroom at the side of the building.

Instead of the usual doortroll, there was a five-foot-tall koala guarding the entrance.

"G'day mate," said the koala. "How may I help ya?"

"Umm ..." I didn't get it. If Abaddon existed in all those cities at the same time, then how could an entirely different creature be guarding the entrance? The concept was making my head hurt. "Where's Tiny?"

"No one here by that name, mate." The koala looked at me with those huge, murky eyes that appeared unfocused and dull.

"I need the door to New York," I said.

"We're closed," said the koala. "This is an employee entrance. Come back tomorrow and make an appointment, eh?"

"I work here," I said. "That is to say, I work for Chulsky. And also for the Watch. We have the right of access to the portals."

"Wouldn't know anything about that," said the koala. "Someone will be in tomorrow morning to sort this out. Well, go on. Don't stand there like you have a roo loose in the top paddock."

I was tired, annoyed, and upset about the way my encounter with Mose had gone. I'd had enough of the uppity doorcreatures with their local color.

"Listen, you oversized discount-bin teddy bear, I don't have time for your nonsense. You pick up that phone, and you call Daniel Chulsky, or Steve Irwin, or Crocodile Dundee, or whoever is in charge of this branch, and you tell them Conrad Brent is here, and he's in a hurry."

The koala bristled—literally. "Crikey, there's no need for that kind of language. You Yanks are so rude. I'm going to place that call now, and if you fair dinkum know Daniel, I'll let you right on through, no worries."

I understood about half of what he was saying. I nodded toward the landline on his desk, hoping he'd place the call before he started drinking Fosters or grilling blooming onions on the barbie, or whatever it was talking koalas did.

The marsupial made that call and nodded as he listened to whoever was on the other end of the line.

"No wukkas," said the koala once he hung up the phone. "You go on through. Sorry mate, I'm just doing my job, deadset. Gotta check to see if the visitor might be a drongo or a crook."

"I didn't know those attributes were still required in order to come to Australia," I told him as I walked through.

I could hear him muttering something about bloody Yanks as I went.

CHAPTER 12

I got to sleep in my own bed that night, but my sleep wasn't restful. The various problems I was dealing with were escalating. I'd never been afraid of facing danger, or standing for what was right, but I liked my challenges straightforward. Hunt down a serial killer. Protect a sacred grove. Encourage a malevolent sorcerer to move their operation outside the boundaries of my borough. Instead, I was wrestling with issues I couldn't fight head-on or bluff my way through.

Mose was as good as gone, leaving a well-meaning but less capable John Smith struggling to lead the Watch. Emersonians terrorized the gifted population of the city with carte blanche from the mayor's office. Angels and demons were preparing to turn the city into a battleground over a disagreement I didn't fully understand. And as if all that weren't enough, only a flimsy armband stood between me and a deferred fae execution.

Those were big scope problems. For the life of me I couldn't understand why Daniel Chulsky had ever thought I'd be a good candidate to constantly deal with such issues on behalf of Abaddon. I felt supremely unqualified, and at a loss for what to do next.

After a few hours of fitful sleep, I felt somewhat better. My problems wouldn't just go away. I needed to address them methodically, take it one step at a time, focus on the parts of each problem I could unravel. At some point, fortune would have to smile upon me, for variety's sake.

For the moment, the problem that seemed the least insurmountable was getting past the cat in the Gravesend Cemetery. If I could break into the Rojas house, perhaps I could then get to the bottom of what it was the angels and demons wanted and scratch a potential armageddon off my list of troubles.

First, I loaded up on artifacts. I didn't know exactly what the cat was: a nature spirit, a poltergeist, or a feline Cerberus guarding the interred. I brought everything I could think of and a few items that were outside the box, just in case.

Second, I asked for help.

Terrie Winter was superb at identifying various kinds of magic, and she had as much experience as me in dealing with the peculiar manifestations of the same. She was also one of the most powerful gifted I'd ever met, save for gods, angels, and other souped-up entities.

"I'm on my way," Terrie said when I summarized the problem for her. "Text me the address. Oh, and grab me an everything bagel with butter from that spot you like. I haven't had breakfast."

Forty minutes later, I handed her the food and a paper coffee cup with a Bagel Beagle logo. We leaned against her Corvette—the convertible was shiny and new but, as best I could tell, not at all magical—and I explained the problem to her in greater detail. I trusted Terrie completely—she already knew that I was a middling and any other secrets I might keep were insignificant by comparison.

"This should be fun." Terrie wiped the corner of her mouth with a napkin. "I love cats."

"I don't think you're going to love this cat." I glanced at the metal fence.

The cemetery looked serene. The accumulation of snow in the street had already melted, leaving only scattered piles of dirty slush. But beyond the gate, the gravestones were still covered in a shroud of pristine white snow.

"Let's see." Terrie held her enchanted staff to the metal bars, poked it through, and examined the lock on the front gate. "An eternal summer enchantment is contained within the cemetery. It has nothing to do with the fence or the lock. Those are both ordinary." She stuck her hand through the bars up to the elbow. "See? Nothing. Guess we have to get in there to activate it."

"Right," I said, remembering my short and ignoble flight over the fence, landing in the street. "Let's be extra careful."

"Always am," said Terrie. Then she climbed the fence and swung one foot over to the other side. "Need a special invitation?"

I followed. We dropped onto the ground inside the fence, and landed in tall grass, surrounded by insects and birds, and a warm summer breeze.

"Sweet!" said Terrie. She looked up at the cloudless sky. "I may have to start coming here to work on my suntan."

I pointed toward the center of the cemetery, where the old tuxedo cat perched atop the same gravestone. It was as though the cat hadn't moved in the days since my last visit.

As if on cue, the cat looked up and studied us with its amber eyes.

I could feel it coming. Like static electricity in the air before the storm. I braced for impact.

Terrie raised her staff, its swirling wood patterns leading up to a fist-sized purple gemstone embedded at the top. A wave of arcane energy rushed forth from the cat, broke against the pulsating gemstone and washed around us like floodwater finding its way past a tall rock.

"Good kitty," she said. "Nice kitty. You can stop this now." The onslaught of energy didn't cease. Terrie's arm began to tremble with effort, the tip of the staff shaking. "Little help?" she asked me.

I activated an ancient Peruvian disc, which the Huari people had used to counter the Tiwanaku war spells long before the Inca dominated that part of South America. It emitted a powerful barrier, capable of blocking most hostile magic.

"This will buy us a few minutes, tops," I said. Huari discs were highly effective but also short-lived. It took both a long time and a considerable amount of magic to recharge one.

Terrie lowered her staff and sighed in relief.

"I'm going to try a psychic link," she said. She focused on the cat, her brown eyes locking with the creature's unblinking stare.

Everything grew quiet. The birds, insects, and even the breeze were silent as the two communed. The waves of arcane power emanating from the cat continued to noiselessly break against the power of the Huari barrier.

After about twenty seconds of this, Terrie gasped and broke eye contact with the cat. She turned to me, looking like a diver who'd finally breached the surface and inhaled a sweet lungful of fresh air.

"How long was I out?" she asked.

I told her.

"Wow. It felt like an hour." Terrie shuddered. "Remind me not to do that again anytime soon."

The arcane energy was steadily eroding the barrier.

"We have maybe a minute left," I said.

"Lady Moody," Terrie addressed the cat, "we mean you and those whose peace you preserve no harm. We're of the Watch. We're guardians. Protectors, like you."

If the cat heard or understood her, it—she?—showed no sign.

"We humbly ask safe passage," said Terrie. "We request the sanctuary of the Gravesend settlement."

I could feel the barrier beginning to give.

"She's not buying what I'm selling," said Terrie. She raised her staff again. "I think a strategic retreat is in order."

"Yeah, no argument from me."

Terrie and I backed a few steps to the fence. Puss-without-Boots watched our hasty retreat. As soon as both of us touched the fence, the cat lowered its gaze, and the attack ceased. Moments later, the remnants of the protective barrier dissipated as well.

We didn't try our luck again, opting to climb fast.

"So, Lady Moody?" I asked when we were safe in the street. The temperature around us was once again within the margin of error of water's freezing point.

"She was the first woman to have founded a village in colonial America," said Terrie.

I nodded. That much I knew.

125

"She was also a gifted, who escaped persecution by the Puritans. When she founded the Gravesend settlement, she made it known that all manner of gifted, heretics, and free-thinkers were welcome here. And they came, from all across the continent. Gifted and mundanes, living in peace, side by side."

"That's nice. Doesn't explain the belligerent feline," I said.

"I'm getting to that," said Terrie. "In exchange for sanctuary, the gifted who lived in the settlement poured some of their magic into protections erected around the village commons."

"And the cemetery is within the boundary of the commons," I added.

"Right. When she was alive, Lady Moody used the accumulated magic to protect the settlement, much like Mose could tap into the nexus under the Watchtower and harness its power to protect the city."

I felt a pang of guilt at the mention of Mose and made myself focus on the present problem.

Terrie continued, "When she died, Lady Moody imbued her power and spirit into her familiar, a cat who passed a few weeks before she did. It became the guardian of the commons. Over time, as the gifted ceased donating their magic, its area of influence shrank until it encompassed only the cemetery."

"She told you all that?" I asked, looking back over the fence. Not that I could see the cat, or any signs of summer, from outside the cemetery.

"Not exactly." Terrie leaned on her staff for support. The ordeal had taken a lot out of her. "I saw flashes. Moments from Deborah Moody's life, moments from the familiar's afterlife. It was a jumble. Postcards mixed with flashes of emotion, out of order. A puzzle I had to put together, and I felt like I'd been at it for a long time before I finally sorted out some of the details."

"We're up against a four-hundred-year-old witch possessing her dead cat. Lovely." I took mental inventory of the artifacts I brought. I hadn't thought far enough outside the box, after all.

"I thought so, too, which is why I tried to reason with her," said Terrie. "But that isn't quite right. Lady Moody transferred her power and will into the vessel she made using the dead cat, but I don't think her mind, her consciousness is there at all. It's just a thing, programmed to keep out gifted intruders. Like one of your amulets, except biological rather than inanimate, if that makes sense?"

"Hmm." I shrugged noncommittally. The explanation made sense. Then again, sense was such a relative thing. "All right, how do we turn off a zombie cat?"

"This isn't going to be easy. Generations of gifted poured magic into the Gravesend commons for over a century," said Terrie. "They kept doing it for a while even after Lady Moody passed away and was buried somewhere in there." She pointed at the cemetery. "They wanted their descendants, and the site of their eternal rest, to be guarded after they were gone."

"Which is why the enchantment hasn't run out of juice," I said.

"Exactly. Since no one is adding more power, the enchanted area has been shrinking, slowly. If you had enough time, you could simply wait it out," said Terrie.

"How much time?" I asked.

"A couple of centuries, give or take a few weeks."

"I don't think that timetable works for me," I said.

We stared at the cemetery. A beat-up Honda zoomed past us, blasting a pop song loud enough to be heard through rolled-up windows.

"Then we're back to square one," said Terrie. "Grumpy Cat doesn't seem to differentiate between good guys and bad guys. It recognizes an intruder, and it tosses them out on their ass."

"A magic-sensitive intruder," I said. "I've seen mundane kids climb over and explore the cemetery before."

"Okay," said Terrie. "How does that help us? Your middling status isn't a free pass either, as we've already established."

"I have an idea. We can't get around the fact that we're gifted, or, in my case, magic sensitive, but maybe we can get around the fact that we're intruders?"

"That's an interesting thought. But how do we do that?"

"What if we're allowed to go in there?" I pointed at the gate.

"Into the cemetery that's been closed for the better part of a century?"

"Hang on." I dialed my cell. "Greg? Conrad here. Good, good. Listen, I could use your help, buddy. I need a key to the Old Gravesend Cemetery. Yeah. Okay, perfect, see you soon." I hung up.

"Who's Greg?" asked Terrie, amused.

"Ten years ago Greg was a rank-and-file Parks Department employee I saved from a werewolf. Today he's still with the department, and he's some sort of a big shot now. Still, when someone saves you from being devoured by a two-hundred-pound bundle of anger and teeth, you don't soon forget that. And when that someone needs an occasional favor, especially an innocuous one, like access to a place administrated by the Department of Parks & Recreation, you just say you'll be there soon, without asking too many follow-up questions."

Terrie grinned. "That's the Conrad I know. Never let a good werewolf rescue go to waste."

I grinned, too. "It'll take him at least twenty minutes to get here. Shall we find some more coffee?"

Greg showed up half an hour later and unlocked the gate. His hair was grayer and he was perhaps twenty pounds heavier than the last time I saw him, about five years earlier. The desk job hadn't been kind to his waistline. Greg still seemed a little in awe of me, and eager to please. He handed me a shiny new key. "I made a copy for you," he said. "Just lock it up when you're finished, okay?"

"You're the best, thanks. I need one more tiny favor. Could you please grant Terrie and me permission to go in there?"

Greg looked at me funny, but he didn't argue. When mundanes learn there's more in the world than they've dreamt of in their philosophies *and* that there are folks who are willing to protect them and their families against the evil things that howl in the night, those people will generally bend over backward to make our lives easier.

"Both of you are hereby authorized to go in there any time you need," said Greg. After a pause, he asked, lowering his voice. "Is this place safe for people? Anything I should know about?"

"Safe as houses," I said, without specifying which houses. The place was perfectly harmless for a mundane, so there wasn't anything for the Parks & Rec Department to worry about. "If that changes at any point, I'll be sure to warn you."

We waited until Greg drove off and then cautiously entered the cemetery, Terrie's staff and my amulets at the ready.

Inside, it was still winter. Our footprints were the only disturbance in the unblemished snow as we walked past the gravestones weathered by age. We approached the one Moody's familiar had perched upon in the magical summertime. Terrie reached toward it, her fingers tracing some invisible pattern around the stone.

"I can feel its presence," she said. "A power that's bubbling under the surface like a dormant volcano."

"Is Mount Catsuvius going to erupt?"

Terrie closed her eyes, communing with whatever magic she tapped into. "I don't think so." She turned away from the headstone. "Looks like your hunch was right. We're permitted to be here, and the guardian is ignoring us. So long as we don't defile the place or attempt to dig up any residents, we should be good."

We walked deeper into the graveyard, to where the headstones were taller and more grandiose. Beyond them lay another fence separating the backyards of the houses in the cul-de-sac from the cemetery.

Approaching the Rojas house, Terrie paused again and traced the invisible arcane patterns with her hand and her staff.

"Curious." She squinted at the fence.

"What?"

"The summerland enchantment and presumably the area protected by the guardian covers the inside of the cemetery," said Terrie. "But here," she pointed at the house on the other side of the fence, "here it extends outward to include the house."

"Huh." As a middling I wasn't nearly as good at reading those subtleties. I suspected that most other gifted wouldn't have been able to detect them the way Terrie could. "I was wondering how they tapped into the cemetery's power. I suppose it was too much to hope that Rojas was stealing a bit of its juice the way people illegally tap into the power grid, and that there was a cable we could cut."

"Maybe this is a good thing. Maybe our status as authorized persons will let us walk right in," said Terrie.

"I'm sure it can help, but the house is using the power it draws from the cemetery to sustain its own protections. The enchantment is masking them, and I bet you'll feel them as we get closer."

We hopped the fence again, this time to end up in the backyard. The tiny lot was covered in concrete. A pair of lawn chairs and a plastic table with an umbrella through the middle occupied much of the available space.

"Oh, boy," said Terrie. "You were right. I sure feel it now."

I felt it, too. The house protections watched us like a pack of irate invisible guard dogs.

"Think we can overcome all that?" I asked.

"Please." Terrie snorted. "I once had to break past the arcane wards at the Voelker Orth Museum. And that other time, I found my way out of IKEA. Compared to those feats, this is a cakewalk. We just have to roll up our sleeves."

And roll up our sleeves we did. We also applied elbow grease, worked our fingers to the bone, and burned the midnight oil. Well, the midafternoon oil anyway. That's how long it took—we literally spent several hours working the problem.

Which doesn't sound all that bad to the uninitiated, but it is. Getting past a magical ward is usually a matter of either brute force or casting the right counterspell. Neither takes very long. That is why a truly effective ward is a Gordian knot of enchantments. Try to break past one with a simple, quick method, and you trigger a dozen more. It takes even greater skill to set up such a complex defense than to defeat it. In those rare cases where one encounters a sophisticated system like that, they're in for several hours of essentially trying to disable one of those movie bombs, where the hero sweats as they ponder which wire to cut and inevitably makes the decision only when there are mere seconds left on the clock.

This is usually not a pleasant experience, and I was considerably perplexed at the fact that I rather enjoyed it.

Despite the stress, despite the danger, there was nowhere I'd rather be than working side by side with Terrie. She was fearless and funny and smart, and the two of us untangling the deadly wards felt so comfortable and right, like an old married couple putting together a jigsaw puzzle on a lazy Sunday afternoon. All my numerous troubles and anxieties receded into the background. The camaraderie made me feel safer than I had any right to be and calmer than I'd been in a long time. It was like the old times, before I learned about the true nature of middlings and got swept up in grandiose events. Life used to feel simple back then.

CHAPTER 13

AFTER several hours of hard work, we finally broke through the house's defenses. The last step was to pick the mundane lock on the back door, which presented little difficulty.

Terrie flipped the switch, and the lights came on. It was warm inside: neither the electricity nor the gas had been cut off since the time of Benicio Rojas's passing. Somebody must've been paying the utility bills.

We walked through the house, turning on lights and examining every room, one by one.

"This looks like a furniture store showroom," said Terrie.

She was right. Although the rooms were furnished, there were no personal effects anywhere. No photos or paintings decorated the walls. There were no dishes stored in the cabinets or even a tube of toothpaste in the bathroom. More importantly, there was no sign of anything magical or unusual; nothing worth going to so much trouble to protect.

"None of this stuff looks like it has ever been used," Terrie said. "Look, there are no scratches or scuff marks on the chairs and table. The bed is made up and the sheets are pristine, I don't think they've ever been through the wash."

I peeked into the nightstand, then opened the wardrobe drawers. "Nothing inside. This feels more like a set for filming a family sitcom than a home."

"Nah." Terrie ran a finger along the drapes. "Sitcom houses tend to have character. This place was decorated in roadside motel chic. Bland and inoffensive."

"I wouldn't say that," someone chimed in. We both whirled, but there was no one there. "It's very offensive, actually," the disembodied baritone berated us with a sexy Spanish accent reminiscent of Antonio Banderas's talking cat from *Shrek*. "You break into my home, track dirt and snow through the house because you didn't have the decency to wipe your shoes off on the doormat, rifle through my belongings, and then have the temerity to criticize my style. How rude!"

Despite his claims of offense taken, the speaker didn't sound angry, not exactly. If anything, he sounded amused.

I gently pushed in the drawers and stepped away from the wardrobe. "Mr. Rojas, I presume?"

"Who wants to know?"

There was a slight edge to those words. The voice was filled with apprehension, even surprise. Did he think anyone capable or passing through his protections might come here on accident?

"My name is Conrad Brent, and this is my associate, Terrie Winters," I said. "We're here on behalf of Abaddon, Inc."

"Never heard of it," said the voice. Try as I might, I couldn't identify where it was coming from. I expected a hidden speaker of some sort, but it sounded as though Rojas stood right next to us.

"We're very sorry for our uncouth behavior," Terrie intervened. "We meant no offense."

"It seems the charming young lady has manners, after all," came the response. "That's a relief. I do so enjoy *polite* company. Polite company of the female persuasion, most of all."

Terrie and I exchanged a glance. It sounded like our invisible host would be more amenable to anything she might have to say. Terrie understood, and took the lead.

"You've done a thorough job of dissuading any visitors, Mr. Rojas," she said.

"Please, call me Benicio," said the voice. "And yes, it was necessary to take certain precautions as of late. Unpleasant and lonely, to be certain, but entirely unavoidable ..." The voice trailed off.

As I listened to the brief back-and-forth with Terrie and Benicio, I came to a realization. Our host appeared to be the sort of man who, when offered a penny for his thoughts, provided his two cents' worth and then threw in another couple of bucks, just to be sure. He needed only a gentle nudge to tell us what we needed to know, but he was understandably cautious about opening up to total strangers who had just broken into his home. All he needed was some reassurance, and he'd sing like a flock of canaries.

I could've spun a cozy lie, but sometimes the truth is best. So I told the truth. I explained that the angels and demons both laid claim to his property, and about our efforts to reach a peaceful compromise. "So you see, Mr. Rojas—err, Benicio—we had little choice but to get past your defenses in order to investigate. We didn't expect to find you here in person, so to speak. We'd been led to believe you were dead."

Rojas chuckled. "Oh, but I am! Therein lies the problem. It is a tale of wonder and woe, and now that I understand your intentions, it would be my honor to tell you all about it. Why don't you make yourselves comfortable in the living room? May I offer you some wine? I regret that I have no other refreshments on hand, but my wine selection is thoroughly agreeable."

We exchanged glances again. "That would be lovely," said Terrie.

"I'm afraid you'll have to help yourselves, as I'm regretfully incapable of performing the duties of a proper host at the moment," Rojas said, forlorn. "The wine cellar is down the stairs and to the left."

Come into my basement, said the spider to the fly, I thought. Was this a trap? Given what I'd learned from both factions, the wine collection, at least, was real. The answers I sought lay down there and, besides, how much more of a risk was walking down a flight of stairs than breaking and entering into a haunted house? I volunteered to retrieve the wine, leaving Terrie upstairs just in case this really was a trap.

I descended into an ordinary, not at all spooky, basement. Downstairs, the vault-like door had been shut but not locked. Beyond it lay what appeared to be a very nice wine cellar, not that I had much basis for comparison. My knowledge of wine cellars was strictly limited to what I'd seen in movies and TV shows. The air-conditioned and climate-controlled room was filled with racks storing hundreds of bottles in a variety of shapes and sizes.

"Please go to the third wine rack on your left and pick any bottle from the top two rows," instructed Rojas. I nearly jumped, as his voice still sounded like he stood right next to me. For some reason, I hadn't expected him to follow me into the basement. "Yes, that's a nice Merlot. It can be chilled quickly. After all, only a barbarian would drink wine at room temperature."

The bottle I grabbed looked relatively modern, but the collection was vast, with plenty of antique bottles. If I wanted to find the booze Bub was after without spending hours in the cellar, I'd need our host's cooperation.

Back on the ground floor, we retrieved an ice bucket from the otherwise-bare fridge per our host's instructions, placed the bottle inside, and rinsed off a couple of glasses from the dish rack. Then we sat in comfortable, brand-new chairs in the dinette and waited for the wine to cool.

"Fifteen minutes is all it will take," said Rojas. "My greatest regret is the inability to drink wine anymore. I shall have to be content with experiencing its joy vicariously through you."

That was his greatest regret? Really? For a man who'd done business with demons, I figured Rojas would identify bigger issues, upon examining his past. But then, I supposed the grass was always greener on the other side of the afterlife.

As to the vicarious experience, my taste buds weren't designed or trained to differentiate a fancy vintage from Two Buck Chuck, but poor Rojas seemed to genuinely enjoy playing host, so I didn't have the heart to tell him.

"Only a tale of wonder and woe could help us endure the wait," said Terrie.

I thought she was only playing along, but she was eyeing the bottle the way I admire a nice juicy steak, so I wasn't too sure.

"Of course," said Rojas. "My story. When I was a young man, I came to New York from Bolivia in order to make my fortune. I was doing reasonably well, I suppose, but my appetites were always large. I appreciated fast cars, gorgeous women, and, of course, fine wine. I lived comfortably, but my tastes were beyond my means. The tragedy of self-made fortunes is that you pay with your time and your health. By the time you have all the money you need, you're no longer in the prime of your life, and are no longer able to properly enjoy it.

"That's when Mammon, Is, & Goode reached out with their offer. I could have everything I wanted, decades before I might've earned it on my own. Life seemed so long then, and my immortal soul so reasonable a price to pay.

"I won't bore you with the details of my meteoric rise in the world of finance, nor with the accounts of my debauchery. Suffice it to say, Mammon, Is, & Goode delivered on their promises, and then some. I lived the bon vivant life I wanted, experienced every pleasure, sought out every thrill that money could buy. It was glorious.

"As they say, nothing lasts forever. I grew older, and the fate of my soul became a more pressing concern. I had doubled my fortune and my benefactors' investment several times over. Surely I'd earned enough to buy out my contract, or to renegotiate its terms. But, as you can probably guess, they wouldn't budge; they stood to inherit most of my wealth anyway. I was not deterred. As in my youth, I sought to find an alternate solution instead of accepting my circumstances. I consulted priests and exorcists and lawyers who specialized in Faustian bargains. They couldn't help me. The deal I'd struck was ironclad. My benefactors had seen every permutation of a mortal trying to weasel their way out of the contract. I wasn't the smartest, or even the richest, client of theirs to try, and fail, to back out of my side of the bargain.

"When I had all but despaired, an opportunity presented itself. I learned that certain factions of On High were amenable to doing business. That a large-enough bribe might buy an indulgence even for a prolific sinner like me. I offered them whatever they wanted in exchange for salvation. Even so, they were reluctant. My soul had been spoken for. My considerable fortune was not vast enough to justify a direct confrontation with their counterparts from Down Below.

"Despondent, I prayed for a miracle, and it seemed the merciful God relented. A faction of On High was willing to accept my bargain: salvation in exchange for my worldly possessions.

"My euphoria didn't last. I'd spent way too long in corporate boardrooms, negotiating with some of humankind's greatest liars, to miss the signs. It's not that the angels were outright deceiving me; it's that they weren't *sure*. They weren't certain it would work, that their claim upon my soul was stronger, that their faction would have the fortitude necessary to contest Mammon, Is, & Goode's counterclaim.

"My soul remained in peril; a fragile flicker caught between forces both immeasurable and indifferent to my ultimate fate.

"Fear is a powerful motivator, however. I threw myself at the problem, considering and discarding dozens, hundreds, of desperate plans. If there was a way to cheat death, I swore I'd find it. But with the marks of two powerful factions upon my soul, my quest seemed futile. No vampire would turn me. No warlock would restore my vigor and youth. Meddling in my fate was not worth the risk of antagonizing such powerful beings.

"Still, I would not yield. I spent what few years remained of my lifespan with my nose in ancient, forbidden texts. I taught myself necromancy, arcane horology, kabbalah, and other disciplines either shunned or deemed too dangerous by most practitioners. It was not the life of excess I'd grown accustomed to, although I still had my money, my gourmet meals, and my wine.

"I was an octogenarian by the time I felt I was ready. My doctors had warned me that my time was growing short. Whether or not my plan would work, I had nothing left to lose in this life and stood everything to gain in the next. So, when the time came, I didn't shed my mortal coil; I upgraded its model."

Rojas paused dramatically, as he waited for us to ask the question. I needed a moment to shake off the spell of his voice and his cadence to oblige.

"How did you do it?"

"I've learned how to transfer my consciousness and soul into an inanimate object," said Rojas. "Technically, I've become undead. In practice, I'm now the house."

"A lich!" said Terrie. "It's possible for a warlock to tie their soul to an object or a place through the use of necromancy and become a lich."

"I prefer a 'genius loci'," said Rojas. "Lich sounds so ..." He searched for the right words. "It sounds much more evil than I'd like."

"There's no need to put labels on this," I hastened to interject. "Point is, it worked, and here we are. I presume doing what you did prevented either faction from claiming your soul. They couldn't be too pleased about that."

"Oh, yes. As you can probably imagine, the process of tying one's soul to an object is difficult, but not altogether revolutionary, certainly not original enough to spend decades pursuing, yes?" said Rojas.

We both nodded. The thought had crossed my mind, but I felt no need to possibly antagonize Rojas by mentioning it.

"The difficulty wasn't in prolonging my existence; it was in doing so without having my creditors showing up to collect what was owed to them. The likes of them could rip my soul from its current place of residence as easily as a person might extract a weed from a garden, roots and all. The process would surely be most unpleasant." Rojas paused, as though considering those infernal implications. "I pondered the subject for a long time until I came to realize that my having struck a bargain with both On High and Down Below could actually work in my favor. I needed to make it difficult for either faction to get at me, where the inconvenience combined with the risk of offending their counterparts and thus upsetting the fragile equilibrium between the factions simply wouldn't be worth the trouble. I sought to create an impasse neither side would care to break, thus leaving me and my soul to our own devices.

"I found and purchased this house because my eventual status as a technically dead person who is interred within the Gravesend Commons would grant me Lady Moody's protection."

"So that's why the graveyard's spell extends to this house," said Terrie with an enthusiasm of a computer geek who just learned about a cool new widget. "That was really clever."

"Thank you, my dear." Rojas continued, "I then added on whatever charms and protections I could muster, turning my once and future abode into a nearly impregnable fortress. Of course, a determined

137

agent from either faction could force their way through. But, again, I banked on it being too inconvenient. I hoped they would either squabble for a very long time, or opt to ignore me in order to avoid rocking the boat. Meantime, the sigils and wards were meant to stop any of the less powerful entities from getting in."

"You don't seem all that upset about us getting past your protections," I said.

"That's because I'd made a terrible mistake," said Rojas. There was an audible sigh, which was interesting in itself, since last I checked houses didn't have lungs. "Don't get me wrong, my research was spot on. I managed to transfer my being and my soul into this house exactly the way I intended to. What I didn't account for is the tedium.

"Being an empty house is not exactly the afterlife I'd imagined. There's nothing to do, no one to talk to. You two are my first visitors in ages! After a few months of isolation, I was beginning to go stir-crazy. You've done me a favor by disassembling the arcane protections. At least now I can get a cable guy in here to install and turn on a few television sets."

"You're assuming the cable guy is going to arrive before a bunch of angry angels and demons do. I'm not sure how much they really care about your soul, but they seem to want this place, bad." I glanced about the unassuming house. Other than its magic protections, the place was unremarkable, inside and out. It was clear to me that the object of their desire was in the basement. What was so special about fermented grape juice? I added, "And they want your wine collection most of all."

"My wine, of all things? I have no clue as to why," said Rojas. "I own many other assets. Investments, properties, money in the bank. More money than either faction knows about, safe in offshore accounts. The factions could split up all those things, and they'd be worth many times more than this house, including the wine cellar. My collection is nice, but its value is only a fraction of my net worth and, frankly, I don't see why either of them would care. I only had it brought here on a whim. Speaking of wine, the bottle should be sufficiently chilled by now."

Terrie didn't have to be asked twice. She popped the cork like a pro, poured two glasses, and swished her wine delicately before sniffing at the contents of the glass. She then took a sip.

"Mmm," said Terrie. "This is great."

I drank from my glass, figuring the odds of it being poisoned were sufficiently low. The wine was nice enough. I couldn't detect notes of nutmeg and vanilla or whatever it was connoisseurs went on about after tasting the stuff. Not wanting to appear the uncultured boor that I was, I nodded my sage approval.

"It gives me great pleasure to watch you enjoy this," said Rojas. "Being unable to eat and, especially, drink anymore makes me feel like the Down Below got my soul after all, and this is their insidious eternal punishment for my audacity. To top it all off, I have an itch in my second-floor staircase that I can't scratch. It's sheer torture!"

"It occurs to me that if we can somehow convince the factions to leave you alone, you could hire people to come entertain you, talk with you, maybe even move in and live here," I said. "Since you can't give up the house, it being your new body and all, would you be willing to let your creditors have the wine?"

"Anything!" said Rojas. "If you manage to broker a deal that gets them to leave me be, they can have whatever they want. And I'd be immensely grateful. In fact, may I offer each of you a bottle as a gift? A down payment, if you will, for your efforts on my behalf?"

In other words, a bribe, I thought.

Terrie took another sip and pointed at the bottle. "I wouldn't turn down one of these. Thank you!"

"Have you got any 1961 Chateau Latour?" I asked.

Terrie looked at me weird, perhaps wondering what happened to the real Conrad and whether my body had been taken over by an evil sommelier.

"You have exquisite taste, Mr. Brent," said Rojas. "You can tell a lot about a man based on his vintage preferences, you know."

I graciously accepted the undeserved compliment.

A short while later, Terrie and I left the Rojas house. She carried the bottle we'd been drinking from, as well as its sealed twin. I held a dusty old bottle by the neck. The vintage Heaven and Hell were apparently willing to fight a war over sloshed within.

CHAPTER 14

WE checked our phones after leaving the house, and we both had missed calls from Aysha. She'd left messages letting us know that Moira was back. Apparently, what our infiltrator had uncovered was bad news all around. Aysha was gathering a war council, and our presence was requested immediately.

Terrie and I barely had time to grab some fast food. We hadn't eaten since morning and couldn't live on wine alone, though Terrie seemed to be willing to give that diet a sporting chance. A couple of lamb gyros later, we drove into the city. I stopped at the Abaddon building to stash the mysterious wine bottle; I figured it would be safest in Chulsky's hands until I could negotiate with the parties involved.

Aysha had used her connections to borrow a meeting room at the main branch of the New York Public Library. The iconic building near Bryant Park was a well-known landmark, seen in countless movies and TV shows. It had been recently renamed the "Stephen A. Schwarzman Building" because the guy had donated a wheelbarrow of money, but who could ever be expected to pronounce or spell a surname like that correctly? New Yorkers shrugged and went on calling it "the main library building" or just "the one with the lions."

The building in question housed a large library of arcane texts and the active group of research librarians who studied them. They were a well-respected and generally neutral bunch, although each individual librarian held their own beliefs and allegiances. Aysha had been among the first to join Herc's irregulars when he stepped up to help protect the city a year prior.

This time around, we headed in the opposite direction from the arcane areas and onto the second floor where a series of meeting rooms were available for research purposes or an occasional book signing.

As Terrie and I approached the meeting room, we saw Herc standing by the entrance, talking to a couple of the irregulars. He was in his late twenties, a kid from Newark made good, and he commanded the sort of respect from many of the gifted twice or three times his age that I imagine had been given to Patton and George Washington by their contemporaries. He'd earned every bit of it. Herc—Hercules Mulligan—had proved himself to be a natural leader. Now that the city's gifted population faced a different threat, he had once again stepped in to fill the power vacuum left by the currently overcautious Watch.

He had been a close friend, once, willing to risk life and limb on my behalf.

I had not reciprocated by trusting him with my secrets, and when I finally told him the truth it was too late. He no longer considered me a friend, and that hurt.

Herc watched us approach and nodded politely.

"Hey," I said, wishing I could instead apologize, again. But this was neither the time nor the place.

"Thank you for coming," Herc told us, politely but without the warmth I remembered. "Why don't you head on in?"

Inside, Moira O'Leary held court. There was none of the self-doubt and vulnerability she'd displayed when we'd come back from the realm of the fae, none of the self-loathing evident in the state of her hotel room a day later. This was the Moira I was used to, wrapped in confidence like a suit of armor, spikes of sarcasm protruding in order to keep friend and foe at arm's length. The gathered irregulars and representatives of the various gifted groups from around the city treated her like an exotic wild beast; dangerous yet fascinating.

Moira was in the middle of telling some tall tale to whoever would listen. When she saw me and Terrie come in, she winked at me and flashed us a grin, but didn't halt her raconteur act. She leaned back in a chair, with a half-dozen gifted hanging on her every word.

"I guess she's fitting in pretty well," I said to Aysha, who'd made her way over to greet us.

"That girl knows how to turn on the charm when she wants to," said Aysha. "When she walked in twenty minutes ago, the reception she got was colder than the weather outside."

Even now, a few of the attendees kept away from Moira and from those gathered to hear her dispense her malarkey. Those folks looked none-too-pleased to be there. They hung back, casting disapproving glances toward the necromancer. Herc's reputation was enough to get them into the same room with her, but they didn't have to enjoy it.

There was a bit of a hushed commotion with heads turning toward the entrance. John Smith entered, immaculately dressed in one of his signature blue Armani suits. Behind him walked Father Mancini in his Catholic priest's cassock and collar. A large cross with sharpened edges hung around his neck on a leather cord.

All but two of the senior members of the Watch were in attendance. As I understood it, Karl Mercado of Manhattan had sided with the Emersonians, and Gord of the Bronx was on the fence; he didn't like the Emersonians but leaned toward supporting the new mayor and the spirit of what he and the Office of Preternatural Solutions were trying to accomplish.

John and Father Mancini nodded politely to the gathered irregulars, and to Terrie and me; our presence evidently far less a surprise to them than theirs was to us.

Herc and his retinue joined everyone inside and closed the ornate doors behind them.

"Thanks for coming, everyone," Herc said without pomp or ceremony. "Our new friend managed to dig up some dirt on the selfies, and the information is about as disturbing as you would expect, with that bunch. Moira, could you please make your presentation?"

"Eh. Presentations involve charts and slideshows, and even I'm not evil enough to use those," said Moira. She never bothered to get up from her chair. "I'm just going to tell you what I sniffed out, yeah?"

No one challenged this assertion. Those among the gifted who've worked corporate jobs probably had their personal wards set up against slide show presentation programs.

"Right then," Moira continued. "It didn't take me very long to find some low-level selfies. They're all over town, like roach infestations, and they've set up a nice racket of legalized robbery. It goes like this. A presentable, well-spoken, self-righteous bastard knocks on the doors of any gifted they can find. He demands they repent their various sins and hand over any illegal artifacts that they've got stashed away. And while he talks all polite-like, there are at least two numbskulls hanging out on the stoop, ready to back up their boss in case anyone gets any ideas about pushing back. The ringleader invites himself in, searches the house for any magical goodies, and confiscates them to be"—Moira made air quotes—"disposed of."

From the looks of them, most if not all of the assembled gifted already knew this. I'd had my couple of run-ins with the Emersonians, but I didn't realize they'd become brazen enough to invade people's homes.

"I made fast friends with one of their crews. They're always on the lookout for more thugs and brigands to act as muscle, and thugs adore the idea of legalized robbery. Someone like me had no trouble fitting right in." Moira grinned. "Except, I hit a snag after that. Turned out, the self-righteous guys in charge? The Emersonian version of the inquisitors? Those are true believers. They wholeheartedly buy into the idea that magical artifacts are evil and that they're saving humanity one home invasion at a time. Those guys drink the Kool-Aid by the bucket. They aren't in it for the money or the power trip, and they weren't going to tell me anything they didn't want me to know, no matter how *persuasive* I chose to be." Moira flashed a wicked half-smile at that, which almost made me feel pity for the hapless selfies she'd encountered. Almost.

"I was willing to bet the people even higher up the food chain would appreciate some real magical muscle. The slack-jawed hooligans in their employ aren't much good in a real fight. So, I waited until we encountered a gifted with a spine and nudged things along to ensure an argument escalated into a brawl. An opportunity for a little show-and-tell to demonstrate what separates a real diamond like me from pieces of coal like them. After I flexed that magic, the true believers wasted no time introducing me to their bosses.

"Emersonians are a suspicious lot, though. The higher up the chain you climb, the less forthcoming they become about their goals and plans. Fortunately, I had just the résumé they were searching for: a powerful Cabal sorceress who'd managed to pull a fast one on *the* Conrad Brent"—Moira winked at me—"and who'd survived against the combined might of the Watch bigwigs. If anything, I was overqualified. It was like Bernie Madoff applying for a middle-management position at a second-rate pyramid scheme."

"Will you at any point quit patting yourself on the back long enough to tell us something useful?" said Zach Shephard. He was among the irregulars who kept well away from the rogue sorceress. One didn't need special powers to read his frown and see how he felt about breathing the same air as Moira.

"I'm getting to that," said Moira peevishly. "In a matter of days, I achieved what none of you managed to learn in months: actionable intel on the Emersonians. And I don't even get to bill anyone for those long hours of hard work. Is a brief victory lap too much to ask for, under the circumstances?"

"We're grateful for your help," Herc interjected. "But the information you brought us is time sensitive, right? Perhaps it would be best to get to the relevant parts? Once the crisis has been averted, I'm sure a number of people here would stand you drinks and listen to the expanded version."

Moira pouted. "Fine. We'll do it your way, Tall, Dark, and Handsome. After many *interesting* events ..." Moira paused to glare in Zach's general direction. "I learned that the man in charge of the Emersonians is named Archibald Grey."

I cursed inwardly. Several people around me cursed out loud, muttered under their collective breaths, or frowned. An equal number of those present looked confused, unfamiliar with Grey's name or reputation.

"Archibald Grey is a powerful warlock who's lived in New York since the late 1700s," Aysha explained, sliding seamlessly into librarian mode, her lecturer voice commanding the room's attention. Unlike Moira, she stood up when she spoke. "A practitioner of dark magic, Grey is rumored to have been responsible for a number of atrocities during the early nineteenth century. However, once the Watch established a strong presence in the city, Grey chose to curtail his activities rather than to directly oppose the guardians. He's been here ever since, doing whatever it is ancient evil warlocks do with their free time."

"He's been trouble over the years, but never in an obvious way. Nothing we could prove, or link directly to him," said John Smith.

"I can tell you what he's been up to," said Moira. All eyes were once again on her. "Oh, I'm sorry, do we suddenly have time for backstory? No? I didn't think so. Anyway, I've met Archibald Grey. He's a creepy old geezer, and that's *me* talking. Due to the nature of my past associations, my tolerance for creepy is bloody damn high. Anyway, he's been super focused on two things lately. The first is staying alive. Keeping that wrinkled sack of bones and contempt he calls a body in working order after centuries of heavy use is difficult, and it's only getting harder with each passing year. But let's get back to that in a moment.

"The second thing the old codger has been up to lately—and by lately, I mean since the Industrial Revolution—is running a secret society dedicated to exterminating all middlings. Yeah, yeah, I know, you can't throw a rock without hitting one of those cozy little clubs. They're as common among the warlocks as the bodegas are on the corners of your loud and sprawling city. But these guys are serious. Their organization dates back to the days of the Roman Empire, under different names and guises, and they claim to have killed at least a dozen middlings over the course of its illustrious history."

I recalled the conversation I'd had with Aysha. Was this organization responsible for organizing the reigns of terror against the gifted in Florence and Paris, or did they merely operate from the same playbook?

Moira went on. "The geezer and his associates convinced Mayor Holcomb that artifacts are the arcane equivalent of automatic rifles. Getting them off the streets and reining in vigilante groups like the Watch would make the city safe for mundanes and prevent another calamity like the middling affliction of last year. Grey recruited an army of religious zealots who are only too happy to carry on this campaign of—I believe the term he used was 'dekulakization' against the gifted. I have to admit, I had to look that one up on the internet. Of course, Grey is a lying liar, and none of what he told Holcomb or his pet Emersonians is even remotely true."

Moira paused again for effect. This time, even Zach patiently waited for her to continue. Satisfied that she had won the room's undivided attention, Moira continued. "Dear old Archibald has discovered a way to remove the stored magical energy from one enchanted item and transfer most of it into another."

"That seems rather pointless," said an irregular I didn't recognize. "If the amount of power is the same, the difference would be purely aesthetic."

"You misunderstand," replied Moira. "Grey is sitting on an enormous pile of artifacts, like a dragon on his hoard of gold. He can take little bits of magic from each one and combine them into a single arcane super-battery more potent than an Atlantean crystal."

The room erupted upon hearing this claim.

"Impossible!" declared Father Mancini. "Magic that powers a ward is different from magic that opens a portal, or levitates an item. The incantations and the user's intent shape raw magic into an appropriate form and purpose, with the Lord's benevolent blessing. You can't just ... squeeze little bits of each into a single bucket like a restaurant recycling half-used condiment bottles."

"Says who?" countered Aysha. "You're capable of both casting a protective spell and levitating an item, Father, are you not? Before any artifact is imbued with power, a gifted capable of using it in a plethora of ways first possesses that power. Who's to say a process can't be developed that converts the imbued power back to its natural state?"

"I've seen it done," said Moira. "The good news is that this process is painstakingly slow. Even a long-lived fossil like Grey would die of old age before he squeezed enough magic juice out of those oranges to make the undertaking worth his while. The bad news is that he's found a way to automate the entire thing."

That revelation shut everyone up. I was too busy imagining all the terrible things someone like Grey could do with that amount of power, and it seemed the others were conjuring up similar distasteful scenarios.

"Elaborate, please," said John Smith.

"Grey has a team of eggheads building a machine for him," said Moira. "It's capable of reabsorbing the magic from a roomful of trinkets at once, and storing all of it in neat little wands, each more powerful than an Atlantean shard the size of a melon."

Moira didn't have that quite right. Atlantean crystal amplified one's own magic, whereas the process she described would create uber-artifacts that could be used by someone like me. Why would an anti-middling cult set out to create something like that?

"The machine is nearly complete," said Moira. "They've had a few test runs and only need to calibrate, or rejigger some thingamajigs, or whatever it is the suspenders-and-pocket-protector types do. They say it should be good to go within a few days."

"And where are they building this Death Star?" I asked.

"A death star?" repeated Father Mancini, confused.

"A powerful device built by evil forces that a plucky band of heroes must destroy in the nick of time," I elaborated.

"It's a movie reference," said John Smith.

"Ah." The priest nodded. "I haven't seen too many recent films."

It took considerable effort to contain the multitude of snarky responses that came to mind. My restraint was worthy of a medal, preferably awarded by a young Carrie Fisher. As no medal was forthcoming, I contented myself with the truism that not all heroes wear capes. Or Rogue Squadron insignia.

"Grey's headquarters is a shuttered dance club in Greenwich Village, just off of Houston Street," said Moira. The Brit pronounced it 'Hews-ton' like the city in Texas, instead of the correct way, 'House-ton.' New Yorkers could reliably identify the tourists that way.

"This club was called Inferno," said Father Mancini. "Modeled after the version of hell from Dante's namesake poem, it had nine descending levels with different kinds of music performed on each floor. It was a den of sin. So much so that the city had shut it down in the 1980s. Archibald Grey subsequently purchased the building."

So the good priest hadn't watched *Star Wars* but somehow possessed an encyclopedic knowledge of the twentieth-century dance club scene? The man was full of surprises.

"Grey, his machine, and a metric ton of artifacts are all on the lowest level," said Moira. "There's no elevator and no back entrance. Only one way in and out, and you've got to get through six underground kill boxes to get to the prize at the bottom of the cereal box."

"And get to the bottom of it we must," said Herc. "Grey can't be allowed to harness that much magical power. That's why all of you are here today. We need to work together, and we need to move against him soon." He turned toward John Smith. "Can we count on your support, John?"

The head of the Watch looked at the eager faces around the room. The irregulars may have picked up a lot of the slack as of late, but the Watch had always been a beacon, an organization that stood firm against the forces of evil. Where John Smith would lead, the irregulars and many other gifted would follow, even if that meant storming an impregnable castle.

"We cannot," said John. "As much as I dislike Archibald Grey and his ilk, they have done nothing to abuse the mundanes. The Watch does not interfere in the affairs of the gifted under any other circumstances. If we were to do so, the ramifications would be terrible. We'd acquire dangerous new enemies, and our members across the globe would be placed at risk."

John sighed deeply. His shoulders slumped under the weight of legacy and responsibility. I knew him well and understood how much he hated to remain on the sidelines. If it were the John Smith of a year ago, the guardian of Manhattan, he would have joined us in an instant, even at the risk of incurring the wrath of Mose. But now that he was the one in charge, he couldn't permit his personal feelings on the matter to influence his decisions.

John took a deep breath and straightened his back. His eyes narrowed and his voice verged on imperious. "Furthermore, no member of the Watch may participate in this attack." He looked directly at me. "I've been lax with some of you, allowing the pursuit of personal goals that are counter to the Watch's agenda. That ends now." He tapped Father Mancini on the shoulder. "Let's go. Conrad and Terrie, come along."

The room erupted. The irregulars thought of the Watch as their closest allies, looked up to our organization in general and to John in particular. The abrupt and rather disrespectful manner in which he chose to leave the meeting grated at them. I was floored as well. When John marched out of the room and my colleagues from Staten Island and Queens followed, I hesitated for only a moment and then rushed after them, not so much to obey John's order but to challenge it.

John marched down the hall at a good clip, then stopped so suddenly that I almost collided with him. He grabbed the three of us and practically shoved us toward the nearby door.

It was a smaller meeting room with runes and sigils hidden among its artwork and decorations.

"Listen carefully, we have only a few moments," said John. "This is a secure room, it should be impossible to listen in on any conversation held here, through science or magic. I staged the outburst so I could get you here."

We stared at John in confusion.

"They have my family," said John. "My sister and her daughters."

"What?" I asked. I'd had no idea John had a family, which in itself wasn't surprising. We took on new names and identities to join the Watch in order to protect our loved ones. In order to prevent the exact situation John was describing.

"Who has them?" asked Father Mancini.

"I don't know," said John. "I can only assume they are forces allied with the Emersonians. They threatened to hurt the girls if I interfere. My family are mundanes. They likely don't even understand why this is happening to them …" John's handsome, usually placid face was blemished by dread. "The kidnappers demanded I stand aside …. That the Watch stands aside and let the Emersonians take over the city. I've done my best to stall, to walk the fine line rather than step over it, to avoid decisions that would irrevocably hurt the Watch while I searched in vain for my family."

I couldn't blame John for his actions. Were I in his shoes, I would probably be doing the exact same thing. Up to and including his performance in the other room.

"You know we'll do all we can to help you find them, John," said Terrie. "What do you need us to do?"

"I want you to hit Archibald Grey with everything you've got," said John. "If these people can get to me, who knows how many others they've compromised. And if our enemies do have ears in there, as far as anyone will know, I've stormed off having done the bidding of my blackmailers, and you subsequently chose to disobey my direct orders."

"Got it," I said. "And another thing. If you're right, and there are spies or unwilling informants in that room, this also means we need to go after Grey immediately, before someone might warn him."

"Yes." John looked at each of us in turn. "I'm sorry to drag you into this. I must continue to play the feckless, indecisive leader for as long as I can. Until I either find the girls, or the kidnappers demand something of me I can't do, not even to save …" He trailed off.

Terrie took hold of John's hand and squeezed it. "Anything you need," she reiterated. "Just ask, okay?"

John nodded. He lingered for an all-too-brief moment shared with trusted friends, then gently withdrew his hand from Terrie's clasp. "Good luck," he said. "Give them hell." Then he marched off to resume his private, torturous battle.

In the larger meeting room, the war council was in full swing. Everyone paused to watch us file back in, some expressing surprise and others with obvious delight.

"We're in," Terrie declared. "Wouldn't miss this party for anything."

"Johnny boy had a change of heart, did he?" asked Moira.

"Screw that guy and the broom he rode in on," I said. I was doing the right thing, but that didn't make me feel any better about pretending to throw John under the bus.

Father Mancini gave me the sort of scolding look best reserved for rowdy Sunday school children. "We're here against Smith's wishes," he said. "It may be wise to proceed quickly, before the Watch or anybody else places additional obstacles in our path."

I spent a lot of time on my phone after that. My first call was to Chulsky. He listened patiently to my report but refused to lend a hand, because of course he did.

"You're still thinking too small, Conrad. What is this Archibald Grey in the grand scheme of things but another minor villain?" The CEO sounded so sure of himself, so convincing. He could've easily negotiated contracts on behalf of Down Below. "Even if the warlock's plan succeeds, and he manages to climb the ranks all the way up to an inconvenience, he has neither the vision nor the power to ever become a major player. You're a step away from preventing an actual apocalypse, but instead you choose to focus your valuable time and insight on Grey. Don't you know that a person is best judged by the quality of their enemies?"

"Yes, yes, I've heard this song before. I even bought the album, downloaded it onto my phone, and set it as my ringtone. I'm not asking for your permission to do this. I'm asking for your help."

"If you were working to prevent a nuclear war between the United States and the Soviet Union during the Cuban Missile Crisis, would you have dropped what you were doing in order to apprehend a shoplifter?" asked Chulsky.

I groaned and ended the call.

My next two conversations weren't any more fun. I'll skip the play-by-play. Suffice it to say neither the angels nor the demons appreciated my seeing through their paper-thin ploys and failing to deliver exactly what they wanted like the good useful idiot they both perceived me to be.

Neither side wanted to breathe the same air as their counterparts, let alone negotiate with each other. I thought back to Zach and some of the others scandalized by the prospect of working with Moira. Self-righteousness and pride weren't limited to humans.

In a span of a few minutes, I had been threatened, inveigled, insulted, cajoled, chided, tempted with a straight-up bribe, and had my better angels appealed to (surprisingly, not by the angels.)

The Archdocent went so far as to claim he'd "sooner level half of this overcrowded, human-infested island than subject myself to the indignity of *negotiating* with those cretins."

"You don't want to level half of Manhattan," I replied. "After all, it's where you keep all your stuff. But if you really must smite something, there's this hot dog stand on 38th Street that really has it coming."

I'd love to claim that my sense of humor had been growing on him, but based on his response—which consisted of yet another admonition to cut the shenanigans, followed by a string of what could only be profanity muttered in ancient Aramaic—I'd be lying.

In the end, I possessed what they both wanted, and they both wanted it badly enough to agree to attend a sit-down. I hoped that they'd behave on Abaddon turf in the presence of Daniel Chulsky, and that, together, we'd find a path forward.

There was one other piece of business with Bub, once we got the unpleasantries out of the way.

"I wanted to check whether you and yours have any connection with Club Inferno," I asked him. "Given its name and all that, I'd like to avoid stepping on any hoofs, so to speak."

"Those poseurs have nothing to do with us," the demon assured me. "Dante grossly misrepresented what Down Below is like. Frankly, his so-called masterpiece smacks of cultural appropriation. It is safe to say that anyone trading upon the imagery and themes from that book is no affiliate of ours."

"That's excellent to know." I was tempted to ask whether he might care to mete out some demonic wrath upon Club Inferno, but I wasn't desperate enough to try to strike a bargain with Down Below, and I didn't want to be beholden to their representative ahead of the next day's meeting. He may have sounded amenable and even friendly, but I knew what he really was, and it only made me more wary. Those who hide their true nature are usually far more dangerous than the obvious hellions.

"I trust whatever your business or pleasure happens to be at that club, it will not prevent you from mediating our settlement with the holy pigeons tomorrow?" asked Bub.

"I'll be there, come hell or high water." I remembered who I was talking to. Did the denizens of Down Below care if one used the word in vain? Did they find the term 'hell' derogatory? I added, "No offense."

Bub chuckled. "Hell will be there, too," he promised. "Get us our due, and it need not be unleashed."

CHAPTER 15

WE launched the attack at the crack of noon. Late enough that a good amount of their people had headed out for the day, to lead the gullible Emersonians on a supposed anti-artifact crusade. Also late enough for us to gather our forces and reach out to trusted allies in the City and for the irregulars to gather from across New Jersey.

John's concern about possible spies in our midst was valid, but there was no way for us to mount an operation so quickly that it would preempt a text or a phone call. We had to balance marshaling sufficient forces to challenge the Emersonians against the fact that every passing hour and every person and group we contacted for help increased the odds of a leak.

We started by launching an insurrection in the Bronx. Herc led a small force of the irregulars and a larger group of eager volunteers to confront the Emersonian squads dispatched in the neighborhood of Belmont. Our allies escalated the conflict by physically attacking the selfies and reappropriating the artifacts these legalized muggers had already collected.

It was important that Herc be seen there. Given his presence, our enemies would view the irregulars' actions as a major act of resistance that they, in turn, couldn't resist squashing. They would thus also be unlikely to anticipate a significant attack elsewhere, without Herc present to act as a rallying point. Much like the Biblical Moses, Herc, who'd led the resistance against the Emersonians for months, would not set foot in their stronghold—at least not until we fumigated it and got rid of the vermin.

We waited long enough for any reinforcements Grey chose to send to the Bronx to have been dispatched. As tempting as it would have been to surveil the club, we decided it wasn't worth the risk. This was going to be a frontal attack regardless; any gifted we could lure away would be a bonus, but confirming their departure was not worth the risk of alerting Grey to our plans.

So, at 12:25 p.m. we converged on the storied location off Houston Street. The squat building retained the Club Inferno sign, with the letter "I" stylized as a red pitchfork, though the awning's once-garish colors were faded. The old sign was weather-beaten and thoroughly crapped upon by the pigeons.

The building's exterior sported a number of magical protections that struck a good balance between stating "keep the hell out" and not inviting curious interlopers like me to wonder about what valuable goodies might be found inside that justified all the defensive magic.

Grey relied on relative obscurity, if not anonymity, to protect him, which meant getting through the front door would be far easier than making it past the protections at the Rojas house. What awaited us within, on the other hand, was guaranteed to be far less pleasant than Benicio the Friendly Lich.

There were half a dozen gifted on the ground floor who, by the looks of them, worked with the Emersonians and might not have been privy to the goings-on under their feet. Most of them took one gander at the well-organized force invading their lair and immediately chose surrender before death. A couple who were made of sturdier stuff remained put and guarded the staircase leading down.

A lone figure stood in between our group and the defenders. Karl Mercado was looking back and forth, seemingly at a loss.

Terrie, his one-time mentor, stepped forward. "You shouldn't be here, Karl. You're mixed up with a bad crowd."

"It is you who shouldn't be here," called out one of the Emersonians guarding the door. "You're breaking laws, magical and mundane both."

Karl appeared torn. He stood there, between the two worlds, frozen by indecision.

Father Mancini stepped forward alongside Terrie. "Search your heart and decide where your loyalties lie," he said to Karl. "Are you still a fellow guardian, or do you stand with those lost, deluded souls?" He pointed toward the Emersonians. "It can no longer be both."

When Karl finally spoke, his words were firm but soaked in deep sadness. "I'm a guardian of the Watch," he said. "And as such, I can no more raise a hand against my friends here than I can against you. Violence against the fellow gifted goes against everything the Watch stands for."

"A conscientious objector. I can respect that," said Father Mancini. "Walk away, and report to the Watchtower. Whatever happens here won't be on your conscience."

Karl nodded. He headed toward the exit, but after taking a few steps he turned toward the Emersonians who stayed to fight.

"Come with me, Chris," he said to the man who'd spoken out earlier.

Chris shook his head. "I'm no quitter."

The fellow looked familiar. I could place him now; he'd been a prospect under Gord's tutelage a year or two back but had never made it into the Watch.

Terrie took another step forward. "Do you know who the Emersonians truly are, Chris? What goes on down there, under your feet?"

"Of course I do," said Chris. "And it's nothing untoward. We're the legal and lawful protectors of this city. Look around you, Ms. Winter. Crime is down. New Yorkers are safer from magical threats than they ever were during the time of the Watch. I mean, sending a sole untrained vigilante to combat all the evil of an entire borough in one of the largest cities in the world—what sort of an insane system is that? Mayor Holcomb has put together an authorized, legitimate, organized force to patrol the streets, and we're making a real difference."

Chris's eyes shone. It was clear he was as much on board with all of this as the deluded fools out there, relieving grandmas of their enchanted heirlooms.

"Emersonians are thugs, terrorizing and robbing the gifted. That is no way to protect the city," said Terrie.

"Excuse me." Moira stepped forward. "We don't have time for a highfalutin debate right now. Every wasted breath lets Archie dig in a little deeper. You," she pointed at Chris, "move or be moved."

"Never. You will have to go through—"

Moira sucker-punched Chris with an arcane attack so powerful, it blasted right past his defenses. He dropped where he stood.

"Have it your way," Moira said. She turned to Chris's one remaining compatriot. "How about you?"

The Emersonian raised both hands palms up and headed toward the front door. We let him pass, and he ran for his life. Karl followed in his wake, at a slower pace so as to salvage what remained of his dignity. Despite singling out Chris earlier, he didn't so much as look back to check on the well-being of his compatriot. I felt the decision to pick the Watch over the Emersonians had more to do with his cowardice than his principles, but I was not overly charitable toward Karl given our past history.

"This concludes the debate club portion of our program," said Moira. "Shall we proceed?"

When it comes to assaulting a stronghold, the defender has a considerable advantage. This wisdom applied to medieval castle sieges and remains true in any operation where a military force has to encroach upon enemy territory. It is even truer when the stronghold has been fortified by magic over the course of decades or centuries. Grey had burrowed deep underground, and we were certain to meet many deadly obstacles on our way in. Fortunately, we'd brought with us some of the strongest gifted in the greater New York area; anything the ancient warlock could muster, we could counter. Or so we hoped.

The only way down was a narrow staircase at the back of the building. A choke point, where two or three people at most could move side by side. We knew from Moira's description that the club was built like a mall, with each staircase on the opposite end of the level. Patrons would have to traverse the length of each hall to descend further. There were no emergency exits, escalators, or alternate escape routes of any kind. It was a wonder the Department of Buildings had ever allowed this death trap to operate, even back in the reckless decades of the '70s and '80s.

We descended to the second level, and through the ornate door at the bottom of the staircase marked with a gilded sign that read LUST. The single spacious hall that occupied the entire floor seemed abandoned. The floor, walls, and ceiling were all painted in garish pink and red hues. Paintings and decorations that looked like they'd been looted from Liberace's most decadent living room adorned the walls. All the paintings depicted orgies in such graphic detail, they would've made the Marquis de Sade blush. Equally garish couches, love seats, and ottomans throughout the hall suggested the floor could serve uses other than just dancing. I would've hated to shine a black light on any of those surfaces.

Our plan was for the advance team to clear each floor; that way our entire group wouldn't be endangered by whatever nasty surprises awaited us. Thus, it was a group of four people who headed in first. Moira, Terrie, myself, and an irregular named Jasleen Singh, who was capable of putting up the strongest and longest-lasting force shields of any of us, Herc included.

The defenses kicked in when we reached the center of the room. Hurricane-level winds appeared out of nowhere and roared, tossing furniture and stripping drapes and pornographic paintings off the walls. The trapped storm slapped at our faces and clogged our nostrils with the salty smell of the ocean. It was a familiar trick; I'd once used the same kind of magic when I released a chinook wind against Moira's mercenaries.

In that instance the wind had been a worthwhile but brief disruption; it escaped the confines of the conference room as soon as the doors were opened. Presently, we didn't have the luxury of such a simple solution; opening the staircase door would unleash the raging winds on the rest of our party.

Terrie and Jasleen quickly erected powerful shields that created a bubble of calm, leaving the four of us disheveled but otherwise unharmed. Broken pieces of furniture slammed against the shields with incredible force. Wood splintered with crunching noises loud enough to be heard over the general din. A single hit from the airborne debris at this velocity could've taken out any one of us had we not acted so quickly.

"A portal," I shouted over the deafening wind. "Open a portal to somewhere over the Atlantic!" I had a portal charm at the ready, but mine led to elsewhere within the city and we didn't want any innocent bystanders getting hurt.

Moira chanted a quick incantation and a portal appeared a few feet away from the edge of the force barrier. The wind rushed through like champagne spraying from a bottle that had just been uncorked. With a sucking *swoosh* sound, the last of the wind escaped and the room was still.

"I was sorely tempted to open the portal to a lower level," said Moira. "Taste of their own medicine and all that."

"We would've had to deal with it again, too," said Terrie.

"My hair would not have thanked you," added Jasleen. She was wrestling her long strands back into place with her fingers, to little effect.

"Sacrifices must be made," said Moira.

We headed deeper into the Inferno, knowing all the while that time wasn't on our side. Surely an alarm had sounded as soon as our attack had begun, summoning all manner of bad guys to Archibald Grey's aid. They would likely overwhelm our forces left to defend the ground floor, and soon we'd be fighting a rear-guard action. We had to destroy Grey's machine before that happened and then, if we were lucky enough, to get the hell out.

The third level was Gluttony. It clearly served as the club's restaurant, where processed junk food was served up in heaping portions at gourmet prices. This level was guarded by a pack of hellhounds, each a tightly wound ball of muscle, teeth, and hate, and vicious enough to overpower a Navy SEAL.

Jasleen erected the force shield and the hulking beasts clawed and chomped at the invisible barrier, leaving saliva marks where their oversized maws made contact, level with our throats. Each hellhound was the size of a Great Dane, the temperament of a Yorkie, and the shape of a Doberman, if that Doberman spent every day at the gym and consumed a steady diet of steroids.

Moira cast spells which had no visible effect on the beasts. "They're magic resistant," Moira said as she kept up her barrage of attacks, deftly varying types and styles, seeking something that might make a dent. She growled in frustration, mimicking the hellhounds' deeper snarls. "I might as well be tossing pillows at them."

Terrie planted her staff into the club floor's lush orange carpet and chanted an incantation. Instead of attacking the hellhounds, she targeted the invisible threads of malicious magic that bound and controlled the beasts. I could barely detect their presence. Scratch that; I would have never detected them had Terrie not revealed those binds by targeting them with her spells. That she was able to sense and interact with those infinitesimal threads was awe-inspiring.

Even Moira was impressed. She ceased her own ineffective attacks and watched Terrie work. "Queens has got moves," she said approvingly. "Guess she's more than just an average-looking face."

Jasleen rolled her eyes. "Next time you bring a friend, Conrad, would you mind vetting them for basic manners?" She spoke without making eye contact; most of her focus remained on maintaining the force shield.

"I make a terrible first impression, and the second impression tends to be worse," said Moira. "But in time, I grow on you. Like a fungus." She turned to Terrie. "Come on, Queens. Time's money, and we're short on both. You dispel that magic resistance and I'll dice up some Chihuahua kebobs." She rested her hand on the hilt of her cutlass.

Terrie ignored the banter, manipulating the sorcerous threads with the steady precision of a neurosurgeon. A few moments later she collapsed the binding spell. The hounds ceased throwing themselves at the barrier. They snarled as they stared at us through the force shield, their bodies tense, their fangs bared.

"Down!" Terrie said firmly. "Sit!"

The pack of ferocious hellhounds obeyed, sitting at attention. They still looked dangerous and scary, but their body language was no longer threatening.

"Shoo," said Terrie. She pointed at the door to what appeared to have been the club's kitchen. "Go!"

The canines obeyed, retreating toward the door. Terrie signaled for Jasleen to drop the shield and walked fearlessly toward the hellhounds. She herded them into the kitchen and locked the door.

Terrie then shook her head at Moira. "Kebobs? Really? Who doesn't love dogs? I didn't have to mess with their natural magic resistance as long as I could remove the enchantment that made them so angry. I wonder if someone should do the same for you."

"Hard pass, Queens," said Moira. "If I ever feel the need to resolve my anger issues, I'll beat up a shrink for fifty minutes."

"Nicely done, Terrie. Let's get a move on," I said. "Who knows what fun stuff lies ahead, and how long it'll take for us to deal with it."

"Oh, it'll be something that tries to crush us, or maybe the walls will close in on us like in the *Star Wars* trash compactor scene," said Jasleen.

"That's … weirdly specific," I said. "What makes you think that?"

"Grey seems to have gone all in on the inferno theme," said Jasleen. "According to Dante, souls were blown about in a violent storm in the second circle, and the third circle was guarded by Cerberus." She observed our blank stares. "Have none of you read Dante?"

"I skipped that day in kindergarten," said Moira.

"The day your weird British kindergarten taught kids about the *Divine Comedy*?" I asked.

"Nah, the day they tried to indoctrinate the little tykes into believing that reading and memorizing nonsense is somehow fun," said Moira. "If I'm going to read a centuries-old book, it better have some extra-strength incantations in it."

"Philistine," I said in my best Oracle of Eighty-Sixth Street impression, and mostly to divert attention from the fact that I hadn't read *Inferno*, either. I'd been there when Moira had told Aysha that she was very well-read indeed. It seemed she couldn't resist making whatever claim might get a rise out of her interlocutors.

"So, the trash compactor?" Terrie prodded.

"The fourth circle is dedicated to the sin of greed, and the sinners are forced to push heavy slabs of stone at each other. Since Grey probably can't make us push stones, I suppose it's likely he will use them as weapons," said Jasleen.

"Right. Watch out for falling rocks. Roger that." I headed down toward the fourth circle, feeling a little like the Roadrunner who knew Wile E. Coyote was waiting for him up ahead with an Acme anvil.

Club Inferno had turned the circle of Greed into the VIP lounge. It had been the champagne room where guests could feel superior to other partygoers by spending outrageous amounts of money on bottle service.

We advanced across the dusty yellow hall, decades past its prime, and no boulders, slabs, or trash compactor walls closed in on us.

"It was a good guess, anyway," Terrie told Jasleen when we made it to the other end of the floor without incident.

"It doesn't seem right," I said. "Why would this floor possess no defenses?"

"We can wait around to find out, or we can take the win. Tock tick." Moira tapped her bare wrist. I couldn't speak for others, but by swapping those two little words around she somehow managed to get pretty deep under my skin.

Terrie gave Moira an annoyed look and I could just tell she was bugged by it, too. "Best we move on," she said.

"What's the next circle?" I asked Jasleen.

"This again?" Moira snorted.

"Doesn't hurt to know. Maybe Grey is lulling us into a false sense of security," I said.

"Wrath. There are all sorts of dangers in that circle as I recall," said Jasleen. "Swamp water runoff from the River Styx, the city of Dis guarded by fallen angels, furies, and a medusa."

"So, the kitchen sink level," I summarized.

"Yeah, I guess. Unless they flood the floor, we're likely to face living opponents rather than wind or rocks," said Jasleen.

"I wouldn't mind testing myself against a Fury." Moira wasn't grinning when she said it. It sounded like the madwoman would actually welcome such a confrontation. "My secret is, I'm more furious than they are."

As we descended the stairs to the next circle of hell, a terrible rumble resonated from above. The entire building shook. We heard screams. Moments later, Zach tumbled down the stairs. His face was bloodied, and his clothes covered in dust. He was carrying an irregular I didn't recognize who was unconscious, and whose arm was badly broken. A jagged piece of bone protruded through the skin of the man's forearm.

"What happened?" I asked as Terrie began ministering to the wounded irregular.

"An avalanche." Zach brushed dust and pebbles off his face. "The second group was crossing the room when rocks fell through a huge portal that opened by the ceiling and tumbled down, filling up the room. We were closest to the staircase. The others ... they didn't make it."

Jasleen gasped. I cursed. We were cut off from the rest of our ragtag invasion force, and we'd already lost several good people.

"He's stable for now, but he'll need medical attention, soon," Terrie said as she rolled up her jacket and placed it under the man's head as a pillow.

"We have to keep going. We won't get another chance. Grey will move his base of operations and disappear," I said.

"Agreed. But I'm going to teleport him out, first," said Terrie.

"Not gonna happen," said Moira.

Terrie whirled on the necromancer. "What kind of a heartless monster—"

Moira cut her off. "Easy, Queens. All I'm saying is, I just tried opening a portal, and I couldn't. The trap is shut."

Terrie tried anyway, and had no better luck than Moira. There were plenty of ways to prevent incoming portals—otherwise, unscrupulous gifted would pop in and steal whatever they wanted, from wherever they wanted, all the time. But preventing outgoing portals was levels of magnitude more difficult.

"No choice, then. Let's move," I said.

I pushed open the door marked WRATH. Beyond, nothing remained of whatever the original setup had been for the circle of Wrath in Club Inferno. This was warlock territory, with runes and sigils drawn in blood on the walls, and with a team of five grim-looking gifted waiting for us. Each of them held in their hands what looked like a baton. Were these the wands made of concentrated magic that Moira had warned us about? Her face went pale, confirming my fears. I'd only seen the necromancer scared of anything but once, when she'd encountered a dragon. At the moment, she looked like a soldier who had just gone up against an AK-47 armed only with a plastic spork.

Jasleen erected a new force shield, and the five of us stepped into the room. One of the warlocks grinned nastily as he pointed his wand at us.

The spell he unleashed felt like something Willodean might have cast at the height of her powers as a goddess of death. A wave of raw magical energy ripped the force shield to shreds and blew the remnants away like so many dandelion seeds. We were tossed hard against the wall. Thankfully, the force shield absorbed the brunt of the attack before it zonked out, or there'd have been nothing left of us, save for a sizable wet spot on the back wall.

It was bad. Really bad. Moira had not exaggerated the danger posed by Grey's new weapon at all. How could four gifted and a middling hope to hold their own against five opponents wielding that kind of power? There was no winning this fight. We had to find a way to escape.

Terrie raised her staff and cast spell after spell at the warlocks. This forced them to use their wands defensively. Zach ran forward, dodging enemy spells to engage them in close combat. He activated a less potent but very portable force shield. It clung to him like a bodysuit, without restricting movement. Moira scowled and threw an assortment of nasty hexes at the warlocks. She was in her element, free to unleash mayhem and violence at her enemies. Jasleen was a pacifist and would not harm or attack her foes directly, but she restored the force shield around the four of us and, in an impressive display of skill, also managed to deflect some of the attacks directed at Zach.

I used those precious moments to study the walls. I was certain there was no winning this battle; not having experienced the levels of power the warlocks were tapping into with their wands. I knew even the strongest among us were no match for them. Something in this room was preventing the opening of portals. I needed to find and disable it, and I needed to do it soon.

Precious seconds ticked by. I almost despaired of failing my team. Zach dodged the brunt of a warlock's arcane attack, but the magic had grazed him and he bled from a wound on his shoulder. Terrie was down on her knee, dazed by an arcane attack that had punctured its way past Jasleen's shields in a spear of blinding white light. Both were still fighting back, casting spells at the warlocks. Thus far,

I'd contributed nothing to the battle, as I focused on our long-shot escape plan. Finally, I saw it: a complex sigil drawn on a wall to my right that prevented teleportation. Except … it wasn't the right one. It prevented people from porting into the building, rather than out.

Moira groaned as an energy bolt hit her square in the chest. She staggered backward and spat out blood but continued to fight back. We all knew it was almost over; at this rate we couldn't last for much longer.

There was still a chance, though. Perhaps Herc was trying to port in, desperate for an alternative passage to us now that the physical path had been blocked. Perhaps he was relying on us to find a way for the reinforcements to reach us. Shutting down the sigil was my only play. I darted to the right, dodged an energy blast, threw myself at the wall, and touched an amulet to the sigil. The quarter-sized cube cut from mammoth bone, with symbols carved into it by the shamans of long-lost Siberian tribes, interrupted the sigil's effect.

I don't know if my companions realized what I was trying to do, but the warlocks did. They focused their attention on me, and Jasleen barely managed to deflect their attacks. With one hand tied up in holding the amulet, I drew on my other trinkets, using up the most powerful magics I had access to at an incredible rate in order to buy us time. The rapid succession of elemental attacks and hexes were all sizzle and no steak, easily deflected or defeated by the wand-wielding warlocks.

My hunch proved right. The cavalry had been waiting for their chance, and a few seconds after I shut down the sigil's effect, a shimmering circle appeared in the air, alongside the opposite wall. I expected Herc, or maybe Father Mancini. Instead, John Smith strode into the room.

Resplendent in his tailored white suit, John stepped toward the warlocks and extended his arms. For the briefest of moments, I wondered if his arrival meant John had finally found his kidnapped family, but it only took one look at him to realize that he had not. His face was a terrible mask of rage, the angriest I have ever seen him in all my years at the Watch. And when he unleashed the ephemeral horrors he was so adept at summoning, *they* were extra angry, too. Shadows comprised of mauve smoke found only in the deepest nightmares, that vaguely resembled oversized bats, fell upon the warlocks, biting and clawing, and gouging. For a moment a flicker of hope welled within me. Could we possibly win?

But even John's magic was only enough to buy us a reprieve. It kept the warlocks busy, but John would be able to keep up summoning his phantasms for only so long.

"The portal is omnidirectional," John shouted. "Go!"

Most portals worked one way, and they were temperamental, delicate things. To open a portal that could be used in both directions required an immense amount of skill and power. It also meant John had even less left in reserves than I'd thought.

"Go!" I shouted to everyone as well.

Jasleen dashed toward the staircase and grabbed the unconscious irregular. He was bigger than her, and she had to drag him, but Zach pitched in, and the two of them got him to the portal. Terrie and Moira covered their retreat, using the last of their reserves to lash out at the warlocks. Then they took positions at either side of the portal, expecting to cover John and me on the way out.

Except I couldn't go anywhere. If I moved away from where I stood, holding the amulet to the sigil, it would reactivate and shut down the portal.

John looked at me. We locked eyes for a moment. I pointed toward the sigil with my chin. John's eyes widened. He understood what I'd done, what I had to do.

He stepped toward me.

"No!" I shouted over the sizzling of lightning bolts and the screeching of bat-like phantasms. "Go! The Watch needs you."

John had sacrificed everything for us. He'd likely forfeited the lives of his sister and her children by joining the fight in order to save ours. It was a terrible choice, and one I was not certain I could make on my best day. But John knew his duty. We were his brothers and sisters in arms, as much his family as those to whom he was related by blood. When we ran out of options, so did he. And now he was ready to trade places with me, to negate the sigil so I could port out.

I couldn't let that happen. My decision was so much easier than his had been. I didn't have to sacrifice anyone else's lives in order to protect my friends.

Only my own.

I resumed my attacks on the warlocks, using up what offensive magic trinkets I could access with my free hand. I'd have no more use for them soon, and I didn't want Archibald Grey's millstone to grind them into concentrated magic flour.

John retreated toward the portal. He took up position directly in front of it, unleashing phantasms at an impressive rate. He looked like the strain of it might kill him. Terrie looked to me with deep sorrow in her eyes, taking full advantage of the extra moment John was buying us to say a silent goodbye. John stumbled, a trickle of blood running from his nostril and down his chin, droplets of it landing on his white suit jacket. He persisted in summoning the phantasms, trying to hurt our enemies with the last of his strength. In the end, Terrie and Moira grabbed him by the arms and pulled him into the portal with them.

As soon as they made it through, I removed the mammoth bone amulet from the wall and the portal winked out of existence. The warlocks dispatched the last of the phantasms and turned toward me as one. After the pandemonium of the heated battle, the sudden quiet was unnatural and foreboding. All of the warlocks had scrapes and bruises and one was down on one knee, but they were all still in fighting shape and they were all pissed.

I tossed the amulet I was holding aside like an empty Coke can and stepped away from the wall and toward my enemies. They trained their wands at me. I stood still, smiling easily at the warlocks.

"Gentlemen," I told them, "there's something very important you should know."

Five pairs of eyes, one with an impressive bruise swelling under it, stared daggers at me.

"I'm not locked up in here with you," I declared. "You're locked up in here with me."

CHAPTER 16

I made it all the way down to the ninth circle of Club Inferno. It just wasn't in the manner I had planned.

Instead of soundly defeating the middling-hating scum and punching their head honcho in the face, Captain America style, it was me who played the role of a punching bag. Also, a kicking bag. The five surly warlocks didn't kill me outright, which seemed like a positive development at the time. Instead, they bound me with their magic until I felt like a mummy, gift wrapped in invisible strips of cloth so tight it took me extra effort to breathe. The bonds did nothing to soften the blows as the warlocks worked me over real good. Kicking and punching a defenseless and immobile man seemed perfectly on brand for them. The beatings continued and my morale most definitely had not improved, but eventually they grew bored and proceeded to unceremoniously shove and push me down the stairs into the lower levels. I acquired plenty of additional bruises tumbling down those steep staircases.

I was hardly in the mood or position to sightsee, but the setup of the bad guys' lair was relevant to my interests and whatever miniscule chance of survival and escape I was harboring at the time. I

167

paid attention to the degree the stars floating in front of my eyes would permit.

The sixth circle was office space. This is where the secret puppet masters of the Emersonians must've conducted their day-to-day business. This floor was filled with computer desks, a few small offices at the far end, and a nice conference room with glass walls and premium chairs. There wasn't a single sigil or pentagram in sight. The place looked like an insurance office or a law firm. It even had a nicer coffee machine than the Watchtower, which added to my state of discontent.

The seventh circle was the warlocks' breakroom. It had couches, beanbags, and flat screen TVs streaming sporting events. A sleek, limited edition PlayStation console was hooked up to one of the TVs, which displayed the load screen for some car racing game. A small shelf of dog-eared paperbacks held a selection of mysteries and thrillers including, improbably, one of the Detonator novels I used to read as a kid. I'd adopted the name Conrad Brent after the series protagonist. The setup might've almost humanized the warlocks for me, if the pain from the recent beating wasn't so fresh, and if I wasn't being dragged like a dead body on an episode of *CSI*.

The eighth circle contained Archibald Grey's private quarters, which I only knew from Moira's report, since the warlocks weren't considerate enough to offer a guided tour. Most of the floor was walled off, with a corridor running along one side. According to Moira, the machine we needed to destroy, and the juiciest artifacts, were stored beyond those walls. I wondered if Archibald ever tried to take a swim in a pile of arcane trinkets like Scrooge McDuck with his money pit.

The ninth circle wasn't the frozen wasteland that my limited knowledge of Dante's masterpiece conjured up in my mind, but it was close enough for discomfort. In addition to the cleaning supplies, pantry, and other various odds and ends one might find in a typical basement, the lowest circle of Archibald Grey's private hell contained a dungeon.

Grey was old-school about his dungeons. Several cells situated along a wall had thick and doubtless magic-proof steel bars, and the torture chamber was complete with a rack and a selection of cutting, sawing, and drilling instruments laid out on the nearby workbench that would've looked wonderfully macabre on the set of a horror flick. The instruments were shiny and clean, but a splatter of brown stains marred the cement floor beneath the rack.

The warlocks dumped me in one of the cells. It was smaller than a Manhattan bathroom and completely bare, except for a single wooden bench. Three of the walls were cement blocks, with the one facing the dungeon made of thick, jailhouse-style bars, with a hinged steel bar door built into them, barely wide enough to shove me through.

The magic that bound me dissipated, and I could move once again. When I did, I immediately regretted it. Everything hurt. The front-row view of the torture rack positioned to be clearly seen through the prison bars really wasn't helping. Which was, of course, the point.

They let me stew for a short while, but soon I heard shuffling footsteps and the sound of a cane. A hunched over, decrepit old man in a black velvet hooded cloak embroidered with gold thread hobbled into view. A pair of younger warlocks followed him, carefully keeping a step or two behind the dotard at all times.

The man stopped in front of my cell and pulled back his hood to get a better look at me.

"How dare you invade my stronghold." His voice sounded raspy and brittle. "You will pay for this insolence."

I expected something more imaginative from the ancient warlock than a Saturday morning cartoon villain speech, but on the list of things to disappoint me, that ranked pretty low, just then.

"Archibald Grey, I presume? Wow, I heard you were ugly, but the stories don't do you justice. There must be a magic portrait of you around somewhere that holds on to all of your youth and vigor."

Grey wasn't merely old, he looked positively antediluvian—as though someone had reanimated a corpse after it had spent a few fun weeks in the dirt, nibbled by the worms. He studied me with sunken, faded eyes.

"Save the pointless bravado, Brent. You have no audience to impress here. You're only alive because a valued ally wishes to personally conduct your *exit interview*." Grey stressed those words in case I was dense enough not to understand the implication. "After that, I'll make certain it takes you a long time to die."

I leaned toward the bars separating the two of us. "Your buddies will get nothing out of me, save for more observational comedy."

Grey wouldn't even dignify that with a response. He scowled at me as if to say, *I've heard that dozens of times before and I wasn't impressed then either.* Then he turned his back on me and began executing the world's slowest exit-stage-left.

"Who?" I shouted after him. "Who's coming for me?" I was going for angry and tough, but the words came off slightly hysterical.

Apparently, the pleasure of seeing my face when he replied was worth the extra arthritis pain, because Grey executed another slow-motion one-hundred-and-eighty-degree turn, faced me, and whispered, "Vaughn."

"Oh, no," I said theatrically. "Not the glorified pencil pusher! Surely the prospect of him boring me to sleep is a fate worse than ten thousand tortures."

"Fool!" Grey squinted at me from under the few sparse hairs that remained of his eyebrows. "Vaughn is the worst thing you will have encountered in your brief, unremarkable life." Then he resumed and successfully completed his slow-motion exit. His underlings followed him with the patience of evil saints.

I had been bloviating for Grey's benefit. I wanted to disappoint and infuriate him. The wicked man was probably impervious to a heart attack on account of not having a heart, but at his age a small upset might cause a stroke, so I'd tried to get lucky. Learning that the centuries-old warlock held Vaughn in such high esteem was a fringe and terrifying benefit, though somehow I was not surprised.

Vaughn had been the puppeteer who'd manipulated a billion-dollar multinational pharmaceutical company into unleashing a genetically engineered plague upon the gifted of New York City. He was now in cahoots with, if not directly in charge of, the Emersonians. I didn't know what his deal was, but I was certain the mousey, unremarkable-seeming man was anything but. Every instinct told me that he was extremely dangerous. Whatever he had in mind for an "exit interview" would not go well for me. Even beside it being the prelude to being tortured and killed. But there was little I could do about it, disarmed and trapped nine stories below ground.

Or ... could I?

Wincing from the pain, I stripped off my trench coat and my shirt. I clawed at the tightly wrapped bandage until my aching fingers gained purchase and unraveled it. Layer upon layer of gauze fell onto the cold cement floor. When it was all gone, Aelfric's plum-purple armband clung to the skin of my left upper arm.

I contemplated the armband and the promise of violent death it represented. How did the fae vengeance magic work, exactly? Would a band of assassins appear out of thin air the moment I doffed the thing? Or would they show up hours later, after leisurely rolling out of bed and first enjoying a nutritious breakfast before a little light killing? Would warlock magic prevent the fae portal from opening within Club Inferno? Grey had said that Vaughn would be here soon. This meant there was another way in past the rubble. They might deactivate whatever magic was preventing a portal, or there was some other devious ingress to Grey's lair, unbeknownst to us. Could Kallan and the fae sniff it out and follow Vaughn inside?

I hesitated. If I ripped the armband off now, the fae might execute me before Vaughn got here. And if I ripped it off upon his arrival, he might be long gone by the time the disappointed fae showed up to find that Grey had finished the job for them. Or would I be on the torture rack, screaming? I was certain I'd welcome their arrival and the release of death then. And what would happen if the warlocks defeated the fae? Would an ever-increasing number of teleporting assassins show up in our dimension, intent on avenging their brethren?

External factors made the decision for me. I heard the sound of footsteps and muffled conversation in the distance.

I tore the armband off and hid it in one of the pockets of my trench coat. Then I tossed the coat over the gauze on the floor and pretended to study my rapidly growing collection of scrapes and bruises. When one of the warlocks approached the cell, we stared at each other in silence.

The warlock scowled at my shirtless self. "A little too warm for you?"

"Just eager to get onto that rack." I nodded toward the torture device. "Figured I'd save a few minutes by stripping naked. You're just in time to watch the pants come off."

"Crazy freak," said the warlock. His scowl deepened. He looked like he wanted to walk away but was also loath to hand me the tiny win.

I maintained eye contact as I began undoing the button on my jeans. The warlock cursed under his breath and walked off.

Inwardly, I was cursing as well. Did this random minion just stop by to check on me and make sure I hadn't suddenly learned how to walk through metal bars? Where was Vaughn? Were the fae assassins on their way?

I heard the warlock talking to some of his buddies out of sight, but I could not make out what they said. No doubt he was thrilling them with the epic tale of the Amazing Stripping Conrad. Their presence on this floor implied that they expected company imminently. But where were Kallan and his warriors? Never in my life did I suspect I'd be so eagerly waiting for my own execution.

The conversation ceased suddenly. Archibald Grey and Vaughn strolled into sight side by side like the world's least charismatic romantic couple. Vaughn looked much like I remembered him: an unremarkable man in a boring suit. It took a little effort to remain cognizant of him being there at all, even when you were looking straight at him.

"Oh," I exclaimed with as much disappointment as I could inject into words. "It's you. I was hoping for someone remotely interesting."

Vaughn looked me over. His expression remained impassive. "Mr. Brent," he finally said. "You somehow possess the knack for being both meddlesome and damfool at the same time."

I glowered at him. "Watch who you're calling a damn fool."

"You're like a piece of gum stuck to the sole of my shoe," the bureaucrat continued. "Aggravating and irksome to scrape off, but ultimately innocuous."

"Were you recently bit by a radioactive thesaurus?" I asked.

"Very well. I shall use smaller words so that your deficient mind can comprehend." Vaughn leaned in even closer to the bars.

I wondered if I might be fast enough to jab him in the eye. I could try an arcane attack—the warlocks hadn't searched me all that thoroughly. There'd be no point with any gifted, who drew upon their inner power for their magic. No one thinks to adjust their security protocols for middlings. But the pair of younger warlocks watched me like hawks. I doubted I would get very far in my attempt. So, I stalled.

"I seem to recall you being reasonably polite in our previous encounters. Did you come all this way just to insult me?" I asked.

"I was polite before you threw away so much power for so flimsy a reason," said Vaughn. "Only an utter halfwit casually discards divinity."

"I had my reasons," I replied. I'd had to burn off my power in order to stop Willodean. In order to save her. I knew better than to expect someone like Vaughn to understand that.

A deep rumbling sound came from above and the entire building shook as if in an earthquake. Grey tilted his head slightly, perhaps listening to some arcane warnings. Had the cavalry finally arrived?

"You've got a problem, Archibald," I said. "And I'm not just talking about your face."

"Whatever it is, kindly go deal with it," Vaughn said without turning around. "I'd like a private conversation with your guest."

Vaughn looked actually pleased by the disruption. He didn't want Grey overhearing whatever it was he wanted to talk to me about, though I couldn't for the life of me imagine what that might be.

Grey didn't argue, nor did he seem put off by Vaughn casually ordering him around in his own lair. Grey and his warlocks headed back upstairs to deal with the threat, be it the fae or Herc and John Smith mounting some sort of a last-ditch attempt to rescue me.

As soon as the others left, Vaughn grasped the bars with both hands and pressed even closer. "Tell me what I want to know, and I will kill you quickly. Demur and I will let the warlock torture you, and then I'll come after your friends. I will destroy everyone you've ever cared about. Do you understand?"

I was pretty sure I could punch him in the mouth before he pulled away. But at this point, I had to know what information the cold bastard was after.

"What do you want to know?'

Vaughn's demeanor changed so completely, I had to fight against an instinct to shrink back. It was as though he dropped his mask and was no longer the bland, insignificant version of himself I was familiar with. His expression turned imperious, his face radiated with a mix of hate and power. In that moment, he looked terrifying—and yet strangely familiar. When he spoke it was in the assured tone of a general whose every command sent legions to their deaths rather than his usual soft, listless manner.

"Where's the Kaladanda?"

I had no idea what this new and disturbingly improved Vaughn was talking about. The term he used was meaningless to me. My first instinct was to throw my ignorance in Vaughn's face, to remind him that he promised to use small, simple words and how that one seemed anything but. I resisted the urge. Whatever this thing was, Vaughn clearly wanted it badly. Perhaps I could find a way to somehow leverage his desire to my advantage.

"Where?" Vaughn prodded.

I furiously brainstormed ways to stall.

"What do you want it for?" I asked.

Vaughn took a few seconds to regain control. He retreated a step from the metal bars and slipped the mask of mediocrity back on so thoroughly that he once again seemed insignificant and forgettable, even as his true visage remained fresh in my mind.

"That is none of your concern," he said. "Rest assured, I have no intention of using it against your friends. They're frankly beneath my notice."

"You expect me to take your word for that? No, you tell me what you want it for, or there's no deal."

Vaughn's eyes narrowed. "You're stalling. Let's see if this changes your mind."

He produced a small yellow gemstone, an opal from the looks of it, and squeezed it in his fist.

A wave of overwhelming, nauseating, incredible agony washed over me.

I'm no stranger to suffering. I've been mauled, stabbed, sprayed with venom, defenestrated, and beaten up. I once died from being shot point-blank in the gut.

This was worse.

I convulsed on the floor. When the pain finally stopped, I couldn't muster the strength to get up. There was a metallic taste in my mouth. I'd bitten my tongue while I writhed and now that smarted, too.

"That was only five seconds," said Vaughn. "The next time I use the stone it'll be for ten seconds, and I'll gradually increase the duration after that." Vaughn pointed at the fancy mechanical watch on his wrist. "No one that I know of has ever survived thirty seconds. The human body shuts down as a defense mechanism. Tell me what I want to know, unless you care to try for a new record?"

"Fine," I managed. "Just give me a moment here. Can't hear myself think through the pain."

Vaughn said nothing. He watched impassively as I gathered myself and, with great difficulty, managed to sit up on the bench. All of my muscles ached, including ones I never suspected I had.

"Have you heard of the Movile Cave?" I asked Vaughn.

"No," he said.

I spoke slowly, as I had to work at uttering every word.

"It was discovered a few decades ago in southern Romania; a naturally sealed cave that's been closed off from the outside world for over five million years." My vocal chords felt like someone had dunked them in boiling oil. It hurt to speak, but I knew it'd hurt a lot more not to, so I pressed on. "There's a sulfurous lake down there, and a completely unique ecosystem that's unlike anything else on the planet. Dozens of species of albino insects, spiders, woodlice, and such that evolved in total darkness, cut off from the outside world. There's—"

"What is your *point?*" Vaughn raised the hand holding the opal.

I took a deep, excruciating breath. "My point, Vaughn, is that a blind albino cave woodlouse that is blissfully unaware of the existence of humankind is more likely to help you in any way whatsoever than I am."

Vaughn rewarded me with another helping of pain from the stone. Each of the ten seconds felt like it lasted an hour. If there had been some way for me to will myself to die, I would've done so without hesitation. I'd like to say that I wouldn't have wished that sort of pain on my worst enemy, but I wasn't that nice a person, and Vaughn was right there.

I was on my stomach, face squished into cold cement. I could barely see my tormentor out of the corner of one eye. He was waiting for me to recover enough of my wits. The bastard didn't even seem to be enjoying my suffering. It was only a means to an end to him, not worth thinking about twice. Like pressing a button to summon an elevator or turning the faucet on to wash one's hands. Even through all the pain, I found it within myself to be offended by this indifference.

Vaughn noticed me watching him. He said, "Let's try this one more—"

There was a loud crash, followed by a bloodcurdling scream and the sounds of combat.

Vaughn stepped further away from the cell and faced the one door leading toward the staircase. I rolled onto my side to get a better view and tried to blink the blurriness out of my eyes.

Archibald Grey appeared in my field of vision. He was backing away faster than I'd seen him move before—which was still at roughly the foraging pace of a geriatric tortoise. He held wands in both hands and kept firing energy beams at adversaries who remained out of my view. Grey was flanked by a pair of warlocks, each armed with a wand as well. Both were bleeding from multiple wounds. Both looked terrified; they were men fighting because there was no other choice left to them. Backed into the corner. Literally, given Club Inferno's architecture.

Three fae warriors appeared in my field of vision. Each was armed with a curved bone knife that I recognized and had grown to loathe thanks to the dearly departed Chad. Each moved faster than a human could, casting disruption spells on the warlocks' force shields while slashing at them with those blades.

Grey pointed one of his wands to his side and a portal began to coalesce within an arm's reach. Before it fully formed, a fae aimed at it, uttering a guttural curse, and the portal disintegrated into blue gossamer threads. They fizzled and dissipated as they floated toward the ground.

Grey growled in frustration. He pointed both wands at the fae who'd disrupted the portal and fired. The fae dodged the shots with the feline grace of an action-film acrobat.

At the same moment, Kallan materialized directly behind the ancient warlock and drove a wicked bone sword into his back.

Archibald Grey froze, staring down in disbelief at the tip of the serrated blade protruding from his belly. He coughed once, a wheezing sound, almost as if he were clearing his throat. Blood-tinged spittle discharged from his mouth. Then he slumped on the fae royal's blade. Kallan pulled the sword back, and the warlock slid onto the ground. Grey had finally lost his protracted foot race with death.

The other fae assassins fell upon the remaining warlocks, who were further demoralized by their leader's demise. They desperately threw up barriers and defenses, but those only served to prolong the struggle by a matter of seconds.

Kallan turned toward Vaughn and froze. His eyes went wide. He clutched his sword tighter and pointed it at the bureaucrat.

Vaughn pinched the nonexistent brim of his absent hat in greeting and smirked as he offered the fae a tiny, condescending nod. He touched one of the buttons on his suit and a portal formed directly in front of him.

Kallan pointed at the portal, undoubtedly trying to disrupt it with the same spell his compatriot had used moments earlier. The portal, which sprung to life fully formed, was unaffected. Vaughn tossed something small at the fae and stepped unhurriedly through the portal, which disappeared immediately afterward.

Kallan parried the marble-sized projectile with the flat side of his blade. It bounced and rolled toward where two of the fae were finishing off the last remaining warlocks.

Kallan shouted a warning but before anyone had a chance to react the tiny artifact flared up with the brightness of a flash-bang. I was lucky to have had only a partial view of this from where I lay on the ground, and my vision recovered soon. The fae nearest to the impact had been immolated. There was nothing left of him but charred remains.

With Vaughn gone and all the warlocks dead, the remaining fae warriors joined Kallan, who finally turned his attention to me. He strolled toward my cell, sword in hand.

I grabbed at the bench and, using it for support, pulled myself upright. Everything still hurt, and getting off the ground was an epic struggle, but I intended to die on my feet. With a savage thrust of his sword, Kallan sliced through the lock. He pulled the cell door open using the tip of his blade, careful not to touch the steel bars with his hand.

I was trying to think of something appropriately snarky and brave to say, to come up with fitting last words that would serve as a heroic epitaph to the legend of Conrad Brent. Kallan spoke first.

"The one who escaped through the portal," said Kallan. "Is he your friend or your foe?"

"Foe," I croaked. Through the pain I managed to add, "Hate that guy."

Kallan looked at me, then at the spot where Vaughn had stood, then back at me again.

"I withdraw the Kra'Ga challenge," he said. "May your continued existence prove baleful to Vahagn the Invader."

He motioned to his warriors, and they disappeared, leaving me behind in the ninth circle of Club Inferno with only the corpses of my enemies for company.

CHAPTER 17

EVEN with the door to my cell kindly forced open by Kallan, I didn't have the strength to get out on my own. I sat, propped myself up against a wall, and faded into something in-between unconsciousness and troubled sleep.

I awoke to find myself being ministered to by Robert Finegold. Doctor Bob used a combination of magic and basic first aid to patch me up.

I was lying on the cold cement floor of the cell, with a rolled-up shirt for a pillow.

"This hospital sucks, doc," I said.

"Oh, please. It's dry, it's relatively clean, and nobody is shooting at us. What's to bellyache about?" said the combat medic. "Plus, you've already got visitors, and there's no nurse to keep them out."

I turned my head. Terrie smiled and waved at me through the bars.

"Come on in, Ms. Winter," Doctor Bob said. Terrie didn't make him ask twice. "He's relatively fine, physically, except for a possible concussion. We'll need to watch for that. Otherwise, cuts and bruises. A bit of bed rest and some ibuprofen will do the trick."

"I don't feel fine," I said, and proceeded to describe Vaughn's opal as best I could.

The doc frowned and examined me again. "It may have aggravated the nerves, or the attack was psychological in nature. Most likely, there should be no lasting damage."

"No lasting *physical* damage?" Terrie clarified.

"I'm not an expert on the other kind, but I can recommend a specialist," said Doctor Bob.

"No, thanks," I said. "I'll just internalize it along with all the past psychological damage. That's a totally healthy way to cope, right?"

Bob frowned again and looked like he was getting ready to lecture me, but I waved him off.

"I'm kidding, okay?" I shifted and groaned in pain. "Please tell me we've secured Archibald's magic extractor thingamajig?"

"It's been scrapped by the mutual agreement between John and Herc," said Terrie. "The machine and the research both thoroughly destroyed so as not to tempt anyone into trying to replicate it. The wands have been secured until our fearless leaders can decide what to do with them."

"I still can't believe you single-handedly took out the warlocks, wands and all," said Bob.

Only then did it occur to me that my allies knew nothing about the involvement of the fae. Kallan and his pals must have destroyed the protective wards, teleported inside the building, and left behind no evidence other than the bodies of the slain warlocks. So, I raised my hand to offer a lethargic thumbs-up. Let the word spread. Let everyone, especially the bad guys, think I performed another impossible feat. So grows the legend of Conrad Brent.

"I'll check in on you later. Just take it easy for a bit, will you?" Bob walked off; given the day we'd had, he surely had other patients.

Terrie sat down on the floor next to me. "You really scared me today. I thought I'd lost you."

Most other people may have said something like, "Why did you have to try to be a martyr," but Terrie understood me. Terrie would've done the same thing.

With anyone else, I would've replied with a wiseass remark, something flippant and droll; a Conrad special people have come to expect. Instead, my hand found hers and I squeezed gently. "It was enough to know everyone else got out."

We sat like that for a time, holding hands like a pair of teenagers. There, on a cold uncomfortable floor of a dungeon, despite the physical pain, I felt a sort of peace I'd rarely experienced.

But something niggled at the edge of my consciousness.

"What time is it?" I asked.

"Five thirty."

I should have been at Abaddon headquarters half an hour ago. There was no time to convalesce, no time to chew on the fact that Kallan knew Vaughn and hated him enough to spare me, even after I'd made him look bad in front of all of his buddies in fairyland. Those were problems for Tomorrow's Conrad. Today's Conrad had an apocalypse to prevent.

"Help me up, please?"

Terrie let go of my hand and gently slipped her arm under my head. She lifted me toward her. Then, she leaned closer and kissed me.

The briefest flash of surprise made way for how right it felt, and how much of a fool I'd been. I knew I'd always been fond of Terrie, but I never dared to classify exactly how I felt about her. I thought back to the hours we'd recently shared trying to break into Rojas's house, and how my heart had melted into the pile of nearby snow whenever she smiled at me.

I realized that I'd carried a torch for her for a long time, a feeling that had grown slowly and tenaciously within me, even as my conscious mind did its level best to ignore it. After all, Terrie had watched me fall in love with Willodean and love her deeply enough to let her go, and she'd never said a word. Terrie knew me better than perhaps anyone alive, saw me for the grifter and manipulator that I was. How could she possibly be interested in getting romantically involved with someone like that? I couldn't afford to jeopardize our friendship over a foolish notion that we could ever be more than friends.

But now that she made the first move, all of that clicked into place. My subconscious no longer had to repress those feelings and lock them away in the deepest recesses of my jaded heart.

I lost myself in that kiss. Demons and angels and armageddons of all stripes be damned. We hung on to each other tight, like a pair of shipwrecked sailors in a maelstrom, neither willing to disengage.

My neurotic doubts and insecurities melted away. In that moment, there was only bliss.

"I think you just broke Aysha's heart," a mocking voice broke the reverie.

We both turned reluctantly, to find Moira watching us, grinning from ear to ear.

"There's nothing between Aysha and me," I said peevishly. "I don't know why you keep needling her about that."

"Because it's fun," said Moira. "Anyway, I came by to check on you. Seems you're quite all right, except for the possibility of brain ischemia, what with all the blood flow diverted to—"

"I'm fine! Thank you very much for checking," I said. "Don't you have somewhere else to be?"

Moira tilted her head. "Don't *you*?"

I groaned. "The mediation. I need to get to Abaddon, fast."

"You're in no condition to go anywhere," said Terrie.

I stared at Terrie's face, tense with concern but no less beautiful for it. It took considerable effort to look away.

"Last thing I want to do is leave right now. But I have to. Which one of you ladies would be kind enough to open a portal to Abaddon for me?"

"Fine, but don't get used to it. I'm not an Uber," said Moira. She spoke an incantation and a portal coalesced in front of the torture rack.

"Would you mind tagging along?" I asked her.

"Me?" Moira frowned. "Wouldn't you rather have Queens go? She could sit on your lap."

"No," I said. "Terrie is much too nice for what I have in mind." I turned to Terrie and squeezed her hand again. "I'll see you really soon. Promise." Then back to Moira. "Come on. I'll explain on the way."

The portal delivered us to the side entrance into the Abaddon building. I'd barely opened the door and limped inside when Tiny the doortroll began to chide me.

"You're late, loudmouth. Important guests are cross with …"Tiny saw Moira walk in behind me and his eyes narrowed. He tensed and a low rumble built up within him, like a feral boiling teakettle ready to pounce on an unsuspecting crumpet.

"Oy, Stringbean," Moira greeted him. "Relax, relax, haven't you heard I'm one of the good guys now? Good deeds, done for free, and all that. Anything I can do for you today? Maybe fetch you a bag of ice, or a pack of frozen peas?"

The first time the two of them met, Tiny had made the mistake of blocking Moira's path, and she'd kneed him right in his trollhood. Tiny wasn't ready to forgive and, based on her comment, Moira certainly wasn't about to forget.

The kettle within Tiny's belly reached a crescendo. Before he did something he would almost certainly regret, I ushered Moira past him and into the building.

Daniel Chulsky waited in the second-floor conference room, alone.

"You're late," he said tersely.

"So everyone keeps telling me. Sorry, I was unavoidably detained. Literally." I looked at the empty chairs. "Are they gone? Did the angels fly the coop?" I was hoping Chulsky had gotten the situation resolved without me and I could just go have a lie-down. I figured karma owed me some kind of a break.

"Oh, they're here. We've kept them away from each other. Both groups have been waiting, and they're none too pleased about it."To his credit, Chulsky didn't chide me for running late because of what he considered an irrelevant side quest. At least, he hadn't yet.

So much for the lie-down idea. I gingerly lowered myself into a luxurious office chair at the head of the table and wondered if I'd be able to get up and greet our esteemed guests under my own power. "Well, let's bring them in, then."

Chulsky hesitated. "Perhaps Ms. O'Leary would be more comfortable waiting in the break room?"

"I've asked her to attend the meeting," I said. "The negotiation will benefit from her unique skill set."

Chulsky appeared unconvinced. He arched an eyebrow.

"You wanted me to do this my way," I reminded him. "If that's still the case, you'll need to let Conrad be Conrad."

"I've spent much of the past hour placating higher beings, yet the idea of letting Conrad be Conrad perturbs me more than their displeasure," said Chulsky. "Take a seat, Ms. O'Leary."

Moira took Daniel's words literally. She grabbed hold of a hefty office chair from one of the sides of the long conference table and rolled it over to the edge, next to mine. Chulsky sat at the opposite end of the table, leaving the two long sides to our esteemed guests.

The Archdocent marched into the conference room, followed by two of the warrior angels I'd met in the lobby of the Department of Natural Philosophy. We rose to greet them. I leaned on the table with both hands in what I hoped was a surreptitious manner.

The Archdocent looked exactly the way he had when I'd first met him. A bearded man dressed in a college professor getup whose stern eyes skewered me from under bushy eyebrows. The two angels had replaced their lab coats with slacks and sweaters that seemed comfortable and wouldn't restrict their movement in a fight. They wore slender, long daggers looped on their belts, without bothering with any sort of sheaths. The Archdocent sat and the angels positioned themselves directly behind him, despite the chairs available for them.

As the Archdocent settled into his seat, the representatives of Down Below arrived. Beelzebub strolled in, looking like a Williamsburg hipster. He wore skinny jeans of purplish hue, and an unbuttoned plaid lumberjack shirt over a Judas Priest T-shirt. Bright-yellow socks protruded from vintage sneakers. A pair of thick-rimmed sunglasses perched on his nose even though it was winter and we were indoors. An orange loose-knitted beanie completed the ensemble. Such an attire tended to elicit the same negative reaction from a certain subset of individuals that a red cloth gets from a bull. I strongly suspected the Archdocent belonged in that subset, along with the majority of Baby Boomers, and a healthy percentage of small-town folks. I also suspected Bub knew this.

Four stern-looking executives in business suits followed in Bub's wake. Were it not for their auras, I wouldn't have been able to tell which ones were demons and which were human lawyers and corporate accountants. In any case, the difference was minor enough to be moot.

Bub and three of his minions settled into the four seats on their side of the table. The remaining human minion made a move to claim an unused chair from the angels' side, the way Moira had done earlier. The nearest warrior angel scowled at him fiercely, in a manner that made him reconsider this action and probably all of his life choices leading up to it. The minion returned to his side with his figurative tail between his legs and stood awkwardly behind his seated associates.

The angels and demons managed to both stare down their noses at each other, which should have been geometrically impossible outside of an Escher painting. Even though no one had spoken a word yet, the room felt like a tinderbox surrounded by a mob of lit matches.

I gave the signal by resting my hand on the arm of Moira's chair. In order to let Conrad be Conrad, I had to commit the unspeakable sin of letting Moira be Moira.

The necromancer ogled the angels the way a toddler might gawk at a sleeping bear at the zoo. "I thought they'd be taller," she stage-whispered at me. As the angels switched some of their mute ire toward the necromancer, she leaned toward the demons and sniffed the air. "Not a hint of sulfur," she said, disappointment dripping from every word. "Just Old Spice."

The higher beings glared at Moira, forgetting their mutual animosity for a moment, united in their opprobrium toward the irritating human. This had been my plan all along. Moira's weaponized abrasiveness would act as a lightning rod, hopefully keeping the factions from lashing out at each other.

"Thank you for joining us, folks," I said. "Please forgive the delay. I've had a run-in with the Emersonians and with Holcomb's stooges who pull their strings."

It was a spur-of-the-moment admission. I figured they'd easily find out if they cared anyway, and it was another point of possible agreement between the parties. No one ever likes City Hall.

"The new administration is preposterous," scoffed the Archdocent. "Leave it to the humans to invent a form of government so flawed that it consistently encourages the dregs of the species to float toward the top. Even so"—the Archdocent stroked his beard—"someone like Holcomb had to have preternatural assistance to outperform the other liars and miscreants in the election. In fact, our sociologists are convinced of this. They wonder who'd stand to benefit." He stared pointedly at his counterpart from Down Below.

"Don't look at us," Bub said quickly. "My firm had nothing to do with that. I mean, sure, we made a small financial contribution to his campaign. We contributed to all the viable candidates equally, as has been our long-standing policy. But to have Holcomb as a client? I think not. Anyone who relies solely on the appearance of success to be successful is not to be trusted."

Moira stretched in her seat and smiled at everyone sweetly. "I used to work for that guy."

She failed to mention that she only did so in order to hoodwink him on behalf of the Cabal, but in her current role as a lightning rod, the less detailed statement was far more effective.

Before anyone decided to smite Moira, I chose to proceed.

"Folks, there are two issues to be resolved here. Each of you laid claim to Rojas's stuff, and also to his eternal soul. Do I have that right?"

Bub's advisers and the Archdocent all tried to speak at once and over each other, gradually raising their voices. I tried to cut in twice and eventually just began banging my palm against the table until I had everyone's attention.

"Look," I said, "I know you're dying to argue whose claim is greater, but you will never convince each other, so what's the point? I've had quite a day, and I can assure you that neither of you is going to sway me, either. So can we please try to do this my way and maybe actually resolve this thing?"

Grudgingly, both sides settled down for the moment, but they weren't happy about it. The tension in the room grew so thick, you'd need a lightsaber to cut it.

"Archdocent, may I ask *why* you want this particular soul?"

The Archdocent skewered me with a sanctimonious gaze. "A deal was struck. An indulgence has been purchased, and the On High do not renege on our promises, mediator." He wouldn't call me by my professional name, but at least he afforded me the courtesy of not using my secret name in front of everyone. I was a mediator, so referring to me by a title would do just fine.

"Except you're not the one to renege," I told him. "It was Mr. Rojas who attempted to manipulate and cheat you. It was Mr. Rojas who engineered a dangerous standoff with the sole purpose of saving his metaphorical hide. Is that the sort of person you wish to reward with a VIP ticket past the Pearly Gates? It seems like that would be an injustice."

"They've let in far worse," Bub muttered.

The Archdocent glared at Bub and both of the warrior angels tensed, their hands grasping the handles of their daggers.

"Stuff it, dude," said Moira the Lightning Rod. "Ain't your turn."

Bub narrowed his eyes at her. "Given your history, it might be prudent for you to be a little nicer to your future hosts."

She shrugged. "I plan to live forever. It's worked out great for me so far."

I cut in. "The way I see it, Archdocent, you only have two reasons to want the no-goodnik's soul. One, is to make sure no one thinks the Down Below's claim can be more significant than yours, and two, because both sides are tying the ownership of Rojas's belongings to the soul thing. I have a solution to these problems."

"Do you, now?" The Archdocent looked doubtful.

"First, can we all agree here and now that Rojas's soul and his estate are two separate assets? He has agreed to give up any belongings either side may want in exchange for being left alone."

The Archdocent nodded, though his expression remained sour. Bub grunted assent. The way both sides agreed to this so easily, only served to confirm my suspicions about their motives. I pressed on.

"Second, Mr. Rojas's soul is presently otherwise engaged. It's in no hurry to proceed to either destination. And as such, if both of you were to withdraw your claims upon it, when it does finally shed what remains of its mortal coil, it could be judged and proceed with no preferential treatment, like anyone else."

"That's going to be a problem for us," said Bub. "It would set a dangerous precedent. We can't be giving our other clients ideas. Or hope. Especially hope."

"I believe it would be in the best interest of everyone involved if no one outside this room ever learned the details of how Rojas manipulated the system," said Chulsky. "Whatever we agree upon today, there will be a non-disclosure agreement preventing Rojas from sharing certain parts of his life story with anyone, enforceable by the combined might of us all."

"Think about it this way," I added. "Where will Rojas's soul end up after all this? Surely in the place both of you agree it ultimately belongs, right? Bub, your entire business model is about playing the long game. What's a few extra centuries if the ultimate outcome is the same?"

The demon nodded. "All right. We agree to this part of your proposal, so long as it has no bearing on the estate."

The Archdocent pursed his lips and tapped his fingers on the conference table. "Very well," he declared. "The On High are amenable to making this concession."

"Wonderful," I declared with the joviality I didn't feel. If the meeting went on much longer, there was a distinct possibility I'd faint and collapse face-first onto the table. "Mr. Rojas is prepared to transfer a considerable portion of his fortune to your respective organizations. Eighty percent of everything he owns, split evenly between you. And before you each complain about the split, this includes a lot of money in offshore accounts and double-blind trusts neither of you knows about or can possibly retrieve without his cooperation. As a result, each side will inherit more funds than they originally expected."

Bub and the Archdocent mulled it over, studying each other like a pair of poker players. Neither was in a rush to accept a deal that was so obviously beneficial to them both.

"You hesitate because you ultimately don't care that much about the money," I said. "It's a fringe benefit and you'll both take it, but this kerfuffle is and has always been about a certain vintage bottle of 1961 Chateau Latour."

I had their undivided attention. I leaned down, a spasm of pain shooting through my body with every motion, and retrieved the attaché case Chulsky had prepared for me. I opened the case and turned it toward the assembled beings. "This bottle."

The room erupted. Everyone was on their feet, eyes locked on the bottle as if it were the Mona Lisa wearing the Hope diamond and holding the Holy Grail in one hand and a box of Brooklyn bagels in the other.

"We had an agreement, mediator," said the Archdocent.

"You promised me that bottle, Conrad," shouted Bub.

Bub's minions and the Archdocent's angels looked like they were about to try and snatch the attaché case. Even though I was certain the bottle was what they were ultimately after, the intensity of their reactions still caught me unawares.

"Calm yourselves," Chulsky's stern voice cut through the commotion. "Sit down," he ordered with so much authority, I would have obeyed had I not already been sitting. "The bottle is here, and we're trying to work with you to resolve this matter. Remember that this is neutral ground, sanctified and designated by your respective masters, and act accordingly."

Chulsky's admonition cooled tempers fractionally. Everyone remained on their feet, but they hadn't rushed me or the prize on display in front of them.

"I've broken no promises to either of you," I said wearily. "I promised to investigate, and as you can see, I'm pretty good at my job. I was able to identify the one and only possession of Mr. Rojas's that you both care about, and I was able to bring it here to you. Now the question is, how do we get you to share your toys? You could open the bottle and drink it together, or—"

"The bottle is ours!" shouted the Archdocent. "We will annihilate this island before we allow the unclean to sink their claws into it."

"I would sooner share a drink with the subway rats than this puffed-up pompous pigeon." Spittle burst forth from Bub's mouth as he stressed every "p" in his alliterative insult.

Two of the minions moved toward the attaché case again. A warrior angel leaped over the table to intercept them, a dagger glinting in her hand.

Moira snatched the bottle from the case. "Stop!" she shouted. She grasped the bottle by its neck, hefted it like a baton and aimed it toward the nearest wall. "If anyone takes one more step, I'm going to christen this conference room HMS *Moira*."

For a long moment, everyone was still.

"If all of you would return to your seats—"

Before Chulsky could finish speaking, the minion nearest to the warrior angel who had leapt across the table drew a thin, razor-sharp blade from the sleeve of his bespoke suit jacket and struck, aiming between her ribs.

The angel dodged, then thrust her dagger at the minion's neck. He parried and they traded blows.

With everyone's attention on the two combatants, the other angel slid toward Moira and tried to snatch the bottle from her hand. Moira twisted out of the way, losing her balance in the process. As she tried to recover, she swung her right hand and the glass bottle smashed against the edge of the table.

The glass shattered, and the pungent red liquid spilled onto the table and floor.

Everyone, including Moira, stared in horror at the pooling wine. And as we watched, a small ampule filled with viscous honey-colored liquid slid from the jagged upper half of the bottle Moira was still holding. It dropped toward the floor.

I had been wrong. The vintage bottle contained treasure worth more than the Mona Lisa and the Hope diamond combined. Before anyone else could react, I snatched the ampule of ambrosia from the air.

"Back!" I groaned. Everyone shrank back as I climbed, painfully, onto my feet.

They couldn't stop me in time. The power of apotheosis was in my hand. A single gulp of the rarest, most valuable substance in the world, and this middling could become a god—again. I could regain the incredible power I'd experienced so briefly once before.

It was the hardest thing in the world not to snap the ampule open and drink.

Angels and demons were prepared to go to war over this prize. What would happen if I claimed it as my own? Would my powers kick in quickly enough for me to fight them off? Would this building be destroyed in the struggle? Would we demolish lower Manhattan? The entire city? Would I cause the very apocalypse I was trying to prevent?

My hand shook. A little persistent voice in my head kept saying: *You've earned it. It's yours. Rojas gifted you this bottle, even if he didn't know its contents.* I struggled to resist the powerful urge. In the past I'd given up this power in order to save the city from Willodean and to save her, the woman I cared for, from self-destruction. How could I possibly justify making a different decision this time? I imagined Terrie's face, thought back to Terrie holding my hand, back to our lingering kiss, and those memories gave me the strength I badly needed.

I faced off against the angels and demons who watched my every move with apprehension. "Daniel told you all to sit your asses down." My voice cracked. It lacked the gravitas of Chulsky's. In fact, it was barely a squeak. But I still held the ambrosia, and for the moment, that gave me all the authority I needed.

Everyone returned to their seats, careful to give me and Moira a wide berth. Moira glowered at them and looked ready to intercept anyone who might try something. She may not have known the value and specific purpose of ambrosia, but everyone's reaction to the ampule was enough to clue her in to its importance. I hoped she wouldn't do anything stupid, like trying to snatch it from me, even though it would have been useless to anyone who was not a middling. She was still Moira, after all. But, for now, she held her ground.

Everyone grudgingly resumed their places at the table. Neither the angel nor the demon who had engaged in a brief duel looked worse for wear. The unfortunate minion who was left without a chair remained standing behind Bub. I allowed myself to relax a little.

"Good," I said. "Now I finally understand why all of you wanted a ten-thousand-dollar bottle of wine so badly."

"Ten grand?" Moira arched her eyebrow. She licked a few droplets off her hand. "It's not bad, I suppose."

"No one cares about the wine," said the Archdocent.

Bub looked like he wanted to argue the point but thought better of it.

"What I don't get, is why you even need it?" I asked. "It's not like any of you were going to ascend. Your superiors would not look kindly upon that." I pondered this. "Wait, is this how one becomes ... like you?"

"It most assuredly is not," said the Archdocent. "We merely wish to keep the substance out of unclean hands. Of course, several of our best natural scientists would love the opportunity to study—"

"That can never happen," said Bub. "My orders from Down Below are to prevent any such experimentation at all costs."

"It sounds like both of you are more interested in keeping the ambrosia out of each other's hands than actually gaining it for yourselves," I said. The little voice in my head grew louder, more insistent.

Bub chuckled. "Oh, so you're going to try and sell us on letting *you* drink it? How noble of you to volunteer for such an arduous task."

I summoned the image of Terrie in my mind's eye and did my best to silence the voice. "No. Not me. But there's someone who could, someone both of you might find palatable and whose godhood may even prove beneficial to everyone here. Someone who can put out the dumpster fire that's raging across the city. You've made your home here. Wouldn't you appreciate it if someone could nudge things back to normality?"

The Archdocent shook his head. "No middling exists that is so wonderful that both On High and Down Below would welcome their ascension."

Bub looked amused. "This ought to be good. I can't think of anyone I'd want to see gain so much power."

I smiled at them. "I think I can prove both of you wrong." I gripped the ampule tighter. I had exactly one good idea, and if they didn't go for it, I'd have to drink the ambrosia after all and deal with the consequences. "I hereby propose the re-apotheosis of Mose."

CHAPTER 18

THEY say the best kind of deal is the one where both sides walk away happy. This can occasionally be true in business, but rarely is it applicable in other aspects of life, and virtually never achievable in politics. The second-best kind of deal is the one where everyone equally feels like they gave up more than they could afford.

Neither the agents of On High nor the denizens of Down Below had been especially thrilled with giving up the vial of ambrosia, but they both could appreciate the fact that letting Mose have it was the least terrible of the options they didn't like. Once they agreed on that, the rest was easy as pie. Or angel's food cake. Or devil's food cake. Frankly, I've had enough of both factions and would settle for a slice of New York cheesecake instead, with a side of extra-strength ibuprofen.

When the deal was ironed out and the mediation finally over, I slumped in my chair, still holding on tight to the vial of ambrosia.

"That was intense," I said. "Great job, Moira. You really came through for us."

She shrugged. "This felt like your typical Cabal meeting, only a lot less violent." Moira kicked back her chair and stretched out her legs, resting them on the conference table, away from the puddle of spilled wine. She pointedly ignored Chulsky's glare, who must've realized this was not the right moment to criticize her manners.

"I could do with a refill of whatever magic Doctor Bob used to patch me up," I said. "Would either of you do the honors?"

Chulsky traced a sigil in the air and studied me intently. "Your body is near the limit of how much it can tolerate," he said. "Propping you up with another magic fix would be incredibly dangerous to your health. You need rest. A guest room and a warm meal will be made available to you."

"I need to get to Australia," I began to argue, but Chulsky shook his head.

"I will send another agent to retrieve Mose. It will be someone he trusts. You must rest. After that, you must finalize the transaction with Mr. Rojas." Chulsky reached out his hand. "I'll keep the vial secure until Mose arrives."

Handing over the vial, I felt like Gollum with the One Ring. I had to apply considerable effort toward unclenching my fist. Chulsky waited patiently for me to do so. Once I did, he snatched up my Precious and slid it into the inside pocket of his suit. He said, "There's no safer place to keep this than the inside of the Abaddon vault."

"What else have you got in that vault?" asked Moira. She held up her hands. "Sorry. Old habits, you know."

Chulsky insisted on personally walking me to the guest room. He told me that food was on its way and was ready to leave when I called after him.

"Hang on. Do you, by chance, know what a Kaladanda is?"

"It's a staff from Hindu mythology," said Chulsky. "According to legend, it is an unstoppable weapon, capable of penetrating past any arcane or physical protections. It can kill any being—living, undead, or ascended."

I wasn't surprised, exactly. It wasn't as though someone like Vaughn would've gone through all this trouble to get his devious paws on an apple pie recipe. Vaughn had proven to have access to nearly unlimited resources. If he needed a weapon like that, he must've been going big-game hunting, up against something even nastier than him.

"It can kill a god?" I asked.

Chulsky looked at me quizzically. "I suppose. Why do you ask?"

"I'm pretty sure the bad guys are looking for it," I said without getting into too many details. Given the way our conversation about him went last time, I wasn't in a rush to broach the subject of Vaughn. First, I really needed to think, and to process all this new information without the distraction of possibly keeling over from pain. "Do you know where it can be found?"

"For once, there's nothing to worry about," said Chulsky. "Kaladanda doesn't exist."

I thought back to Vaughn revealing his true face. He had been certain this weapon was real, and suspected I'd know where to find it. But, why? Was it my status as a fellow middling? My brief experimentation with godhood? My affiliation with the Watch? My recent trip to fairyland? There simply weren't enough clues for me to hazard a reasonable guess.

"How can you be sure it's a myth?" I asked.

Chulsky thought it over. "I suppose there's never a definitive way to prove a negative. Still, if something that powerful existed, I would have been aware of it."

I wondered if he was lying to me, but there seemed little enough reason for him to do so. "All right," I said. "Thanks."

"An exemplary job today," said Chulsky. "Now, rest." He left the room.

I stretched out on the made-up bed in my clothes. So, Vaughn's end game involved killing a god, or someone nearly as powerful. But which one, and for what purpose?

I was in no condition to figure it out. I needed to get hold of Terrie, to talk to her about what happened earlier. It was difficult to focus on anything else. The pain was making it difficult to think at all. Even my eyeballs hurt.

I rested my eyes for a moment, and was asleep before the food arrived.

It was still light outside when I woke up. I felt considerably better. Practically good as new. A quick glance at the clock made me realize my error: it was *already* light outside. I'd slept for over sixteen hours. This was my second such recuperative hibernation in a few short days, and I vowed not to make a habit of it, at least not until I became a senior citizen.

The tray of food someone had brought in the day before was still there. Ravenous, I polished off a handful of cold French fries and washed the aftertaste of salt and oil down with a bottle of spring water.

Someone had also placed a white linen shirt, a pair of black slacks, socks and underwear all neatly folded on the nightstand. Everything was brand-new, with tags still on. Whoever it was had made a decent job at guessing my sizes. I imagined Tiny the doortroll on a supply run to a nearby Target, trying to decide between boxers and briefs. The thought gruntled me.

I used the landline in the room to call Terrie. She wasn't picking up. Was she busy, ignoring an unknown number, or just not ready to discuss whatever-it-was between us over the phone? I tried my best to push the thought away. There were a million other things vying for my attention, but I permitted myself the luxury of a hot shower and a shave. I felt I'd earned at least that much. All the supplies, from shaving cream to cologne, were available in the suite's bathroom. I had to admit, Hotel Abaddon provided five-star accommodations, even if the day-old fries tasted a little stale.

By the time I left the guest quarters, I felt human again. Dressed in slacks and a button-down shirt I looked like a supermarket-brand version of Chulsky. The only thing missing—

"Mr. Brent!"

I turned. A fellow in his early twenties smiled at me.

"Mr. Chulsky is currently indisposed, but he will return this afternoon. He requests that you inform Mr. Rojas of the negotiated settlement today. He also recommends that you stop by the armory on your way out."

"Yes, wonderful." A way to defend myself was exactly what I was missing, especially now that we'd poked at the Emersonian wasp nest. "Where would that be?"

The polite young man led me to an unadorned door, held it open, but didn't follow me inside.

The armory was a vast hall larger than my entire Brooklyn apartment. And while it did offer a superb selection of armaments—from automatic rifles to pistols to bladed weapons of every conceivable shape and length—most of the room was occupied by an extensive array of magical artifacts. Wall-to-wall cherry-wood shelves were stuffed with meticulously cataloged trinkets of every kind. The variety and sheer volume would turn magic vendors like Steve and Mordecai green with envy.

I looked for some kind of a curator, but I was alone, in the company of millions of dollars' worth of artifacts. Was there some etiquette to this? Some version of a ten-items-or-less limit? Did I need an Abaddon library card to check the artifacts out? This had to be one of the perks of working for this organization. Perhaps Chulsky sending me here was even meant as a gentle nudge, an extra carrot to entice me into full-time employment. I felt like a sticky-fingered kid in a candy shop as I helped myself to a full arsenal. Soon, my pockets felt heavy and I wore enough rings, chains, and other trinkets to star in my own rap video. I left the armory as well-stocked as I had ever been.

I walked over to the Manhattan Municipal Building and descended into the Watchtower. The usually quiet, sparsely populated office was bustling with activity. Just about everyone from the support staff to the cleaning crew were running around like reanimated chickens in search of their cut-off heads.

I waved at one of the desk jockeys who was wrangling an overflowing storage box. A little potted cactus perched precariously atop stacks of thick manila folders.

"What's going on?" I asked.

"Moving day," he said. "We're clearing the building."

"What? Why?"

He merely shrugged, got a better grip on the box, and pointed toward Mose's office with his chin. "John's orders. Ours isn't to question why, but if you really want to know, the boss's in there." He carried off the folders and the cactus to wherever their new home might be.

I entered Mose's office. John sat stooped over the massive desk, his expression pained. He halfheartedly lifted his hand in greeting, then dropped it onto the pile of papers in front of him.

197

"Good to see you on your feet," John said with a sort of morose earnestness.

"Thank you," I said. "And thanks for the assist earlier. Any word on your family?"

John raised his haunted eyes at me. "No progress, but the kidnappers claim they're still alive."

I pulled a visitor's chair to the desk and sat down across from John. "Claim?"

"They were furious about the raid on Inferno, and the role the Watch played in it. I sincerely thought my sister's life was forfeit ... . Shortly after the raid began, while you and the others were still in there, we received an official decree from the mayor's office, giving us forty-eight hours to vacate this building, and ordering us to immediately cease all operations in New York City." John lifted a stack of legal-sized sheets of paper bound with a paper clip and dropped them back onto the table with distaste, as if they were covered in something foul. "Five minutes after the documents arrived by courier, the kidnappers called. They issued threats and admonitions, but the short of it was that they wanted me to accede to Holcomb's demands. The same 'or else' as before."

"It makes sense," I said. "If they ... do anything drastic, they lose their leverage over you."

John sighed. "They promised to provide proof of life after we vacate the Watchtower. So here I am, doing their bidding against my better judgment. Again."

I looked our tormented leader straight in the eye. "Don't beat yourself up, John. You stood up to them when it meant saving lives. *Our* lives. As for the rest? The Watchtower is just a place. The Watch is its people, wherever they are. We'll find a way to bring Holcomb and Vaughn down even if we have to operate out of a Holiday Inn across the Hudson."

John leaned on his desk with both elbows and rested his chin on the interlocked fingers of his hands. "Throughout the centuries and across many different cities, this will be the first time the Watch has ever been unceremoniously booted out," he said bitterly. "And I'll be the one presiding over the greatest embarrassment in the organization's long history." He went back to staring at a pile of paperwork in front of him.

"The greatest embarrassment in the history of the Watch had to have been leaving that phoenix cage unlocked in Chicago in 1871. I can't believe they blamed the resulting fire on a cow, of all things. You, on the other hand, are making the best of a very difficult situation. So, chin up. Literally."

"We'll be handing them the nexus," said John.

The Municipal Building had been erected atop a powerful source of raw magical power. Mose had been the god of the nexus, guarding it from all threats, and drawing upon its energies when necessary to help defend the city.

"Temporarily," I countered. "I come bearing good news. I can't tell you the entire story, but there's an excellent chance Mose might be coming back soon." I performed the mental math, calculating how long it'd take Abaddon's agent to reach Mose in the outback. Once Mose drank the ambrosia, he could teleport back on his own. "Perhaps even before our forty-eight hours are up."

John looked at me. This time there was hope in his eyes. "Really? That would …" He trailed off, then refocused with visible effort. "I'm afraid, Conrad. I'm afraid of what I might be willing to do while the lives of my loved ones are at stake. Short of finding them, I can think of no greater relief than to hand the responsibility and the power back to Mose."

"The bad guys must think you're in charge," I cautioned. "If they find out that Mose is back and if they feel you're no longer of use to them …"

I didn't have to finish the sentence. We both understood the implications.

"Knowing salvation may be within reach is enough for me," said John.

My cell phone had been a minor casualty of the battle against the warlocks. I procured a replacement from the Watchtower's supply room before its contents were packed away, and loaded my contacts from the cloud. My first call was to Terrie, but she still wasn't picking up. We needed to talk about that kiss.

I sent a message to all my top contacts so they'd have a number where they could reach me. The phone rang almost immediately, but it wasn't Terrie as I had hoped.

"I made inquiries after that meeting yesterday, and your girlfriend caught me up on that Rojas bloke," said Moira. "I want in."

Girlfriend? Was that what Terrie would want? A single kiss was no guarantee she would, and my neurotic brain unhelpfully imagined scenarios where she already regretted taking our relationship into this new, unexplored direction. I hoped the two of us would get to discuss it soon, but I wasn't about to express any of that to Moira.

"You want in on what, exactly?" I asked.

"The novelty of being a good person is starting to wear thin," said Moira. "Don't get me wrong, it's been great fun, and I do enjoy the camaraderie. No one has tried to stab me in the back even once, no matter how much I aggravate them. Problem is, I haven't been paid. Like, at all. I've got to come up with an alternate plan to support the lifestyle I've grown accustomed to. Rojas is rich, and we're helping him. You do the math, yeah?"

"He's about to give up his wealth as part of the settlement," I reminded her.

"Eighty percent of his wealth. Which leaves—let me see, adjust for compound interest, carry the seven—enough to get me properly reimbursed for all the selfless deeds I performed this week," said Moira.

"I'm going to buy you a dictionary for Christmas, so you can look up the definition of the word 'selfless.' Meantime, you absolutely may *not* rob that guy."

"Rob him? Oh, please. That's only my backup plan. Introduce us, and I'll make him an offer he can't refuse."

"That doesn't sound all that much better."

"Not like that. He'll be awestruck by my idea, even if he doesn't know it yet." Moira batted her eyelashes at me, which somehow seemed more terrifying than her past threats. "Pretty please?"

Moira's moral compass may have been right twice a day on a good day, but I did owe her after everything she'd done for me and my friends lately. I nodded grudgingly.

"Look, I have to go see him anyway. You can come along, but I expect you to be on your best behavior."

"The bestest," said Moira in that sweet tone that made me very nervous.

I was already beginning to regret my decision.

We drove into Brooklyn to find the streets and sidewalks empty and people huddling within their homes. Many buildings had scorch marks on their façades and other structural damage.

The sight shocked me. Moira filled me in on the events of the past day. I had been so busy dealing with what Daniel Chulsky would describe as "real problems" that I was unaware of what was happening in the streets.

Our assault on Club Inferno had triggered a chain of events whereby my city found itself in the midst of an arcane civil war. Civilians who had been previously uninvolved in the conflict between the irregulars and the Emersonians saw our attack as a rallying cry.

Although these people had magic, most of them were nothing like the guardians of the Watch or the Cabal sorcerers. They were accustomed to living quiet, peaceful lives, like their mundane neighbors. Lives that had been uprooted by Holcomb and his ham-handed and misguided campaign of oppression against the gifted.

The gifted were tired of being bullied and mistreated. They'd had enough of Holcomb's schemes to make them shoulder the responsibility for solving all of New York City's problems by tapping their magic through forced labor in the guise of volunteerism. They were angry about having their artifacts and family heirlooms confiscated in the name of city government; of being simultaneously asked to give more than everyone else, and treated as though they were somehow less.

The mayor wasn't ready to throw in the towel, however. As a businessman, he'd built a brand that relied on the appearance of success, even if actual success may have been present only some of the time. He had to win, no matter the cost. As a politician, he'd convinced the world that New York City was thriving thanks to his brilliant and unorthodox policies, which made him an appealing candidate for an even higher office. Holcomb couldn't allow the sandcastle of presiding over New York City's miraculous recovery and economic boom to be washed away by the flood wave of his gifted citizens' discontent.

Holcomb called in the mercenaries.

Mages of fortune, ex-Cabal operatives, arcane military contractors, borderline criminals, and thugs of every stripe poured into New York. Paid from the city coffers, they suppressed and intimidated the very people whose labor and magic had filled those coffers in the first place. Holcomb squandered a fortune earmarked for all the shiny projects meant to benefit residents of our city, programs he lauded in his campaign speeches, all in a vain attempt to save face and to keep the gears turning on his fatally flawed machine.

The mercenaries had clashed, repeatedly, with the irregulars and with the allied gifted, while Holcomb gave press conferences about doing everything he possibly could to quell the latest wave of gang violence in his city.

The violence, the skirmishes, and the damage made our modern, civilized city seem like the collapsing Yugoslavia of the early 1990s or Syria of the late 2010s. How could a stable society degenerate into such a quagmire so quickly? How could it scrub off the veneer of civility in the blink of an eye? It hadn't even been twenty-four hours. I suppose people unfortunate enough to have found themselves in similar predicaments throughout history had been equally stunned and dismayed.

I had to finish the business with Rojas, help John find his family, and have that conversation with Terrie. But after that, I vowed to do something about the mayor and his cronies, even if I had to bring down both the Holcomb Tower and City Hall to do it.

CHAPTER 19

AS we drove past the Gravesend Cemetery toward the Rojas house, Moira pasted her face against the car window, practically salivating at the view.

"So much latent magic. Such exquisite sorcerous threads running all across this place like a spiderweb!" Moira appeared happier than a necromancer in a natural history museum.

As a middling, I couldn't see what she saw. Without the help of some clever trinket, all I perceived was rows of weather-beaten, snow-covered gravestones in various states of disrepair.

"I could raise a private army of top-shelf ghouls from those—"

Moira yelped mid-sentence and shrank back, as though she had just touched a live wire.

"Something there really doesn't want me sticking my nose into its domain," said Moira.

"That would be the cat," I said.

Moira shot me an inquisitive glance but didn't press for an explanation.

"The same cat who protects the Rojas house," I added.

I was pretty sure Moira wasn't planning on doing anything too underhanded, but a gentle warning couldn't hurt, could it? She pondered my words as I pulled the Oldsmobile to the curb.

Rojas's house was a much more welcoming place this time around. Although I could still detect a sensible amount of arcane protections, the place no longer bristled with them like a rolled-up hedgehog. A video doorbell was now installed at the front door, but before we could ring it, a smart lock clicked open.

"Come on in," Rojas's cheerful voice emanated from the doorbell speaker.

Inside, the house looked much the same as during my previous visit, except every room now had a security camera. Brand-new television sets murmured from various rooms, each one set to a different channel.

I briefly dwelled on how the disembodied lich managed to conduct his affairs. He must've had a trusted associate or an employee who could physically handle the payments. Being wealthy easily assuaged most of his problems as well as any form of magic could.

"Hi, Benicio," I said. "I see you've been busy."

"Welcome back, Conrad! You've done me an enormous favor by breaking down my protections and inspiring me to live my afterlife instead of cowering in fear. Thank you!"

"It's my pleasure," I said, trying to remember if I'd actually said something inspiring the last time I was here. "I bring good tidings."

I told Rojas about the meeting, skipping the part about his bottle of wine being priceless. Some people would hold a grudge over losing an item of considerable value even if they never knew of that value to begin with. I exaggerated my role in getting him off the hook with the powers beyond mortal comprehension, but it was only a slight exaggeration, well within the acceptable parameters. Moira winced at my embellishments but didn't contradict me. Perhaps she appreciated the need for some good posturing, or she wanted my cooperation in pitching whatever madcap scheme she had in mind.

"And again, thank you so much. I can shed those worries and focus on the future and the possibilities that are open to me in my current state," said Rojas.

I glanced toward the assorted electronics. "You seem to have made a lot of improvements already."

"I don't know how anyone could stand binding their soul to a building back in the old days, but now is the golden age for disembodied individuals," said Rojas. "Smart homes are the solution! I've had these cameras installed in every room so that the contractors think I'm at work, talking to them through an app on my mobile phone!" The lich chuckled.

No one else seemed to be around. "I don't mean to pry, but how did you unlock the door for us?" I asked.

"A lich has a limited capacity to manipulate physical objects. Ones that are a part of the structure their soul is bound to," said Moira.

"Yes, quite so. A door lock, for example, is a part of the house, making it possible for me to control it. Appliances that are merely plugged into the electric grid, like a fridge or a roaming vacuum cleaner, are not extensions of myself, however. I'm still learning; experimenting with the limits of my abilities. The young lady is as sharp as she's beautiful. Aren't you going to introduce us, Conrad?"

"Moira O'Leary," said Moira with every bit of flair she could muster. "An expert on all things undead."

"We prefer the term 'differently extant,'" said Rojas.

"And I prefer the term fizzy pop to soda, but in the end they're the same bunch of chemicals, barely fit for human consumption and diluted in carbonated water," said Moira.

Rojas chuckled politely. "I suppose a cut rose by any other name is just as wilted. You always keep such fascinating company, Conrad."

"My brusque friend here actually insisted on coming to see you," I said.

"Oh?" said Rojas.

"I've got a proposition for you," said Moira.

"Oh?" Rojas repeated. "If I were corporeal and a few decades younger ..."

"Slow your roll, Grandpa Four-Walls," said Moira. "I'm here to talk business."

"By all means," said Rojas.

Was it my imagination or did he sound like an indulgent uncle, steeling himself for whatever nonsense might pass through the lips of his allegedly precocious niece next? Did he feel he owed it to me to hear Moira out, because I'd literally saved his non-corporeal bacon from the fires of Down Below?

"I've got nothing but time, now," Rojas added.

"Therein lies the problem," said Moira. "What good is all the time in the world when you're stuck in this unremarkable little dwelling? Whiling away decades watching drivel on television and listening to podbooks and audiocasts and whatnot."

After decades of constantly risking life and limb, I couldn't help but think that might not be such a terrible existence, especially for an introvert.

"It's a problem to which I've been giving serious thought," said Rojas. I suppose I shouldn't have been surprised. After all, from what I knew of our host, he had been a lot more like Hugh Hefner than Howard Hughes when he was alive. "I was thinking of letting a family move in here. Given the rent prices in Brooklyn, I shouldn't have any trouble finding some willing housemates. That way I'd always have someone to talk to."

"Right idea, wrong execution," said Moira. "Adopting a pet family is a long-term commitment, and there's no guarantee you'll bond with the ones you pick. They might not be properly housebroken. They are bound to scratch up your nice furniture. And if things go really wrong, I hear it's pretty difficult to evict a tenant in New York City, even for a supernatural being."

"Hmm." I could practically hear Rojas mulling this over. "What do you suggest, then?"

Moira grinned like a used car salesperson talking to a live sucker who's shown interest in the rusty Yugo Deathtrap at the back of the lot.

"I know of a beachside resort for sale in Costa Rica that has scenic views and is absolutely perfect for binding a human soul. Instead of being cramped in these four walls"—Moira waved about with as much disdain as she could muster up for what seemed like perfectly serviceable walls to me—"you could be entertained by the lives and adventures of over a hundred suites filled with guests. And those guests would be coming and going. Then there's the staff, the entertainment .... Never a dull moment!"

"Is that even possible?" he asked earnestly. "Could my soul be unbound from one building and rebound to another? I've never heard of such a thing being done." I didn't have to be a lich whisperer to realize how much this prospect might appeal to someone like Rojas.

"It is a delicate and complex procedure, but it can be safely performed by a world-class necromancer." Moira's grin widened. "Someone as skilled in the dark arts as she is astute when it comes to international real estate."

"How?" Rojas pressed. "Walk me through it."

Moira launched into a detailed explanation of the proposed soul transplant. I quickly became lost in the technical details, but it seemed Rojas had truly done his homework as he was able to keep up with Moira. They discussed and argued over the details of the necessary rituals and I could tell both were equally excited at the prospect of moving forward with this endeavor.

After listening to their disturbing necromancy banter for a time, I felt increasingly like a third wheel. At the briefest lull, I managed to interject. "It sounds like you two have this well in hand. If you don't mind, I will take my leave."

"Thank you so much, Conrad," said Rojas. "You saved my soul, and it seems now you've also saved my sanity by introducing me to your clever friend. How can I ever repay you?"

"All in a day's work." I was glad to have discharged my duty to Abaddon. I could now focus on the Watch without juggling so many impossible problems at once. "Unless you happen to know how to prove Holcomb stole the election and depose him."

I said this on a whim, not expecting any useful input from someone who had spent the recent months cut off from the world, hiding out in a magically booby-trapped house.

"I had some dealings with Bradley Holcomb back in the day," said Rojas. "You are ambitious at picking your enemies, Conrad."

"I don't so much pick them as tend to attract their unwanted attention the way an outdoor cat picks up fleas," I said.

"With much love and respect, I wouldn't be so sure which one of you is a dangerous predator and which is merely an annoying insect in this scenario," said Rojas.

I shrugged. "What can I say? Tilting at windmills is my specialty. Just call me Dumb Quixote."

"If you're really serious about going after Holcomb, there's only one person I can think of who has both the talent and the *cojones* to uncover the evidence you seek. Mitch is the most talented computer hacker I've ever encountered, and a brilliant forensic accountant. He lives right here in Brooklyn. I trust you don't have any problem working with nonhumans?"

I'd never heard of this Mitch, but Rojas was no fool, and he was providing a stellar endorsement. Which quite possibly meant the hacker was exactly as good and discreet as advertised. It couldn't hurt to try.

"None whatsoever," I said, wondering what sort of a magical creature might make a forensic accountant. A sphinx? A dragon? I already knew that some vampires were good at math and were running a hedge fund. "What should I know about this Mitch?"

"He's a highly peculiar individual, but don't let that throw you," said Rojas. This sounded evasive to me, but I doubted the lich would be inclined to send me into any sort of a trap. "Mitch seldom takes on new clients anymore, but he owes me a few favors. Tell him I sent you, and bring him a bottle of Grand Constance from my cellar, and he will find the digital needle in the virtual haystack for you."

I plugged the address Rojas had given me into my phone's GPS and headed to Cypress Hills.

I called Terrie again as I drove, but my call went to voicemail. Was I reaching the limit of how many times one should call and just wait for her to call me back? There were plenty of reasons Terrie would be too busy or otherwise unable to talk, given the state of our city. All I could do was to agonize and wait.

I arrived at an unassuming single-story house overdue for a paint job. Its front yard was paved over and bare, save for a few trash bins lined up alongside a decorative metal fence. The place looked and felt normal, for lack of a better word. If there were wards or other magical protections, I couldn't detect them.

There was no doorbell, so I knocked and waited. I could hear someone moving inside, but the door was solid plate metal and lacked a peephole. I looked up at a pair of security cameras pointing at me from above the doorframe and waved.

"Password?" spoke the voice from inside the house.

"Rojas sent me," I said, rather lamely. My incorporeal friend never mentioned anything about a password. "Benicio Rojas?"

My interlocutor uttered what sounded like a noncommittal grunt.

"Rojas said you could help me," I said. "To obtain certain information. He said you know him."

"I know him," said the voice, which presumably belonged to Mitch. "I don't know you. Anyone can claim a mutual acquaintance for their own dubious reasons."

I drew a dusty bottle of red wine from the plastic shopping bag I was holding. Its plain white label was torn and marred in places but the text, inscribed in a font that looked like handwritten script, was still legible. It read, *Grand Constance 1820.* I'd followed Rojas's instructions to locate this bottle in the cellar. "This is a collector bottle, too old to drink. I preferred vintages I could taste. When I was alive, that is," he had told me.

I held the bottle up, its label facing the camera. "Rojas said you would want this."

There was an audible gasp and several loud clicks as Mitch manipulated locks and deadbolts.

Once again, everyone around me was going nuts over a container of spoiled grape juice. I wondered what might be hidden inside this one? A holy grail? A treasure map? The world's first cereal box toy?

"Come in." Mitch opened the door just wide enough for me to squeeze through. As soon as I was inside, he set about relocking and dead bolting the door, which gave me a chance to finally get a good look at him.

Mitch looked like a love child of Cousin It and a string floor mop. He was nearly seven feet tall, with thick vines of gray braided hair cascading down past his waistline. He wore a plain white T-shirt decorated with a plethora of stains, and a pair of bright-purple shorts over his hirsute frame. The T-shirt was a bit tight around his beer belly. A pair of pink bunny slippers completed the ensemble. His hair obscured much of his face, but I could glimpse enough of the high forehead, powerful jaw, and elongated facial features to know that Mitch was a sasquatch.

He was a rare breed of magical creature, native to the cold, mountainous areas across the globe—called Bigfoot in some places, the Abominable Snowman in others—I'd only encountered them in New York City a handful of times.

His house looked like a bachelor pad that hadn't been cleaned in weeks. I could see into the kitchen where empty pizza boxes and two-liter soda bottles were piled high upon the counter and the garbage pail overflowed with takeout containers. It probably didn't smell very fresh either, but I couldn't tell because of the overpowering scent of wet dog emanating from my host.

As soon as he finished locking up, he reached out a hairy, longer-than-human hand. "May I?" he asked.

I handed over the glass bottle. Mitch the sasquatch examined it with the enthusiasm and yearning of a glutton on a strict diet staring at a double-filled jelly donut.

"Benicio gave this to you?" Mitch asked.

I nodded.

"He must really like you," said Mitch. He turned the bottle this way and that. "I've tried to convince him to part with this treasure many times, but he always rebuffed me."

"Fortunately for both of us, he's recently learned valuable lessons about things that matter more than earthly possessions."

"Indeed?" Mitch's fingers reverently caressing the frayed edges of the label. "Do you know what makes this bottle so special? This is Napoleon's wine. It was his favorite vintage, and he drank it every day during his exile on St. Helena. Boxes were shipped from a vineyard in South Africa, and only a handful of bottles remained after the emperor's passing. I've been wanting to add this to my collection for years."

"And you might soon," I said. "This is not a gift. It's a payment, should you be able to render the services I require."

Mitch grinned, showing off his oversized teeth. "But of course. Step into my office, Mr. Brent, and tell me what you need."

He turned and headed for another room. I rushed to keep up. I was a bit surprised at hearing my name, since I hadn't introduced myself. Still, it wasn't unreasonable for a magical resident of Brooklyn to recognize a guardian of the Watch.

"You know who I am?"

Mitch didn't respond. I followed him into a room filled with computer monitors. Several of them displayed photos of me. Others showed various documents, including my Midwood apartment lease.

"Conrad Brent of the Watch," said Mitch. "Couldn't have picked you out of a lineup until you knocked on my door. This is what I was able to pull up in under a minute. Current address, various photos, criminal and credit history going back two decades. Given how abruptly those trails disappear at a certain point, it's safe to assume you've switched names, but I didn't dig further. Oh, and your credit card bill is due tomorrow. Don't forget to pay it, the interest those companies charge is usurious."

"Under a minute, eh? Impressive, and more than a little scary," I said.

I've always found it annoying how so many films and TV shows portray hackers as modern-day wizards, who are able to seamlessly bend electronics of any type to their will. Real hacking, as I understood it, is nowhere near as flashy. Mitch, on the other hand, appeared to be the genuine article.

"I don't mean to intimidate you," said Mitch. "But I am very good at what I do. I find this sort of demonstration makes potential clients eager to avail themselves of my services. And eager to pay promptly and in full, though you're way ahead of the curve on that score."

"I bet," I said, eyeing all the data the sasquatch had managed to gather so quickly. Did his species have some sort of a special predisposition toward computers? He appeared to be using no magic at all, at least not from what I could tell. "Look, I have two difficult problems and if you can help me solve them, the bottle is yours."

Initially I was only going to ask him for kompromat on Holcomb, but Mitch seemed far too eager to get his hands on the expired bottle of booze.

"Very well," said the hacker. "What would you like me to do?"

211

Mitch the sasquatch told me it would take him a few hours to solve both of my problems. That sounded overly optimistic, but given the speed with which he'd managed to give my personal data a digital colonoscopy, I wasn't about to dismiss his claim as mere bragging.

Besides, I had things to do, and uncomfortable conversations to have. I returned to the City. The recent clashes among the gifted kept all but the most foolhardy civilians indoors. I only caught a glimpse of a few moving vehicles along the way. Driving down empty streets was a surreal experience for a New Yorker.

Chulsky was in his usual spot, watching the world through the oversized windowpanes of his office. He turned and smiled at me when I walked in.

My own expression was more somber.

"I can't accept your job offer," I told him without a preamble.

For the briefest of moments, Chulsky's pupils widened in surprise. He cocked his head. The smile fled from his face, though he remained amicable enough.

"Why not?"

"We are allies. I hope we always will be," I said. "But our philosophies are too different. You once told me that I can do the most good by shrugging off the plethora of minor cases I deal with protecting my borough as a member of the Watch, that I should focus all my attention on the greater threats where my efforts might potentially save millions."

Chulsky nodded. "I stand by those words. I believe the logic of doing so is unassailable."

"Spoken like an immortal being who has watched the teeming mass of humanity ebb and flow for thousands of years from the lonely apex of this office," I countered. "I can't operate like that. I can't *think* like that. A person who loses someone to a werewolf attack or the actions of an unscrupulous gifted won't just shrug off their grief and accept the greatest-good line. To them the welfare of their loved one is as important as saving the world, and far less abstract."

"No one is suggesting we should abandon such people and deprive them of the protections granted by the Watch," said Chulsky. "I merely posit that others can step in and handle those tasks. People who lack your level of experience and skill, freeing you up to undertake the challenges they aren't qualified to handle."

I shook my head. "And who decides the importance of those tasks? Had I followed your advice and ignored the threat posed by the Emersonians, we would have never uncovered Archibald Grey's plot which surely rises to the level even Abaddon couldn't possibly ignore." I didn't even bring up the fact that Chulsky had miscalculated when he'd assumed Grey was only capable of becoming a minor inconvenience. "The accident of birth that made me a middling, the aftereffect of ascension that left the faint stink of divinity around me—those things haven't burned out my humanity."

"A caterpillar must evolve into a butterfly," said Chulsky. "And a butterfly can't shed its wings and crawl again, even if it wanted to."

I pointed to the window showing the bird's-eye view of Manhattan. "Those are my people down there. They're fighting for their freedom and their rights against a wannabe autocrat. I tend to doubt myself on many things, but I'm certain about this one. My place is crawling in the muck with them, for better or for worse."

Chulsky sighed, the weight of the world almost visible upon his shoulders. "Very well, Mr. Brent. The doors of Abaddon are always open to you, should you change your mind."

We nodded our goodbyes, but I couldn't shake the feeling that something irrevocable had passed between us. It was as though Arthur had tossed the sword back into the lake, as though Christopher Robin had walked out of the Hundred Acre Wood. Had I spat in the eye of destiny and if so, what would it cost me down the road? I tightened my trench coat against a sudden chill. Whatever the cost, I'd made the right decision. I'd given up godhood in the past; surely giving up a position at the right hand of Daniel Chulsky was less drastic by comparison.

I headed out into the streets, where after months of being persecuted and bullied by the Emersonians, the gifted of New York City were standing up to their oppressors. I'd been a middling outsider for decades, but this was the fight where I belonged.

CHAPTER 20

I gave up the power, the connections, and all the fringe benefits of working for Abaddon, Inc. in order to remain with the Watch—an organization whose recent leader still hadn't returned from a self-imposed exile in the Australian outback, whose current leader was being blackmailed by the Emersonians, which had been evicted from its home office and which, on at least one occasion, had fired me and robbed me of all of my artifacts. Also, the office coffee was terrible.

Frankly, I felt pretty good about my decision.

Sure, the Watch had fallen on some hard times lately but, more than anything else, it was an idea. A belief that there are those among the gifted who will stand up and protect mundanes against magical threats, not for money or power or glory, but because it's the right thing to do. People like Terrie, who will risk their lives to save others without hesitation, without stopping to consider balancing the scales or keeping powerful entities placated, or whatever other important but ultimately political details Daniel Chulsky and his subordinates focused on.

While I pondered these things, my legs carried me toward the Watchtower. I knew my compatriots would be long gone, but I felt the need to descend its steps and stand within those hallowed halls one more time.

When I got there, it didn't prove to be the solitary experience I was expecting.

There's an Eastern European proverb that says: "a sacred place is never empty." The Watchtower, abandoned by the Watch for the first and only time since the Manhattan Municipal Building was erected over the nexus of power in the early 1900s, had been re-claimed before Holcomb's people even got the chance to change the locks. The Watchtower was bursting with activity, filled with throngs of irregulars.

John had had our people empty out the vault, pack the com-puters and the paper files, but they'd left just about everything else behind. Perhaps he couldn't be bothered to deal with the additional logistics on such short notice, but more likely it was a minor act of defiance, a shout into the void saying, "We'll be back here before you know it!"

The office furniture remained in place, the lights were on, the wi-fi routers were still connected. The vintage copy machine and the world's most mediocre coffee maker were both operational at their full, if underwhelming, capacity. The sigil of the effulgent eye, drawn on the cement floor steps away from Mose's private office, persisted in its proper place.

Herc's irregulars had turned the Watchtower into their com-mand center, using laptops and phones to communicate with their members and allies on social media, directing their forces in clashes with the remaining Emersonians and Holcomb's mercenaries.

In the center of it all was Herc himself. He issued orders and answered questions, all in an unassuming and businesslike manner that made his followers love him and his enemies respect him. He didn't grandstand, didn't seek glory or power. He simply did what he had always done, first at the Watch and then on his own: he stepped up when others needed him to.

We exchanged a brief glance. I navigated my way through the of-fice that was currently busier and more energetic than it had been in all my years with the Watch, and I knew from the way Herc looked at me that despite our fighting on the same side, despite our goals and aspirations being so aligned, he still hadn't fully forgiven me for betraying his trust.

I nodded in a polite greeting. "I see you've made yourself at home."

"Just keeping the seats warm for your crew," he told me. "Well, most seats." He waved toward the door that led into Mose's private office. "We left that one alone."

I looked at the closed door and the sigil in front of it that looked like it was painted yesterday, contrasting with the shabby chic aesthetic of the Watchtower. Where was Mose? Had he refused the ambrosia? No, that seemed wildly out of character, especially considering the withdrawal symptoms he'd been experiencing while forced to live as a mortal. Had he survived his re-ascension? The process of apotheosis was fraught with danger, even for someone like Mose. Or perhaps …. Was he in there now, hiding from the world in his office, having invited the irregulars here while he planned the triumphant comeback of the Watch …?

I walked over to the office door as if some force drew me there, leaving Herc somewhat rudely behind, though he was probably too busy to notice, surrounded as he was by his lieutenants.

The room was empty. I shut the door behind me, cutting off the noise and stood in front of the oversized desk. That moment of solitary reflection I'd come here seeking was finally upon me, and I found it wanting. It was just an office. Just a desk. Without Mose behind it, larger and more intimidating than life, it was merely furniture. As I'd said to John, the Watchtower wasn't the Watch, its people were. We would maintain its mission, what it stood for, no matter from where we had to work.

Which also meant I should get over the nostalgia and be out there, protecting people and patrolling the streets. After one last look, I walked out and asked Herc where I was needed most.

I was on The Bowery, helping to protect a group of demonstrators marching against the mayor and his policies, when my phone rang.

I badly wanted it to be Terrie, to hear her voice and know that she was all right, but I'd since learned that my fellow guardians were busy transporting and securing the dangerous and expensive contents of the Watchtower's vault. They'd maintained radio silence, as per John's orders, and would continue to do so until our treasure trove was safe at some undisclosed location. Reinforcements were coming in from the Watch branches in Philadelphia and Boston. They'd beef up our numbers until the artifacts could be properly secured and until the situation in the city was once again under control.

The number was marked as private, and when I picked up, Mitch was on the other end of the line.

"Do you want the good news first, or the bad?" asked the sasquatch.

"Hit me with the bad. I've grown used to that by now," I told him.

"Holcomb didn't steal the election," Mitch told me. "He won it, fair and square. Yeah, I was surprised, too, but the paper trail doesn't lie, and no one at the city or state level is good enough to manipulate the numbers in such a way that I wouldn't notice."

"I'm not angry, I'm just disappointed," I said. "Well, okay, I'm also a little angry. People of our city genuinely chose that guy to lead them?"

"A person is smart. People are dumb, panicky, dangerous animals and you know it." Mitch was quoting *Men in Black*, and my already considerable respect for the slob hacker went up another notch. "Wouldn't be the first time people collectively made a really questionable decision."

I looked at the demonstrators, chanting and carrying signs. Clearly not everyone bought into Holcomb's message. Then I wondered how many of them might have voted for the man, only to experience buyer's remorse later.

"I found plenty of dirt on the guy," said Mitch. "His tax records show a considerably smaller net worth than he's claimed, shady transactions via offshore accounts, bribes paid to facilitate his real estate deals, hush money paid to ex-mistresses. The list goes on."

"That might dislodge him from office, but not quickly. His lawyers can tie up any investigation for years," I said.

Mitch sighed. "Sorry it's not what you wanted. I'm going to send you everything I found and hope you can figure out a way to use this information."

"You did say there would be good news," I prodded.

"This was actually the more difficult job," said Mitch, "but I found where your associate's family is being held. They're in a house on Staten Island that sits on a sizable plot of land. I'll text you the address."

I breathed an enormous sigh of relief. This is where my personal philosophy diverged sharply from Chulsky's. In the grand scheme of things, proof that Holcomb stole the election might have been more useful, might have better served the greater good. But given the choice between getting my hands on that proof or an opportunity to save John's family, I'd take the latter every damn time.

"Thank you. If we find them, you will have earned that bottle for sure."

I stared at the text Mitch sent me and committed the address to memory, just in case. Then I sent a text of my own to John's burner phone, feeling well-justified in breaking the radio silence. *I know where they are. Meet at the Bowery Hotel. Bring whoever you can.* I headed down the block to the rendezvous point I'd designated, and called Moira. I figured we could use the extra muscle.

John ported onto the sidewalk by the hotel entrance when I was still a few dozen steps away. He kept the portal open for the rest of the guardians to step through. Moira arrived seconds later through a portal of her own, nearly colliding with Gord.

I practically ran over to Terrie, who stepped through the portal and toward me, a smile blossoming on her face. We embraced and held each other tight, then kissed right in front of the rest of them, heedless of their opinions on the matter. That kiss was much too brief and yet worth all the pain and suffering fate had slung at me recently, and then some.

It was with great difficulty that I pulled away. The remaining guardians watched us impassively, while Moira gawked at us with a wolfish grin. I just knew she was biting back a dozen snide comments.

"If you're all here, then who is minding the shop?" I asked.

"The cargo is in a secure location," said John. He glanced sideways at Moira, and I knew without it having to be said that he wouldn't disclose that location within her earshot on pain of death. "Everyone else is there."

Given the stakes, I couldn't blame him for leaving only a skeleton crew behind. I told the team about the house in Staten Island where, according to Mitch, John's kidnapped sister and her kids were being held.

"I'm not aware of any arcane activity in that area," said Father Mancini. He frowned, as if the hostages being held in the borough he protected was somehow a mark against him.

"Wouldn't be much of a safe house if it drew any sort of attention to itself," said Moira.

"What are we waiting for?" asked Gord. He hefted his sawed-off shotgun.

All the guardians were armed to the teeth. I was still flush with the plethora of artifacts from the Abaddon armory. Chulsky had never asked for them back, which was kind of him. I knew him well enough by this point to assume it wasn't an oversight.

John opened another portal and said, "Once more unto the breach." And unto the breach we went.

The people guarding the hostages were mundanes. They had no auras, no magical trinkets, nothing but guns to defend against six of the most powerful magic users in all of New York. The bad guys' desire to rely on anonymity in this case was understandable; even if they employed some sort of a gifted mercenary force, they'd be hard-pressed to find someone capable of holding off several pissed-off guardians of the Watch.

The swarm of phantasms John summoned streaked through the house, mauling the kidnappers' faces and rending their flesh. Bullets passed harmlessly through the phantasms' ethereal forms, but their claws and teeth became solid and sharp whenever they connected with human flesh.

We followed the phantasms into the spacious grand room of an old mansion where a dozen kidnappers were screaming and running and dying. We left them to the phantasms, barely pausing to activate some force shields against the stray bullets, and then followed a couple of villains who were smart or lucky enough to outrun the summoned horrors and retreat upstairs. There, a middle-aged woman huddled with a pair of tween girls. I don't know if the remaining kidnappers meant to harm them. We never gave them the opportunity to try.

It was rather anticlimactic. These were dangerous people, trained killers armed with guns they were proficient with and didn't hesitate to use. There were fifteen of them between the two floors, and that entire group stood no chance whatsoever against a few gifted. It's possible John might have been able to handle them on his own; let his phantasms do the job for him. This was exactly why mundanes needed an organization like the Watch to protect them from malicious magic users. But these people didn't deserve our protection. These people had dared to harm the family of one of our own. We let the phantasms dispatch vengeance, if not justice.

John stepped toward his older sister and the kids, tears rolling down his face. She called out his name—not John, but his real name, which the rest of us simply pretended not to hear. The four of them embraced and held each other tight.

Then the walls caved in on us.

The house rumbled like a great beast that had woken from its slumber and rose toward the sky, shedding bricks and shingles and chunks of concrete, severing electrical wires and metal pipes. It began to collapse in on itself, as though a giant squeezed it in an enormous fist; as though a black hole had opened up at the center, sucking in drywall and furniture and floorboards.

We activated force shields against debris and whatever malevolent force was crushing the mansion. Several of us attempted to open portals to no avail. Sigils of enormous power flared up on the crumbling walls, disrupting and countering our magic.

The mundane guards had never been meant to stop us. They were merely bait, there to lure in whoever showed up before the trap sprung. Powerful artifacts were built into the foundation of the building, sigils written in its walls, its floor, its ceiling. Through the shattered glass of disintegrating windows, I could see even more malevolent magic activating across the property that surrounded the mansion.

Our unseen enemy had gone to enormous lengths and expense to set up this trap. I could think of only one possible culprit.

Vaughn.

We struggled mightily against the trap. I burned through artifact after artifact, but multiple layers of malicious magic countered my efforts with ease. None of the others were faring any better.

John, Father Mancini, and Moira managed to combine and strengthen their force shields, creating a bubble the size of a minivan around us. The girls screamed and their mother whimpered while we fought to sustain the shield against the layers of debris and dust that clung to it from all directions, pushing relentlessly inward.

Slowly, inexorably, the force shield shrunk, pressing in until the area it protected was barely large enough for any of us to move. Soon, we could no longer move at all.

I had survived incalculable close calls, cheated death any number of times, only to get compressed to a bloody pulp by a magical compactor, along with most of my friends, along with Terrie, and there was nothing I could do about it. Fate had a sick sense of dark humor.

It became difficult to breathe and I could feel the physical pressure building against our ball of human flesh. I could feel my ribs beginning to crack. Pain surged through my body. I tasted coppery, salty blood on my tongue. I had many regrets, but no time to voice them or sort them out. I drew upon the magic of my talismans to help maintain what was left of the shield.

There was no time for self-reflection or self-pity. We all used every bit of magic we had, every bit of strength, to hold back the compressive force, to buy our friends a few extra seconds of life. Just because we couldn't win, didn't mean we'd stop trying. We were made of sterner stuff than that.

I literally fought until my dying breath. It was the least, but also the most I could do.

I found myself on the shore of a wide river. The air was warm and thick and fragrant with the aroma of wildflowers. Crystal clear water flowed slowly past. A few yards downriver a fisherman chewed on a stalk of grass and lounged lazily next to his fishing rod, which was planted in the soft dirt of the riverbank.

Something felt off, and it wasn't just an idyllic setting. After a moment, I realized that, for the first time in days, I felt no physical pain.

I gawked about like a tourist in Grand Central Terminal, trying to figure out where I was and how I got there.

"We had such hopes for you," said the fisherman. "Such plans. It's a shame things turned out the way they did."

The fisherman looked to be a vigorous older man, stocky and muscular, with olive-toned skin and short, gray hair. He seemed at ease, which appeared to be the only natural state suited for this place.

I had so many questions, so I began with an easy one. "Where am I?"

"A place of eternal rest which you've earned through your earthly deeds," said the fisherman.

I gaped at him. "Heaven? You're telling me this is heaven?"

The fisherman shrugged and leisurely adjusted his fishing rod, its thin line cast far into the waters. "If you say so."

"No way," I said. "I've been dead before. This is not what being dead feels like, at all. What kind of game are you playing at?"

The fisherman smiled in a most grandfatherly fashion. "Ahh, the fallacy of youth. The young always think they know everything." He pointed toward a grove of fruit-laden trees in the distance. "If you taste an apple once, will you presume all other fruit are also apples?"

This was ludicrous. My friends were in serious trouble. I was probably experiencing one of those hallucinations conjured up by a dying brain. The strangest part was that I couldn't summon up the sense of urgency this required, didn't feel sufficient panic, or fear, or anger. All those emotions dwelled within me but were somewhere very deep in the background, and I could only think of them logically. The chemical factory in my brain that pumped out adrenaline and dopamine and every other "-ine" that made me human seemed to have shut down for a holiday.

"How do I go back?" I asked. "I have to go. Now. My friends are suffering."

"Suffering?" He arched an eyebrow, like some beach-vacation variant of Mr. Spock. "Try spending centuries regrowing your liver every night, only to have it devoured by birds the next day, then come talk to me about suffering."

I gaped at the fisherman. "Prometheus?"

The ancient trickster god smiled kindly at me. "It's nice to finally meet you, Conrad. I wish it were under better circumstances."

"Can you help me? Can you save my friends? Please, there's not much time—"

He waved me off.

"Time is like this river. It flows at different speeds in different places."

His words made me think of the fae realm. If this place wasn't on Earth, would every minute spent here equal moments or centuries?

"Some things can't be rushed," he continued. "You've got time enough for a brief chat."

"Okay," I said. "We can chat. But after that, will you help me?"

"Aren't you tired of being helped?" asked Prometheus. "It must be exhausting, having to rely on beings more powerful than you to save you from other beings who are more powerful than you."

I was inclined to point out that this was exactly what I did, every day. I saved mundanes from warlocks and monsters, because mundanes were powerless to save themselves. But I wasn't looking to get into a philosophical debate with a trickster god. I was foolhardy, not foolish. Instead, I said, "I'm not proud. I'll take help where I can find it."

The sly grin on Prometheus's face grew wider. "But what if you could help yourself?"

"How?" I asked. Did he want something from me, or was he just having a bit of fun? Paradise could get pretty boring, I supposed. "I'll do anything."

Prometheus must've sensed my increasing impatience. He got up, stretched, and walked over until we stood face to face. "There's a way," he said. "And you have a choice to make."

"I'll do anything," I repeated.

"The spark within you is dormant, but not extinguished," said Prometheus. "Normally, you'd need another dose of ambrosia to reinvigorate it properly. But here, in this realm, it's possible to rekindle a tiny portion of it for a brief moment."

Hope welled within me. If I could tap into divine power, I could surely defeat the trap Vaughn had sprung upon us. For all of his extensive preparation, his powers as a middling were no match for a god.

Prometheus held up his index finger. "I know you're in a rush to play hero, but take a moment and consider the implications. First, you'd be able to tap into an infinitesimal fraction of your power. It may not be enough to save your friends. But you could teleport yourself and perhaps one other away."

That stung. I could save Terrie and myself at the cost of everybody else's lives. I was certain she wouldn't choose this, wouldn't want me to do that, but I couldn't discount the option outright. It was the world's shittiest version of the trolley problem.

Prometheus wasn't done. He held up another finger. "Second, no matter the outcome, no matter whether you survive or perish in this trap, you will never again be able to return to this place." He pointed toward the water, sunshine sparkling off its surface. "No man ever steps in the same river twice. Leave here, and the gates of paradise will be forever closed to you."

I thought back to angels and demons, squabbling over a soul.

"You mean it's sulfur and brimstone for me next time around?"

Prometheus shook his head. "The universe predates the Christian afterlife dichotomy. No, it won't be Hades for you, either. Your fate shall be worse. It will be oblivion. The next time you die, you'll simply cease to be."

It should've been a difficult decision, or maybe an easy one, depending on how you look at it. What did my actions and decisions over the course of a mortal life that might last a century matter compared to an eternity in paradise? I inhaled the floral aroma. The air tasted sweet as honey.

"Well, I wouldn't want to be tortured forever anyway," I said. "And if I choose not to save the people I love, then I don't deserve paradise."

Prometheus flashed me another of his wry smiles and somehow I knew, without a shadow of a doubt, that he was certain I'd choose to do precisely what I did. What was that he said about vastly more powerful beings helping out? He wasn't hanging out in my designated paradise because the fishing was good. He was here to nudge me in the right direction, for reasons of his own, just as his underling Dolus had manipulated Willodean and me toward his inscrutable purposes. For once, I didn't mind being a pawn in the game of gods, as long as the players moved me in the right direction.

"So, how do I rekindle the spark? Send me in, coach."

Back in the house-turned-kill-box no time had passed at all. I guess it's true what they say: an eternity in heaven doesn't last longer, it just *feels* longer.

With my expanded senses, I could feel the others; still alive but suffering, life literally being squeezed out of them. Gord and John were the only ones who still had the strength to maintain their force barriers and I was amazed at their resilience.

I had divine power again and I felt like a blind person regaining his sight, like an octogenarian rejuvenated to the strength and vigor of their prime years. I felt like I could do anything.

The malevolent magic crushing my body had other ideas.

I strained against it like Sisyphus, heaving the boulder up that hill. And as with Sisyphus, the boulder was getting the better of me, pushing back with the determination of an immovable object that didn't believe in the concept of an unstoppable force.

They say in times of great peril a person might tap into reservoirs of incredible strength, like a mother lifting a car to rescue her baby. Those stories are told by mundanes, and the mother was probably an ogre or a troll or some other creature capable of lifting a car. Eyewitnesses explained her feat in a manner palatable to their mundane brains.

I was operating in actual god mode at the moment, and I was still losing.

Worse yet, I could feel my powers beginning to fade. The reignited spark would be snuffed out again at any moment.

There was still time to cut and run. I could save Terrie. I'd hate myself forever after that, but Prometheus had made it clear that my forever would last only a lifetime anyway.

I shoved that traitorous thought into the deepest recess of my screwed-up brain. There had to be another way. I took a second to think. To examine the spell with my celestial senses and find its weakness.

The solution was there. I would've seen it sooner had I not opted for the idea that if brute strength wasn't solving the problem, I wasn't applying enough. In this case, it was the opposite. Vaughn's trap combined several powerful and ingenious spells that sapped whatever force was being thrown at it and turned this force against the opponent, like a judo master.

I marshaled the fleeting dregs of my power and hit the spell with everything I still had from the outside.

An enormous boom reverberated through the bubble. I could feel the shaking in my teeth. The sound of it might've burst my eardrums had they not been so thoroughly blocked by layers of debris around the force shield. The pressure eased, then let off as the force shield expanded to its original size, shrugging off chunks of rock and clumps of dirt like a wet dog shaking off water after a bath.

Moments later, the force shield collapsed. I lay on the ground, trying to breathe. I was sure a number of my ribs were broken. Chunks of drywall bit painfully into my back and I was covered in dust and what very well could've been asbestos. Each breath hurt. My bruised body ached all over. Someday soon I hoped to go an entire week without getting thoroughly beaten up by someone or something unpleasant.

Worst of all, my powers were gone. I felt the hollow pangs of withdrawal that had haunted Mose so badly. I couldn't heal myself or the others. I shifted my head slightly so that I could see my friends out of the corner of my eye. Each looked like they'd suffered broken bones, or worse. Wouldn't it suck to die from internal bleeding, after all that?

"You really are more trouble than you're worth, Conrad," spoke a familiar voice.

It took a lot of effort, but I lifted my head and opened my eyes. Dolus was standing over me, frowning at the dust that had landed on his expensive shoes.

The trickster god looked annoyed. It was as though someone had rung his doorbell and he'd had to get up from under a warm blanket and throw on a robe and a pair of slippers just to tell a stranger they'd got the wrong house.

"Remember that it was my master who saved you and your friends," said Dolus. "Remember it, because a time will come soon when we will ask for your help."

Did Dolus show up to be a glory hound and claim credit for what I did? It didn't seem likely. By the looks of him, Dolus didn't even want to be there. I wondered if Prometheus had sent him as backup, in case I didn't manage to save myself and needed rescuing—to look after their investment in my survival. What possible use could someone of Prometheus's power have for me? This was a problem to ponder and possibly lose sleep over some time in the future.

I tried to say something snarky, but only managed to gasp like a fish out of water.

Dolus waved his hand and the pain disappeared. I was able to sit up, as were my companions. He healed the entire group effortlessly, as an afterthought.

"Dale?" Moira stared at the god wide-eyed. She'd only known him when he'd toyed with us in Europe, pretending to be a middling.

Her astonished reaction brightened Dolus's mood. He grinned, winked at Moira, and winked out of existence.

"Who the devil was that?" asked Gord, earning a disapproving look from our priest.

"That was my buddy Dale. We backpacked through Europe together," I said. "Nice of him to keep in touch."

This earned me an array of annoyed looks. I ignored them, got up and walked over to Terrie, who was sitting in the rubble. She was covered head-to-toe in dust and grime, same as the rest of us. I didn't care. I sat beside her, and we leaned against each other like it was the most natural thing in the world.

Events had conspired to keep us apart since that moment in the dark heart of Club Inferno. There was nothing I wanted more than to spend some time sitting like this, next to her, and forget about apocalypses, uprisings, and other calamities for a brief respite. Except, an unpleasant, incessant thought needled the back of my mind. Reluctantly, I spoke.

"If Vaughn was behind this trap, and I believe he was, he must've had a reason that extends beyond mere malice."

John's brow furrowed at my words. He wrapped his arm protectively around his sister's shoulder. His frown deepened. I could tell that he was reaching the same ugly conclusions as me. "The Watch artifacts," he said. "They might have done this to draw us away!"

He gently let go of his sister and opened another portal, despite Moira's presence in our midst.

This time I followed him in without a wiseass remark.

CHAPTER 21

WE arrived at a two-story house similar to the one that had had the temerity to collapse in on us minutes earlier. The land lot was smaller, but the property made up for it with a magnificent view of the Hudson River. Later, I learned this was Tarrytown, a quiet village nestled between its famous neighboring village of Sleepy Hollow and the on-ramp to the Cuomo Bridge.

We were quite a sight, covered from head to toe in dust and dirt. We headed toward the house, while Father Mancini stayed behind with John's sister and the girls, just to be on the safe side.

The front door was ajar.

"There should've been guards," said Terrie. "Where are the guards?"

We picked up the pace. Moira rested her palm on the hilt of her cutlass. Everyone else clutched their weapons tighter.

Inside, the signs of a recent sorcerous battle were everywhere. Scorch marks on the walls, broken windows, wooden shelves smashed into pulp. A dead man sat propped up against a wall, his glassy eyes open. A combat wand appropriated from Archibald Grey's warlocks earlier lay next to his unclenched fist. A trail of blood marred the carpeted stairway that led to the second floor.

In the middle of it all, towering over the furniture like an adult who'd wandered into a jumbo dollhouse, stood Mose.

The leader of the Watch and god of the nexus gazed at us, his expression filled with pain and regret.

"I arrived too late," he said. "I wanted to … needed to deal with the violence in the city. If only I had come here first, I could've stopped him."

"Are they all …?" I couldn't bring myself to finish the sentence. As I spoke, I realized that the dead man propped up against the wall wasn't a combat sorcerer; he was the same office grunt I'd talked to the other day, the one carrying his pet cactus out of the Watchtower.

"Not everyone," said Mose. "He let those willing to walk away go in peace. Some … too many …" Mose's booming voice cracked. "Stayed and fought to the end."

"Who?" asked John. "Who did this?"

I already knew the answer. Mose's confirmation was a handful of salt poured over a fresh wound.

"Vaughn," he said, steel in his voice once again. He spat out the name, and on his lips it sounded like a promise, like a pledge. Mose would fight half the world for a shot at revenge against him. "It was Vaughn."

Of course it had been Vaughn. The unassuming bureaucrat with a forgettable face who was lurking behind every dastardly scheme, hiding in every shadow. He'd been playing his chess game and manipulating lesser villains to attack the Watch for a long time. At one point, we'd come to believe he was after the ampule of ambrosia Mose was safeguarding in the Watchtower, but clearly that hadn't been it. After Mose had given me the precious substance, and Nascent Anodynes International had been taken down, Vaughn had ingratiated himself with Holcomb. With Mose out of the way, he manipulated events so that he could force us to move the contents of the Watchtower vault into the open where he could finally checkmate us and come after what he wanted.

Terrie arrived at a similar conclusion. "He did all this to steal the artifacts from the vault?" she asked.

"Just the one," said Mose. "Our most valuable and dangerous weapon."

"The Kaladanda?" I asked.

Mose shot me a surprised look. "Yes. The weapon capable of killing any living being, no matter how powerful. The weapon against which there's no known defense," he explained for the benefit of the others, who seemed no more familiar with the damn thing than I had been up until recently. "Except he didn't steal it. He destroyed it."

Mose reached for a shelf unit that had survived the recent violence, and picked up two broken halves of a short staff. Each piece was roughly two feet long, jagged edges revealing a hollow compartment inside.

"He took the gem that powered the staff," said Mose. "An intricate artifact that works on the same principle as the Atlantean shards, but is many times more powerful. It is said to have been forged by Prometheus himself."

Prometheus? What was his role in all this? There was absolutely no chance his meddling in my affairs and his connection to the artifact Vaughn had been after all along was a coincidence.

"Without the gem, the staff is useless," Mose continued. "But the gem is equally useless without the staff. Unlike the Atlantean crystal, it won't work on its own. I don't understand why the bastard wanted it. Why go through so much trouble and cause all this pain?"

An engraving on the Kaladanda caught my eye. "May I see it?" I asked.

Mose handed me the two halves of the staff. I rotated them to get a better look at the design. The staff was inlaid with jewels and gilded, and so over the top it would feel at home as a prop in the schlockiest of fantasy movies. Yet, the engraving looked familiar to me. Where had I seen it before?

Others were talking, saying something urgent and important, but I tuned them out. The realization pawed at the edge of my memory, until my conscious mind grabbed at it with both hands and yanked it into the light. I sucked in my breath and nearly dropped the Kaladanda fragments.

The design engraved on this weapon was the same as the one on the gauntlets of the god of war that Kallan and his fae warriors had banished from their realm centuries ago.

I focused my mind's eye on the god's face. I could see it so clearly, now that I'd made the connection. It was Vaughn's face, as a much younger man. Before time, age, and toil had weathered it into its current, unremarkable shape.

Vaughn was a god.

Correction. Vaughn *had been* a god. Even the weakest of gods wouldn't have to go through the sort of trouble Vaughn had gone through to get his hands on the Kaladanda. With Mose gone, no one else at the Watch could stand against even the weakest of deities. Vaughn could've walked right in and cracked our vault open like a ripe watermelon. No, he was most definitely a middling now. Which meant that somewhere, somehow, he'd had his divine spark burned out of him the same way mine had been extinguished as a result of my struggle against Willodean, a goddess of death.

What was it Kallan had called him? *Vahagn the Invader.* His pronunciation had sounded off at the time, and I had assumed it was merely his pattern of speech as a fae.

Mose didn't know what Vaughn wanted with the Kaladanda's power source, and neither did I. But if I'd learned anything at all during my unfortunate acquaintance with the cold bastard, the crystal he now possessed was a means to an end, another step toward his ultimate goal, whatever it might be. And I was certain that his achieving that goal wouldn't bode well for anyone.

I looked at my friends, struggling with grief and shame over what had happened. I'd need to tell them—I'd made a promise to myself that I wouldn't keep secrets from them anymore, not if I could help it. I was trying to find the right words when Karl Mercado strolled into the house.

"Oh, thank goodness it's true!" he said. "I heard you were back, Mose. I had to see it for myself."

Somehow, it didn't surprise me in the slightest that Karl had been among those who took Vaughn up on the offer to walk away and live. Whereas a true guardian rushed toward danger, Karl had done an awful lot of the opposite.

Mose turned to greet Karl, but his expression suddenly hardened, his oversized hands balled up into fists.

"You," he roared. "It was *you!*"

Karl looked like he'd soiled his pants. He took a step back and almost tripped over his own feet. "Wh … What are you talking about?"

"You revealed the whereabouts of this safe house to Vaughn." Mose loomed over Karl, his nostrils flaring, his fists clenched tight. "I can smell the stink of betrayal on you. Look!" He pointed at the dead man in the corner. "Look at what you've done!"

Karl noticed our murdered comrade for the first time. His face, already pale with fear, twisted into a horrified mask. His shoulders slumped. He took a few uncertain steps toward the dead man, ignoring Mose as though several hundred pounds of muscle and rage didn't threaten to squash him at any moment.

"They're all dead," said Mose. "Everyone who stayed behind."

Karl's feet failed him. He slumped to the floor, tears rolling down his cheeks. His anguish was genuine; there was just no way he was that good an actor. As much as I hated the man for what he'd done, I couldn't help but pity the poor wretch on some level.

Terrie stepped between Karl and Mose and shooed our boss away. I was more than a little shocked when Mose complied and stepped back. Terrie leaned down and looked Karl in the eye.

"Why?" she asked. "Why did you do it?"

Her tone was gentle rather than accusatory. Terrie was a saint, too good for any of us, especially me. Her approach cajoled a response out of Karl, even when Mose's rage couldn't.

"They said no one would get hurt. They said they needed this one artifact. That if they could get it, they'd leave all of us alone, and we'd be safe. Maybe the rest of you would even be permitted to return to the city if the mayor could be convinced." Karl raised his haunted eyes to look at us. "I did this for all of you."

"Yeah. You're the real hero in all this, shithead," said Moira.

"The traitor has to pay for what he's done," said Gord. He pointed his shotgun at Karl.

"No," said Terrie. "He's not an evil man, merely a weak one. He has to live with what he's done, with the damage he caused on his conscience. That is punishment enough."

Neither of their opinions mattered and we all knew it. Everyone looked to Mose, who had calmed down somewhat, although the veins in his neck still bulged.

"Get out of my sight, traitor," said Mose. "And make certain to stay away. Should we ever meet again, you will not find me so charitable."

It took Karl a moment, but he gathered himself and marched to the door, desperately trying and failing to hang on to some shreds of his dignity.

"Fine," he said through tears and snot. "Fine, I don't need the Watch, anyway. I'll go where I'm appreciated. I'll help the mayor restore New York City to its former glory. I'll be protecting our city while you're all banished to suburbia."

Terrie rested her hand on Mose's forearm, which may well have saved Karl's hide. We watched him go in opprobrious silence. Karl tried and failed to slam the door behind him.

"He's in for a surprise," Mose said after the traitor was gone from our midst.

"How do you mean?" asked Gord.

"I told you I was late in arriving here because I was restoring order in the city," said Mose. "I've had a heart-to-heart chat with Bradley Holcomb."

He had our undivided attention.

"I told him I was back, and I was retaking the Watchtower, whether he liked it or not. I also told him that if he continued on his current path, the Watch would alter its long-standing policy and become directly involved in the conflict. That I'd clear out his mercenaries and his flunkies personally. Then I offered him the one alternative where he could avoid making an enemy of me while the city regained the support and protection of the Watch. And he took it."

Terrie crossed her arms. "What alternative, exactly?"

Mose's lips stretched into a humorless smile. "Effective immediately, the Holcomb administration has fired Vaughn, disbanded the Office of Preternatural Solutions, and ended any and all attempts at trying to force the gifted to perform forced labor for the city. In fact, Holcomb is to have nothing whatsoever to do with the affairs of the gifted. He's to run the city as any mundane mayor would and leave it up to the Watch to handle any arcane threats."

"You mean he gets to stay in power?" asked John. "That's outrageous. You don't know how bad it's been, the damage he's done while you were away! He has to go."

"That is the accord we reached," said Mose. "We protect the mundanes. We don't interfere in their affairs. And we certainly don't pick and choose their leaders. That would open floodgates we never want to unseal."

"But he stole the election," said Moira. "Conrad hired a hacker to find proof."

"He didn't." I forced the words out, hating every moment of it. "He merely hoodwinked enough people into voting for him."

I told them about my dealings with Mitch and all the dirt the hacker had uncovered about Holcomb.

"May I see it?" asked Mose.

I handed him the burner phone, containing hundreds of pages of incriminating evidence Mitch had uploaded to me.

Mose frowned as he scrolled through the data, his massive fingers somehow managing to manipulate the tiny phone. We all waited for his verdict.

"None of this has anything to do with the Watch," said Mose. "We will keep to our principles and leave the people free to make their choices, even when they make bad decisions."

"He's a monster," said John. "We have a moral imperative to do something."

Mose stared his second-in-command down as he clenched his fist around the phone and crushed it into bits with a muffled crunch. "I forbid any member of the Watch to pursue this further. We need to focus on protecting mundanes from supernatural threats. Mundane affairs are outside our purview. Is that clear?"

No one was happy about this. We looked at each other, waiting to see who would contradict our leader first.

"Leaders and governments are imperfect," said Mose. "I'm imperfect. So is everyone who has ever been in charge. If we make excuses today to take Holcomb down, then who will it be tomorrow? Where do we stop? Who is going to check our power? The Watch was created to prevent the few people with our outsized gifts from using them to make decisions for everyone else. We can't ever cross that line, no matter how much we might wish to."

I thought about his words. What was the term Chulsky had used? Kakistocracy. The government by the least capable. Sure, Holcomb's administration fit the definition. But then, what power structure didn't? No tyrant, general, or freely elected ruling body has ever been perfect.

I thought about the fae who might have overrun and murdered us all if not for their rigid and inefficient feudalist government. About angel academics who were so focused on their "cutting edge" research into natural philosophy that they failed to realize science had left them behind centuries ago. About demons who were so intent on a wing-measuring contest with the angels that they failed to get much of anything accomplished. About Chulsky who was so laser-focused on the big picture that he couldn't zero in on the really important details. He was so concerned with protecting humanity as a whole, that he was in danger of losing his own humanity, or soul, or whatever it was his creators had imbued him with that ultimately made him a decent, if fallible, person. Finally, I thought about Mose, freshly returned from a self-imposed exile, still largely out of touch, and yet making a decision that was clearly difficult for his entire senior staff to swallow. But what if we didn't obey? What if we chose to challenge Mose's authority and then to challenge the authority of the mayor's office? If we took those steps, how long would it be until we ourselves were the kakistocracy in desperate need of being eradicated?

I stepped forward. "Mose is right. I accept and support his decision."

The others turned to me, shocked, surprised, and maybe even disgusted.

I had been away, in fairyland, for months. That made me the worst person to make this call, save for Mose himself. Even so, it wasn't a united front anymore. The ice had cracked. Terrie flashed me a half smile.

"I agree," she said.

The rest still didn't like it. But they accepted the imperfect decision by an imperfect leader, so that all of us could move forward together, for the greater good.

After that, I was able to finally have some time alone with Terrie. The two of us were a sight, disheveled and dirty, strolling along the quiet suburban street.

Our long-delayed conversation went as well as I could've possibly hoped.

Three days later, Moira came to see me at the Watchtower.

I'd been spending way too much time there, way too much time in Manhattan, and I didn't like it. There were mundanes to protect in my borough, problems to solve, monsters to keep in line. But there was even more work to be done in restoring the Watch to full operational capacity, especially given all the good people we'd lost.

Herc and the irregulars were extremely displeased with Mose's mandate, and, if anything, it probably widened the rift between me and Herc even further. I had to hope time and my actions would gradually bridge it. Regardless of hurt feelings, we offered the irregulars all the support we could. We worked around the clock to throw out the mercenaries and thugs who didn't have the good sense to leave on their own once Holcomb cut off their funding. We redoubled our efforts to protect the people of our city. That had to count for something.

I had an office to call my own now, and I hated that fact with every fiber of my being. Sharing what infrequent free moments I had with Terrie counterbalanced all of that, and then some.

I was hunched over the desk, squinting at the computer monitor, when Moira walked in.

"Have you decided what you're going to do next?" I asked her. "Have you considered my offer?"

"I'll stick around New York City for now." Moira reclined in the visitor's chair across the desk from me and took a sip from the cardboard cup she had filled from the office coffee maker. She made a face and abandoned the cup on the edge of my desk. "It's not entirely boring here, and Aysha has been kind of fun to hang out with." She raised her index finger. "If you tell her I said that, I will murder you in your sleep."

"Aww, you've made your first friend. How adorable."

Moira ignored the barb. "I've been thinking a lot about what you said to me when we returned from the fae realm. This karma stuff, doing the right thing all the time, you really make that work for you, don't you?"

"Karma?" I asked.

"Take Benicio Rojas for example. You literally saved his soul, and you never even asked him to pay you, even though the lecherous old bastard is wealthier than several of the countries where I'm wanted by the authorities."

I knew Rojas was well-to-do, but not quite that wealthy. Perhaps I should've charged something—but then, this was a teachable moment for the recovering necromancer, so I wouldn't express my regrets. "I wasn't working for Rojas. I was working for Abaddon. And they did pay me."

"A pittance! Anyway, my point is, you did your good deed, which punched the karma piñata just right, and the information about the hacker that you would never have been able to find or afford otherwise just happened to fall out. You do this over and over again, and, improbably, things work out for you."

"Like I told you before, if you hang around good people and do good things, you will make friends and allies who are not out to stab you in the back. Joining the Watch would be a perfect opportunity for you to do this. Given our current predicament I think we can convince Mose to ignore your past Cabal affiliation and—"

"I've decided against joining the Watch," said Moira.

"Oh?" I was disappointed. She had been making real progress in the past two weeks.

"I've decided to give this karma thing a shot, though. To do good deeds and see if maybe karma will reward me in unexpected ways, too." Moira smiled in that special way I'd come to recognize and to dread.

"What did you do, Moira O'Leary?" I asked in my best imitation of a schoolteacher's voice.

Her smile widened. "I helped our friend Rojas move into the much nicer digs in Costa Rica, and he paid me handsomely for it. But instead of my usual shopping spree, I decided to spend that money on a charitable cause. I figured I'd use some of it to feed orphans, or puppies, or maybe feed orphans to puppies. Whatever it is rich people do to make themselves feel good about being rich, you know?"

I frowned at her and waited for the punch line. It was clear she was dying to tell me, and verbal sparring would only forestall the reveal.

"Then I came up with an even better idea," Moira said brightly. "I went to see Mitch and paid him an obscene amount of money to purchase all that blackmail material on Bradley Holcomb that he had collected for you."

"You plan on blackmailing Holcomb?" I asked.

"Heavens, no. The old me would've done it in a second, and I'd be lying if I told you I wasn't tempted. But I'm trying the karma thing, remember? So instead of profiting from all that juicy, scandalous information, I gave it away for free."

"Gave it to whom?" I asked.

"Oh, you know, the usual people. *The New York Times. The Daily News.* Several international websites who publish documents on the web and whose servers are outside of US jurisdiction."

"You leaked all of Holcomb's dirty secrets?"

"Got it in one!" said Moira. "It should have gone public right around the time I walked into the Watchtower." She was positively beaming. "I don't know whether people are going to carry him out of City Hall tarred and feathered, because New Yorkers tend to be a little too civil for that. But I'm being told by some very nice chaps over at the *Times* that his chances of reelection hover in the vicinity of absolute zero."

I had to admit, the news didn't exactly upset me.

"Mose is going to be pissed," I said. "He expressly forbade us to do this."

"Ah, but remember what he said." Moira perched at the edge of the chair and leaned with both arms on my desk. She imitated Mose's deep voice: "'*I forbid any member of the Watch to pursue this.*' Except, I'm not a member of the Watch, am I? And I ain't even applying to join."

I thought back to three days ago. Mose had always been careful with his words, and Moira was *right there.* Did he intend for her to leak the information, thereby keeping the Watch's hands ideologically clean? How could he possibly know she would develop a large enough conscience to forgo a wheelbarrow of money? It didn't pay to second-guess a god.

"I can't speak for karma," I said, "but *I* approve."

Moira didn't stay long. She intended to bask in the glory of her altruism, and that meant there were many new friends for her to visit and brag to, among members of the Watch and the irregulars alike.

As soon as she'd left, our chief archivist knocked on my door. I waved him in. He shuffled inside, carrying an ancient-looking leather-bound tome in both hands.

"I've researched your query, Mr. Brent. I believe this is the most comprehensive volume available on the subject in the English language."

I thanked him kindly and cleared the space in front of me to make room for the large tome. The old leather felt pleasant to the touch and emanated that hard-to-describe old book smell familiar to anyone who spends a lot of time in libraries. I gently flipped it open to the fancy title page. The archaic font read:

Vahagn the Dragon Reaper:

Myths and Legends of the Armenian God of Fire, Thunder, and War.

I flipped the page and began to read.